THE DEVIL IS A PART-TIMER!

21

SATOSHI
WAGAHARA

ILLUSTRATION BY ■ 029 (ONIKU)

MgRonald

CONTENTS

THE DEVIL IS A PART-TIMER!

21

SATOSHI WAGAHARA

ILLUSTRATED BY ■ 029 (ONIKU)

YEN ON

NEW YORK

THE DEVIL IS A PART-TIMER!, Volume 21
SATOSHI WAGAHARA, ILLUSTRATION BY 029 (ONIKU)

Translation by Kevin Gifford
Cover art by 029 (oniku)

This book is a work of fiction. Names, characters, places, and incidents are the product of the author's imagination or are used fictitiously. Any resemblance to actual events, locales, or persons, living or dead, is coincidental.

HATARAKU MAOUSAMA!, Volume 21
© Satoshi Wagahara 2020
Edited by Dengeki Bunko

First published in Japan in 2020 by KADOKAWA CORPORATION, Tokyo.
English translation rights arranged with KADOKAWA CORPORATION, Tokyo, through Tuttle-Mori Agency, Inc., Tokyo.

English translation © 2022 by Yen Press, LLC

Yen Press, LLC supports the right to free expression and the value of copyright. The purpose of copyright is to encourage writers and artists to produce the creative works that enrich our culture.

The scanning, uploading, and distribution of this book without permission is a theft of the author's intellectual property. If you would like permission to use material from the book (other than for review purposes), please contact the publisher. Thank you for your support of the author's rights.

Yen On
150 West 30th Street, 19th Floor
New York, NY 10001

Visit us at yenpress.com
facebook.com/yenpress
twitter.com/yenpress
yenpress.tumblr.com
instagram.com/yenpress

First Yen On Edition: March 2022
Yen On is an imprint of Yen Press, LLC.
The Yen On name and logo are trademarks of Yen Press, LLC.

The publisher is not responsible for websites (or their content) that are not owned by the publisher.

Library of Congress Cataloging-in-Publication Data
Names: Wagahara, Satoshi. | 029 (Light novel illustrator)
illustrator. | Gifford, Kevin, translator. | Steinbach, Kevin,
translator.
Title: The devil is a part-timer! / Satoshi Wagahara ;
illustration by 029 (oniku) ; translation by Kevin Gifford;
translation by Kevin Steinbach.
Other titles: Hataraku Maousama. English
Description: First Yen On edition. | New York, NY :
Yen On, 2015–
Identifiers: LCCN 2015028390 |
ISBN 9780316383127 (v. 1 : pbk.) |
ISBN 9780316385015 (v. 2 : pbk.) |
ISBN 9780316385022 (v. 3 : pbk.) |
ISBN 9780316385039 (v. 4 : pbk.) |
ISBN 9780316385046 (v. 5 : pbk.) |
ISBN 9780316385060 (v. 6 : pbk.) |
ISBN 9780316469364 (v. 7 : pbk.) |
ISBN 9780316473910 (v. 8 : pbk.) |
ISBN 9780316474184 (v. 9 : pbk.) |
ISBN 9780316474207 (v. 10 : pbk.) |
ISBN 9780316474238 (v. 11 : pbk.) |
ISBN 9780316474252 (v. 12 : pbk.) |
ISBN 9780316474252 (v. 13 : pbk.) |
ISBN 9780316302658 (v. 14 : pbk.) |
ISBN 9781975302672 (v. 15 : pbk.) |
ISBN 9781975302696 (v. 16 : pbk.) |
ISBN 9781975302719 (v. 17 : pbk.) |
ISBN 9781975302733 (v. 18 : pbk.) |
ISBN 9781975316327 (v. 19 : pbk.) |
ISBN 9781975316341 (v. 20 : pbk.) |
ISBN 9781975316365 (v. 20 : pbk.) |
ISBN 9781975340902 (v. 21 : pbk.)
Subjects: CYAC: Fantasy
Classification: LCC PZ7.1.W34 Ha 2015 | DDC
[Fic]—dc23
LC record available at http://lccn.loc.
gov/2015028390

ISBNs: 978-1-9753-4090-2 (paperback)
978-1-9753-4091-9 (ebook)

1 3 5 7 9 10 8 6 4 2

WOR

Printed in the United States of America

PROLOGUE: THE DEVIL HEADS FOR WORK

The moment she stepped away from the Gate, Emeralda Etuva smiled and immediately began spewing sarcasm.

"How to puuut it, you knooow…this place is kinda naaaauseating."

"Yeah, hold back, why don't you?" Urushihara winced. Emeralda didn't let it faze her. She couldn't be blamed—this was Devil's Castle and, by extension, the demon realms. This was the lair of her sworn enemy, more or less.

"What are you even here for? Aren't you busy? 'Cause I sure am."

This demonic headquarters had, just a few hours ago, returned to the demon realms for the first time in several years. It contained Maou and his crew, all busy with preparations for their upcoming assault on heaven, and at its base were crowds of local demons, elated to witness their triumphant return. Between this, that, and other things, Urushihara and everyone else had their hands full.

"Oh myyy, yes, I *am* busy. Thanks to a certain king, I'm so preoccupied that I've hardly had time to sleep these past three years, how about that, hmm?"

Emeralda shrugged, all but blaring out that she was well aware of that. Since before the summit, she had grown noticeably sharper around the demons, and she wasn't about to let up here, either.

"N-now now, Lady Emeralda. What has happened, if I may ask?" Camio stepped in, attempting to intervene. "Devil's Castle has only just returned. It will still be some time before we storm the heavens."

Emeralda's sarcastic smile instantly disappeared.

"Lord Camio, the Devil's Regent," she said, suddenly serious. "I know the human world is not your primary concern right now, but there is something I must confer with Emilia about right this minute. Would you be able to find a quiet place for us to chat?"

"Ahh. In that case, her chamber may work. It is not large, but it does have a table and chairs sized for human beings. Come with me."

"Thank you." Emeralda nodded, suddenly polite—whether it was because she had no direct beef with Camio, or she simply wanted to show respect for the elderly, none could say. Just then, Emi—no longer sporting her holy sword or Cloth of the Dispeller—ran in from a Devil's Castle corridor.

"Sorry, Eme! I was all sweaty, so I changed my outfit. I didn't think you'd be coming so quickly. What's up? Something going wrong?"

When they launched Devil's Castle up from the Central Continent, Emi had propelled herself into the air in pursuit of it, a streak in the sky fast enough to escape Ente Isla's gravitational pull. If it resulted in nothing but a few sweat stains, that showed how praiseworthy—or how scary—her strength was. But Emeralda declined to comment on it, instead taking some folded papers out from her robes.

"Wellll, things are ultra-chaotic around the world right now, so I'd like to get the paperwork squared away as soon as I can, you know? Our account ledgers would be easier to fudge right now as well, soooo..."

Emeralda flashed a wicked grin while Emi casually took the papers, skimmed through them, and nodded.

"Eme, this is..."

"While we have the chaaance, you see? Oh, and Lucifer? I think you'll be seeing Amane here before too much lonnnger, okay?"

"Huh? That's rare. Is she coming over here of her own accord?"

"Yes, she contacted Bell about it. And she's taking someone from Chiho's place, too, you know."

"From Chiho Sasaki's place? What's that mean?"

"Oh, I don't know for *sure*; that was just what I heard from Bell. Maybe a third Yesod child showed up or something perhaps, hmm?" Emeralda had little interest in addressing Urushihara's query.

"Now, my dear Regent Camio, can you guide us to her chamber, by chance? And Emilia, if you could sign that there without thinking too deeply about it for me, pleeease...?"

"Um, all right...?"

"Very well. This way, please."

Guided by Camio, Emeralda, like a con man on the street, pushed Emi along.

"Eesh," Urushihara grumbled. "Try to keep me more informed on this stuff, okay, guys? Who's she taking up here? If it's another Earth Sephirah, that'll be *such* a pain..."

About an hour after that whining, Amane Ohguro arrived at Devil's Castle. She had two people with her, in fact. One was Sadao Maou, looking pale and not at all in full health. The other was...

"Uh, who're you?"

Urushihara immediately blurted this out when he saw...this person. One who looked exactly like him, just standing there, smiling.

"Now, Emilia, listen to me, pretty please. Even if you refuse to accept this, I'm still going to do it, all riiight?"

"But isn't this too much?"

"No, it's not toooo much at all! If you consider that Saint Aile participated in the summit, unofficially or not, this is *almost* too little, you know."

"...This is so weird."

"No, it's not weird at all! This is the just reward that you deserve, Emilia, my dear—"

"I don't mean that." Emi peered at the papers then into the eyes of her valued, diminutive friend seated next to her at the table. "I mean, it's weird that we're having this talk *here*, of all places."

Emeralda nodded, quickly picking up on what Emi had left unsaid.

"...Well, all it means is that our opponents this time were the demons and the Devil King's Army, you know?"

"You think so? If I was fighting one nation or another in Ente Isla, do you think we ever would've been friends?"

Emi and Emeralda exchanged another look. Then they sighed in tandem, the smiles gone from their faces. Grinning would be an affront to all the people who'd lost their lives as part of the "war" Emilia and her friends had fought in. So she turned back toward the papers, eyebrows down.

"But," the Hero groaned, "if I'm getting this much, what will I even use it on? I have no idea."

"You're free to decide, my dear."

"Free...?" Emi skimmed the text once more, puzzled. Something in her was compelling her to refuse this, no matter how rude she had to be.

"Eme..."

"Yessum?"

"So, much of this was beyond my control. I mean, really, there's no way I could have received *this*, you know? Not if we were fighting anyone besides the Devil King's Army."

"I imagine you're onto something, yes, but then, nobody expected that you would be coming to terms, more or less, with the Devil King at the end, you know?"

"Well, no, I mean...I can't help but feel like I'm just putting out the fire I set myself. And if everyone in the summit found out about this, do you think they would all accept it? I don't."

Emeralda, again reading between the lines, scowled. "...Yes, my dear, I'm sure Lord Cervantes and that old biddy up north would try to take advantage later."

"Don't call her an 'old biddy.' And besides, there's at least *some* chance Dhin Dhem Wurs will find out from the Malebranche— that, or she'll extract it from Chiho somehow. So, Eme..."

Emi spread the papers out on the table once more.

"I think...this could end up becoming a weapon."

"A weapon...?"

"Yes. And he said it right in front of me, too, didn't he? Like, this could become a 'new power.'"

Emi smiled—a little strained but backed by conviction.

"So look, Eme. Even if the world changes... Even if, after this battle, we lose our holy force and my sword leaves me...I will still be the Hero. No matter how much the world changes, that truth never will."

*

The summit: This was the meeting where all the major players of the world worked out a plan to integrate demons into the human world of Ente Isla. A gathering arranged not by the Ente Islans, not by the demons, and certainly not by the angels, but by a single teenage girl from the faraway land of Japan. This was Chiho Sasaki, the only person in this world who could deal with Ente Islans, demons, and angels as equals. A girl who loved the Devil King and Hero on fair and equal terms...and who, despite irresponsibly wielding a godlike perspective over it all, still remained a faithful third party.

Her (in a way) selfish refusal to step away from the Ente Isla she loved allowed her to unite the prevailing regions of the planet, although it was still limited to just a certain number of regions and leaders. The Ente Islans had accepted that. Although Chiho was just a thoughtless teen who wanted everyone to get along, they still accepted her wish. On paper, at least, they accepted this world they had never thought to step into before, because, while they knew it was the right thing to do, it would inevitably involve a terrifying amount of difficulty and sacrifice to make happen.

A lot of this had to do with the presence of the Devil King and the Hero, who were both as powerful as an entire nation's military force. They should have been crossing swords to decide the fate of the globe and its people, but instead they were raising a child in another world—a wild truth that, for better or worse, had helped push this world's leaders into cooperating with the assault on heaven.

Thus, the summit members had worked with the Devil King's

Army to put on a performance convincing enough to deceive everyone. Then, later, they decided that they would spread three pieces of news across the planet.

One: Devil's Castle, a foreboding symbol of the demons' legacy, had blasted off and disappeared into the skies.

Two: Emilia Justina, Hero and savior, had pursued the structure into the stratosphere, seeking to eradicate it for good.

Three: The Crusade launched by the Church had succeeded, supported by comrades and Heroes across the Land of the Holy Cross.

This spate of good news—not the whole truth, but not an embellishment, either—excited the world. This, in turn, caused the people of Ente Isla to show their willingness to unite as one.

And then—from the Yesod fragment in Chiho Sasaki's possession, the trigger behind all this—a new "life" was born. This life, one that all of Earth's Sephirah tried to send off to Ente Isla the moment he was born, looked exactly like the fallen angel Lucifer—aka Hanzou Urushihara.

It all happened that night, a night when everything seemed to be coming to a close; a night in June, when the summer heat was just beginning to make its presence known.

◊

A cheerful, smiling presenter on the TV weather forecast that morning called for boiling heat and sunny skies across Japan. But if you lived in the roasting neighborhood of Sasazuka that day, feeling the light through the window, you didn't need the reminder.

"What's with this sunlight? I'm indoors, but my eyes still hurt."

Yes, it was the end of July, but "midsummer" didn't seem like an oppressive enough word to describe the rays stabbing down from the sky. But there was no point complaining about it; this had been an especially hot summer, and the news kept talking about people taken to the hospital for heatstroke.

Squinting, Sadao Maou lumbered to his feet to take his breakfast plate back to the sink.

"This kinda weather all the time seriously hurts my appetite."

His morning meal had consisted of a piece of toast and some leftover miso soup from yesterday he found in the fridge—a pretty out-there combination. But with this heat, no matter what kind of food they put in the fridge, it would start showing signs of rotting the following day. He had gotten into the habit of sniffing his meals before taking a bite.

"...They said they sold a ton of iced coffee yesterday, didn't they?"

With a sigh, Maou took his phone out of his pocket. Smiling a bit at the sight of his beloved daughter on his lock screen, he went back to a frown as he brought up another app and called the number at the top of his history.

"Hey there. Sorry to call you so early. You think we could stock up on one-liter take-home bottles from you? Yeah, we had a ton out the door yesterday. If I wait for the regular deliveries, I think we risk running out. Sure. Thanks. I'll punch in the numbers over here. Right, have a good one."

Ending the conversation, Maou looked at the clock hanging on the wall. It was six in the morning.

"Great, six already? I wasted too much time on breakfast."

He picked up the pace of his morning prep. Taking out a baseball T-shirt from the folded laundry (his way of preventing sunburn), he put on some soft, functional jeans, and in his backpack, he stowed the dress shirt, tie, and work slacks he'd picked up from the dry cleaner the day before. Then he grabbed the remote on the low table in the middle of the room.

"I'll be back to change after work, so six hours ought to be okay."

Quickly and deftly, he set the timer on his air conditioner for later and turned it off. The moment the cool breeze came to a halt, Maou could already feel the sweat form under the hair on his skin. It made him roll his eyes, but the clock was still ticking. It was time for work.

"And this is even hotter..."

Picking up the pack, he took the open-faced motorcycle helmet from the shoebox by the front door, strapped it on, and lowered the visor. Then, he put on a pair of brown leather shoes, stepped outside, locked the door, and jiggled the knob to make sure the latch was engaged.

Lifting his head back up, he leaned over to the neighboring door and gave it a knock.

"Hey, I might be late today, so give me a call if something comes up, okay?"

There was no reply. Maou shrugged, expecting this, and pushed through the heat as he jogged down the outdoor stairwell.

His next stop was to approach the silver object broiling under the sun in the bike lot. Removing the silver cover, he was greeted by the sight of a scooter, deep yellow in color. He neatly folded up the cover, slid it into the seat-rack storage, and climbed aboard.

"Ugh, this is burning my butt..."

Pushing the scooter off the gravel and into the street, he felt the seat sear the denim, already cooking in the early morning heat, as he held the brake and turned the key.

"Well, MgScooto, time for another day of work."

The engine revved up as Maou listlessly spoke to his ride, slicing through the hot air as he set off into Sasazuka.

So began a midsummer morning, three years after the battle in heaven.

THE FALLEN ANGEL CLAIMS HIS RELIC

The man whom Amaned had dragged in showed up in Room 201 of Villa Rosa Sasazuka, just as Devil's Castle was back home and preparing to hurtle toward heaven for one final battle.

Thanks to what had happened right after the summit, Maou was in bad shape. He'd been living with Emi for a while, but now that she was back in Ente Isla, he was relishing life by himself in Villa Rosa once more. When he saw the figures awaiting him at the door, Maou could only assume that his illness was now giving him hallucinations.

"Wow, that's a rarity. You got a cold or something?" Amane asked.

Ignoring the jab, Maou tried his hardest to support his heavy body as he spoke. "Urushihara… Why are you…? Aren't you supposed to be in Devil's Castle in Ente Isla…?"

"Sorry to break this to ya with no warning, but I'm not Urushihara. I'm a Sephirah child, born of the person who has laid out a direction for the people of Ente Isla."

"…Um? What?"

"But there's a reason why I came out like this. And I do share a lot of bodily traits in common with Lucifer."

"W-wait a sec. I'm having trouble keeping up with you. You're *not* Urushihara? A Sephirah child? So are you the one who's supposed to be born later, or…?"

"Oh, you know about all that? Perfect. Yeah, that's me. I'm the Da'at of Ente Isla."

Out of the jewels that compose the worlds, the Da'at—the eleventh Sephirah—was known to come after its other brothers and sisters. Maou had heard about that. But that wasn't all he was concerned about.

"What do you mean by, 'born of the person who has laid out a direction,' blah blah blah?"

The words of this Da'at posing as Urushihara compelled Maou—too ill to stand up straight before—to keep his knees unbent.

"I'm talking about Chiho Sasaki, of course. Thanks to the way she handled the summit, Ente Isla's people have unified into... Whoa, hey now."

"You... Don't you *dare* do anything else to Chi...!"

"Look, my dude, I didn't show up because I *wanted* to bother her. But the thing is, all of you people... The king of demons; the emperors and kings and generals and high priests of mankind; the Hero, even... None of them could treat the inhabitants of Ente Isla as *Ente Islans*, so to speak. None of them except an average teen from another world."

"...Ngh..."

"Besides, *you're* the one who got her involved in the first place, aren't you?"

His astute observation sapped Maou of his vigor. His knees were starting to buckle on him again.

"Maou, what's *wrong* with you?" Amane asked. "Do demons even get colds? What's your live-in butler doing, even?"

It was such a pitiful sight that even Amane—who hadn't missed the opportunity to needle Maou about his roommate—extended a concerned hand to him.

"Oh, wow, you've got a bad fever. Here, get back in your futon. Do Yusa and Ashiya know you're like this?"

"I'm sorry... Ashiya doesn't know. Emi and Alas Ramus are in Ente Isla, launching Devil's Castle, too, and...I didn't wanna use her stuff without asking, so I came home."

Maou lay back down as Amane offered a helping hand. He kept his eyes on the Da'at.

"Well, wouldn't Yusa's place be a lot more convenient for you? You're so obstinate that way. Inflexible." Amane opened up Maou's fridge as she spoke. "At least you're eating, judging by the fridge. Oh, but even without Ashiya, you still got Libicocco here, don't you? But still…that body's human, you know. You don't have the flu or something, do you? Have you seen a doctor?"

"No, um, I'm pretty sure a doctor couldn't help with this. It happened on the way back from Ente Isla last time, so it's not the flu…"

His vague excuses weren't about to work against Amane. Her eyes sharpened upon him, as if she could tell Maou was hiding something.

"Well, if it's a disease from over *there*, that's a problem, isn't it? That's something Yusa or Kamazuki ought to check up on for you. If you start bringing alien viruses to Earth, I'm not gonna take that sitting down, understand?"

"N-no, it's not that. It's not a disease."

"What? How do you know that?"

"I—I mean, I know the cause of it, and, uh, medicine doesn't work on it, and I think I'll be fine once I get some rest."

"Again, how do you *know* that?"

"H-how? I mean…"

Amane usually took a fairly hands-off approach with the demons, but she was being oddly coercive today. That Urushihara-shaped Da'at must have had something to do with it. Maou glanced at him again. He had a vague sort of smile on his face—maybe out of pity, or maybe out of rebuke.

It brought Maou to a realization: This man, born from the Yesod fragment in Chiho's possession, knew exactly why he was ill.

"Weird, isn't it?" the Da'at said. "Maybe it's the biology of you demons. Is it because you're dealing with a human being, maybe? Or just because it's *her*?"

"You…!"

"What are you talking about?" Amane wondered. "Well, anyway, what a pain. I had no idea you were in such a sad state of affairs, Maou. *Now* what're we gonna do?"

If Amane found out the true cause of Maou's illness, he'd doubtless never hear the end of it from her for the rest of his life. But she seemed to have several things weighing on her mind today, so she wasn't paying close attention to the two men's conversation.

"What's...gotten into *you*, though, Amane?" Maou deflected. "Why did you bring this guy over?"

"Like I keep telling you, I don't want any trouble with the Sephirah from over there. I want you to take him over to Ente Isla for me...but if *this* is the shape you're in, I guess I'll have to ask Chiho or Rika instead..."

"W-wait a minute, please. So you want me to send this fake Urushihara to Ente Isla? Well, right now, over there—"

"You're launching Devil's Castle, fending off a rising crusade, and don't have a lot of safe spots for him, right? Well, I don't care. I want you to ferry him off this planet."

"Why are you in such a hurry? It's not like Alas Ramus and the rest are—"

"The Da'at is different. And if he's the twin of Urushihara, that, along with everything else we know, is *way* too much to mess around with. It's gonna be nothing but trouble for all of us."

Her tone was light, but her emotions were real.

"...All right. I'll take him there. I have a few days off work anyway."

"Huh? Are you sure you'll be all right?"

"I'd be a lot more anxious about leaving this mystery guy with anyone else. Also, I'm already going to the demon realms. I was just thinking that I probably need to recharge my demonic force over there to get back to health."

"You're probably right. We're on the same page," the Da'at agreed smugly.

"Shut up." Maou resented the implication. "Do you have a name?"

"Not right now. You gonna give me one?"

"Are you messing with me?"

Maou had anticipated that he might not have a name, but he didn't expect the Da'at to ask him for one.

"You don't have to act all defensive. I could christen myself, for that matter, but my first choice would be to have Chiho Sasaki do it. After that, I'd prefer either you or Emilia Justina do it, I think."

Maou opted not to ask how he'd come up with this order.

"…Copy-hara."

"Are you serious, Maou?"

Amane quickly voiced her complaint at the rather tasteless suggestion.

"Copyhara, huh? Copyhara… Not bad. I like it."

On the other hand, it didn't seem to bother the person being named at all.

"Okay, you're Copyhara now. We can worry about your first name later. Also…"

"What's this? Hair wax?"

The pomade Maou casually tossed his way made Copyhara raise an eyebrow. Maou listlessly pointed at his own forehead.

"You look *way* too much like the real Urushihara. It's too confusing, so part your hair on the opposite side for me."

Summoning all his resolve to sit up from the futon, Maou wrote a quick note for Libicocco. Then he called for Acieth, who was over in the landlord's house, and after that, he sent a text to Chiho detailing his future plans, including what he'd do with Copyhara. Finally, he set off for the demon realms with Amane and Copyhara.

Being unable to use an angel's feather pen, the already sickened Maou required a Herculean effort to open his own Gate—he nearly lost his lunch a couple of times inside it, too. But back in the demon realms, looking up at Devil's Castle looming high over the red sky and terrain, he could feel the demonic force in the air work its way into his body, like a relaxing hot spring bath. In just a few moments, he felt palpably better.

"You look distressed about something," Copyhara noted.

"Can you read people's minds, or…?"

"A little."

Copyhara sure wasn't being shy.

"It's not like I'm trying to invade your privacy, though I need some training before I can manage to avoid hearing anything I don't need to."

"I can't believe you were born looking and speaking like that…"

Maou almost wanted to believe he was Urushihara's long-lost twin brother. Then:

"Devil King? Weren't you under the weather or… Hey, who's that?"

"Your Demonic Highness! If I'd known you were here, I would have come to greet you… Who is that behind you?"

"…Uh, who're you, dude?"

Emi, Ashiya, and Urushihara, all stepping up to greet Maou's arrival in the demon realms, were all suspicious, in their own respective ways, of Copyhara standing behind him.

✳

The day after Amane and Maou dragged Copyhara to the demon realms, the group returned to that mysterious laboratory deep underground, preparing to kick off the final phase of their assault on heaven.

Countless bodies, the remains of an army of mechanical soldiers, could be seen lying in the cracks running along the ground. Beyond them lay a legion of enigmatic machinery, crafted by unknown hands during an unknown age. It was all reminiscent of Satanas Arc, the ancient city Satan had discovered, which once served as the demons' stronghold in this realm. But this did not evoke good memories for Maou or Emi. Even as they returned here, moving through this graveyard of soldiers—as well as through the demonic power-sucking entrance that had stymied Maou and Camio before—kept Emi on high alert.

"Well…I really don't think they'll attack now, the way things are. No point in being too anxious."

"Wasn't it the same last time, though? And Alas Ramus has been kind of unstable lately. The time may come when Acieth's power no longer works against them."

Maou shrugged at Emi, who seemed ready to believe there were enemies in all directions. His guard wasn't down, though. The first time they'd journeyed down here, the only true fighters in their party had been Emi, Camio, and himself—and being robbed of their demonic force meant relying on the strength of Emi, Acieth, and Kinanna. But in addition to the members from before, they had Urushihara, Gabriel, Amane Ohguro, and also a certain other person tagging along. It seemed safe to assume they had a firm foundation to work with.

"Damn. This place is gross."

Urushihara winced as he ran a hand down his hair. Passing through that entrance had taken all his demonic force, as expected, so now his hair and eyes were back to their "angel" versions. But as a fallen angel, he was still capable of using power resembling any other member of his kin. (Maou and Camio, just like before, were also forced to retreat into their respective human and chicken forms.)

"If I may ask… How come I wound up like this, but Laila's still got the same coloring?"

Fairly recently, Laila had experienced the opposite transformation from Urushihara—going from silvery-blue hair and brilliant red eyes to a purple hue for both. They believed this happened after Maou had healed her injuries in Japan, but considering the entrance here sucked demonic force away from physical bodies, no one had expected this to happen.

"I don't know… Maybe, unlike you, my magical force isn't an integral part of my life systems or something."

Laila didn't give it much more consideration than that.

"Well, maybe *you're* fine with that, but…what about *him*, then?"

Urushihara, still unconvinced, turned toward another figure next to Amane. Ignoring the stare, the Da'at flashed a breezy smile exactly as Urushihara would.

"Well, you know, it wasn't an *acquired* thing like it was with you. I've been like this from the start, dude. Isn't that right, Amane?"

"Don't ask *me*. I'm not a Sephirah child, so I wouldn't know."

Amane was oddly evasive as she sized up Copyhara's statement.

It was rare for her emotions to come to the surface like this, especially when you considered she knew he was born of a Yesod fragment, which meant he couldn't have been her enemy.

"So what's the big deal, huh? These things happen sometimes."

"Jus' like Lushiferrr! So weird!"

The two other Yesod kids weren't afraid of Copyhara at all. Thus, the denizens of Devil's Castle decided to allow the interloper's presence, despite not being entirely on board with him.

"How *we* are doesn't matter right now, does it? You guys have a job to do," Copyhara reminded them.

"Ugh... My work's ninety percent done now that Devil's Castle is back down safely, so why do I get all *this* guff, dude? Because this feels a *lot* grosser than you think it does," spat Urushihara, apparently disgusted by the relaxed smile of the man with an identical face. "Don't start any crap with me, dude, or I'll make you regret it."

"Well, I'm here right now because everyone trusts me, y'know? Despite having your mug."

Whether he was a Da'at born from a Yesod fragment or not, why was Copyhara tagging along to a place that had caused Maou and Emi so much strife? It was mainly because he claimed that if they could put this facility into operation, it'd make it far easier to attack heaven than what Maou's plans called for. What's more, activating things down here required not only the four relics of the Devil Overload Satan, previously used to operate Devil's Castle as a rocket ship, but Urushihara himself.

"Copyhara, are you *sure* you know how to run this whole thing?"

"Of course. But don't *you* know, too, Lucifer? Like, this whole operation?"

"I *really* don't like that 'Copyhara' name, dude! Just hearing you use it drives me crazy. Do I really *sound* like that?"

Urushihara was complaining about something else entirely. But he didn't deny the question.

"Like I keep telling you, most of my memories about my life have been pretty vague for a while. What I think…or at least what I recall…"

He was now pointing to a set of five capsules of various sizes, set up at one end of the large mechanical facility. His finger was aimed at the central section, where Kinanna and the Nothung had been the last time.

"…is all of that belonged to me."

Hearing this, Copyhara flashed an implicating smile, just like Urushihara always did. "That's right. Everything here belonged to you. That stuff, and the *real* relic hidden here."

He must have been referring to the Devil Overlord's relics. Maou and his cohorts had initially searched for them so they could launch Devil's Castle away from Ente Isla; they hadn't been looking for anything else, apart from replacing things that were broken when they'd touched down for their attack on humanity. In fact, until Copyhara had suggested activating this facility, the best plan they'd come up with was to launch Devil's Castle from the demon realms, then follow an orbital path toward the heavens. That idea was fraught with danger, but no one had any better suggestions—they had debated it many times, since before the castle launch, and that was what they'd concluded.

According to Copyhara, however, bringing all the relics they'd collected back to the lab would put their fears to rest. Maou's gang had been dubious at first, but with Urushihara talking about the relics again as well, they decided to give it a shot—and now, every last relic was here.

"Hey! You done yet, Amane? This spear's heavy! Can't we haul it in?"

The Spear of Adramelechinus, significantly larger than any of the other relics, was being carried by Gabriel, who was currently griping from near the entrance.

<"Well, then… Time to begin the polishing…">

Jewel in his throat shining, Kinanna carried the magical sword Nothung on his shoulder as he toddled in.

"Wait, Kinanna! We haven't finished any of our *peep* preparations!"

"Cheep-cheep! Don't climb on the machines!"

"Hey, big sis, do not pull the tail of chicken! With chicken, you grab by neck—"

"Gah! *Cheep!*"

"No, you two! How many times do I have to tell you? Camio is *not* a chicken!!"

Alas Ramus and Acieth were running around underfoot, chasing after the hapless chicken Camio, as Laila tried desperately to stop them.

"After everything that's happened, why isn't everyone a little more...tense?"

Emi, watching them carry on like usual, began to feel a vague sense of anxiety about all this.

"All right, outta my way, please; we got big cargo comin' through. Keep the little kids back, mm-kay? Oh, don't hit the top part! Can you handle the back?"

"You're not a moving crew."

Ignoring Maou's jab, Gabriel worked the giant spear above, around, and through the chamber, finally ensconcing it inside the largest of the five capsules. All the other relics fit into their own capsules as well, like keys in keyholes; now only the central capsule was left.

"Boy, so big! Chiho, she score that spear, yes?"

"'Score' isn't exactly the word I'd use, but yeah, I won't forget that day for a while... Also, why are you eating that dried squid, Acieth?"

Emi raised an eyebrow. Acieth's mouth was full of shredded dried squid, a popular Asian snack, as she spoke. Her gluttonous habits hadn't abated, but she tended to require less food in Ente Isla than on Earth, so a plastic bag of squid she'd purchased at a store was tiding her over well enough.

"They say if you chew a whole lot, it taste real good."

"Oh..."

"By the way, this not actually the squid. It is the gummy candy, with shape of squid. You eat, too?"

Emi looked at the bag for a while, wondering who thought this product would sell and how the people at the manufacturing plant even crafted it.

"I'll pass."

Unfazed, she turned it down. In the midst of this, all the preparations came together.

"Okay, everything's set up like you instructed. Is something gonna happen now?"

<"Finally, time for some real polishing.">

Responding to Gabriel's call, Kinanna began deftly operating the panel connected to his capsule, just like before. There was a loud roar as all the machines in the chamber activated at once. When Kinanna heard it:

<"I have waited a long time... A very long time indeed.">

Wagging his tail, he stepped into one of the empty capsules.

"...And?"

The sword, spear, and magic gear were all genuine relics. That must have meant that the jewel in Kinanna's throat really was the Astral Gem after all. But even with all the Devil Overlord's relics in one place, it seemed like nothing else was going to happen. Across the room, everyone's gaze fell on Copyhara...but it was Urushihara who looked despondent.

"...Do I *have* to do this, dude?"

"Yep."

"Listen, how much do you know anyway?"

"I am a Sephirah that has taken your form. I think I have most of your memories, and being a Sephirah, I can remember things a lot further back than you can."

"Oh. Well, I think you probably know, but *my* memory isn't all that great, and I'm not totally certain what I'm about to do is the right thing. But when Gabriel talked to me about the relics, for the first time in a while..."

"Oooh, yeah. That was a real hot day out, huh?"

"...Well, I didn't want to pay the inheritance tax, you know what

I mean? I think it's already burned into my DNA...like, how if I receive these relics, it's gonna be this massive pain in the ass."

With that, the still despondent Urushihara slowly walked forward. Then, just as Kinanna did, he stepped up and into the only empty capsule remaining.

"Close it from the outside for me, Maou. And...*you*. You operate it, okay? You know how, right?" Urushihara asked.

"Can't you call me Copyhara? He's the one who named me."

"I'd rather die, dude. Come up with a more Sephirah-like name."

"Um... So close it? Like this?"

As instructed, Maou closed the lid on the capsule, blocking out Urushihara's voice. At the same time, Copyhara placed his index finger on the control panel.

The next moment:

"Huhh?"

"*Cheep?!*"

A torrent of light and vibration, nothing like the roaring from before, filled the eyes and ears of everyone in the room. As it did, they could all feel the entire underground facility traveling farther downward.

"Is this whole place an elevator?!"

"We—we can go back, right?"

"Don't worry, mm-kay? I have my feather pen if we get in trouble."

"Great, but what about me and Camio and Kinanna?!"

"Mommy!!"

Amid the din, Alas Ramus's voice shot out more sharply than the rest.

"Someone...is here."

Not something, but *someone*. That put everyone on edge, but when they saw who that "someone" was, it made them all put on quizzical looks.

"What...is that...?"

When the room quieted down, they found that the wall facing Urushihara had opened wide. They all peered in, curious about what lay beyond. There, they found an even larger laboratory, complete with the capsules Urushihara and the rest had stepped into—except they were several dozen times larger. Even compared to the giant capsule holding the spear, these were still about five times as big.

"...It wasn't this huge, but I think I've seen something like this before..."

Stiffening up, Emi sifted through her memories as she examined the new chamber. There, within the gigantic space even deeper in the underground facility, they could make out an enormous, enclosed jar. It was about half-filled with soil, extending out from which was a withered stump, its shape twisted. A soft light shone down on the container, and a thin layer of moss covered the soil's surface.

"Right. It's a terrarium."

"Tera... What? What's that?"

This was, in essence, a blown-up version of a terrarium—a glass container with a small natural environment inside, often kept for decoration.

"A terrarium. You know, those small containers with plants and stuff you put in the window. A lot of people make them for fun using stones and small branches and moss. If you do it right, you can create a self-sustaining ecosystem inside."

"So it's kind of a gardening thing?"

"It just *looks* like that, I mean. But..."

Upon further inspection, it seemed to be sealed away—locked in an underground facility, to be opened only by Urushihara and the Devil Overlord's relics.

"If this only opens after you collect the Devil Overlord Satan's relics and lost child here, it can't just be some hobbyist bonsai. Maybe you can turn it into a great weapon, or... Huh?"

As they stood there, unable to fathom what the container could really be:

"Asseth, that's us."

"Yeah. It is. We were here."

Alas Ramus and Acieth whispered to each other, apparently aware of what it was. It made Acieth drop her bag of gummy squid.

"Alas Ramus? What do you mean? When you say 'we'… Are there still Yesod fragments in there?"

"No. That's us."

"Emi, why don't you put the fragment in your holy sword up to it? Then we can see if there's some in there or not."

"Y-yeah… Um, Alas Ramus, if you have a minute?"

"Okeh."

At Maou's suggestion, Emi remembered to summon her holy sword. Alas Ramus disappeared as she did.

"Hey, are you sure this is all right? I don't know anything about this place. And besides giving Alas Ramus to Satan, I didn't leave any other fragments in the demon realms…"

"If there's no guiding light from the fragments, it won't react at all. We've made it this far. We need to test out everything we can."

"That's true…"

Quieting Laila's concerns, Emi—as she had done many times before—held her holy sword aloft, infused it with holy force, and released the power of its Yesod fragment. If another shard was near, they would see a beam of purple light connecting the two. If not, the sword would instead react to the next nearest fragment, the one in Acieth.

"…Did it just shake a little?"

"It did. That didn't feel like an earthquake…"

But everyone standing there could feel a vibration cross their bodies.

"Yes. Because of that."

Acieth pointed at the stump inside the giant terrarium.

"Wait, was *that* there before?"

Maou squinted at it. At first glance, it definitely looked like a withered tree stump. Now, however, a whisker-thin twig had sprouted atop it, with a young bud fully spread out from its top.

"It call me and my big sis, Emi. Saying 'Let's go home.'"

"Go home…? Ah?!"

Suddenly, a much larger tremor rocked the entire space.

"Hey, Gabriel…"

"Ah, um, yeah. You're probably right. But I can't say I really predicted this, or, um...like, how *big* it got is kind of a surprise. On the other hand, it would also be unexpected if it still worked at *this* size..."

"Laila! Gabriel! What are *you two* so convinced about? What's all this shaking? And what's in that stupid jar thing?!"

Recovering from illness, drained of magic power, and exposed to a train of improbable events, Maou was tired of it all. He pressed the two archangels for answers. They turned toward him, showing more bewilderment—plus a tiny amount of excitement—than he typically ever saw from them.

"I think we probably won't immediately get what's going on, even after we leave here, but..."

"But we can tell you what this is, yes."

Laila walked over to Acieth, standing next to her. She hadn't picked up her bag of gummies, nor had she moved on to another snack. As Laila patted her on the back, all she did was gaze at that lone bud from the stump.

"This is not the end of something...but yes. Very long..."

"You're right. I'm sorry we made your wait so drawn-out."

"...So this is something related to the Sephirah?"

"More than just related. This is literally a root from it."

"Heh-heh!"

Gabriel giggled a little after Laila said that—just a casual snicker, as if someone had just inadvertently made a pun.

"The one we knew was a lot smaller than this. Small enough that a grown person could lug it around. But...yeah. Considering how much time has passed, this is still pretty puny."

Laila, holding Acieth by the shoulder, looked toward Emi's holy sword.

"I'm sure the same question must have crossed your mind. Out of the ten Sephirah, why was it that only the Yesod shattered into pieces?"

That hadn't been a passing thought, no. Ever since Erone, born from Gevurah, appeared, the regulars at Villa Rosa Sasazuka Room 201 had always kept that concern in the back of their minds. Emi even asked Laila about it once. Why fragments? Who broke it, and how?

"Well, here's your answer. Long ago, Satanael cut this from the Tree of Life. Maybe the other Sephirah would have shattered if he'd cut off anything else. That's how this works."

The solemnity of Laila's voice was not lost on Maou and Emi. It was the first time they'd ever felt that from her.

"This is one of the roots that supports the Tree of Life. There are eleven in all on Sephirot, each corresponding to its own Sephirah, and this is the ninth."

Listening to her mother's voice, Emi couldn't help but tighten the grip on her holy sword.

"The Yesod Sephirah's root…"

◊

"Huh?"

Under the shade of the awning, Maou spotted a woman carrying a sunshade over her head. Noticing the sound of his engine, she lifted her head and waved at him.

"Sorry. Did you wait long?"

"Good morning. Oh, right, the manager starts in the afternoon today, right?"

"Yeah. I'm just helping out in the morning. Lemme open it up for you. It had to be hot out here!"

"Yeah, it's so early, but I can't believe how scorching it is just standing here!"

The woman looked like she was sick of it.

"Lemme have the key, president! I'll go in and start the AC for you."

"Sure, sure."

Maou gave the woman who'd casually called him "president" the key case from his pocket. Well acquainted with this process, she opened the entrance with the key and rushed in, sending the old-fashioned bells that hung over the door dinging away.

Parking the scooter at the far end of the parking lot, Maou took a look around the building. He glared at a small collection of cigarette stubs that had appeared overnight, but otherwise everything seemed well. After a quick check to make sure there was no dirt on the sign, he opened the door and went in.

Today, as usual, it was time to prep the Eifukucho flagship location of Yesodd's Family Café.

Enjoying the dim, cooled air inside, the woman from before greeted Maou as she came in from the back.

"We sold a lot of bottled coffee yesterday. Do we have enough? Oh, here's the keys."

"Yeah, I placed an order for more before I left home. They'll bring them over."

Accepting the key case from her, Maou pointed outside.

"Also, Shoji, sorry to work you this early, but outside..."

"Oh, the cigarette butts again? Ugh! Don't they get businesses to put up NO SMOKING signs 'cause they don't want that sorta thing?"

Kaori Shoji, a member of the part-time staff, was dressed in her standard uniform—white shirt, denim cutoffs, chic black salon apron. As she fumed a bit, her tied-up black hair swayed around. She took a trash bag from under the register and went outside.

"Oh, right, Maou! I mean, president!"

Then she came right back.

"So, I saw that the manager's coming in this afternoon on the shift schedule. Are you off after that?"

"Yeah. I'm getting together with someone afterward."

"Oh, a date?!"

"Huh?"

Hearing that word from out of nowhere, so unrestrained, made Maou widen his eyes. He thought for a moment, then nodded his assent.

"Well... It's not that it isn't, I guess?"

"Not so inactive after all, huh, prez?"

Then, for some reason, Kaori's face lit up. Maou knew that

whenever she looked up at him like this, something bad was about to happen.

"Hey, stop picking on your elders. What's *that* supposed to mean?"

"Well, the manager told me that you've been really busy lately, so I figured, maybe you just don't have it in you, so..."

"Don't have it in me? I sign your paychecks, you know."

"But today you've got plans, huh? That's really impressive. And if you're leaving before lunchtime, are you dining out, then? Maybe eating at the airport?"

"Well, yeah, lunch, but... What? The airport?"

Maou winced at the second unexpected keyword.

Now Kaori looked puzzled. "Weren't you going to Haneda Airport? Or are you meeting up at Hamamatsu-cho or somewhere?"

"Haneda? Hamamatsu-cho? What are you talking about? I don't have any business there."

It may have just been the glare from outside, but Kaori's face suddenly took on an aura of terrifying darkness.

"Oh, you don't? Ahh, I knew it. *Tssh.*"

"What? Hey, Shoji! Why're you talkin' like that to the president?"

"I swear, all you workaholics..."

Watching Kaori leave after that tirade, Maou thought to himself for a moment.

"The airport...? Hang on... I didn't hear anything, but maybe..."

And as his mind came up with an assortment of ominous scenarios, Kaori began cleaning the tables. "I'm done outside," she declared, "so I'll start in here."

Based on the way she was acting, Maou was now sure he'd messed something up.

"Look, I didn't know, okay?"

The muttering was nothing but a lame excuse, so he went back to his own duties. No matter what was happening with him, or the world, he had to get this café up and running. He was president of The Maou Company, Ltd., operators of the Eifukucho location of Yesodd's Family Café, and they were opening in ninety minutes.

THE
DEVIL
KING'S
ARMY
MOVES
THE
MOON

That day, the chief astronomer at Sankt Ignoreido, headquarters of the Church, submitted a very strange report.

The chief astronomer's job was to observe the movements of heavenly bodies, craft weather forecasts and calendars, and divine good and bad fortunes. His words and predictions would occasionally carry more sway than even input from the Six Archbishops of the Church. What he reported to Archbishop Cervantes Reberiz and the assorted bishops and cardinals of the headquarters was so unusual that, at first, it made everyone doubt their ears. But perhaps the chief astronomer had anticipated this disbelief. And that was why he concluded his report with the following statement:

"There has been no error made in this observation. All observational equipment is in full working order, and all personnel involved with this observation are of sound mind."

＊

"Ur, urgghh…"

When Urushihara all but fell out of his capsule, everyone staring at the "root" of the Yesod Sephirah suddenly shivered and turned toward him.

"Ahh… I think the reason I get carsick so easily is because I've got an extreme case of claustrophobia."

"After holing up inside that closet for half your time there? C'mon… And don't scare us like that."

"Look, there's three aspects to claustrophobia, okay? Fear of dark places, fear of tight places, and fear of being constrained. I'm the last one—I feel sick if I'm in something I can't get out of on my own volition. I think."

As he made this rather sensible-sounding statement, Urushihara flapped his arms out, stretching all the joints in his body.

"Did… Did you know this was here?"

He winced at Emi. "I told you a million times, dude. I forgot about this entire setup. All I remembered was that my dad hid this relic, or *something*, around here."

As everyone watched, Urushihara slowly gazed up at the Yesod root and the small bud growing from it.

"Or maybe I was right all along. He never told me how to claim this relic. Like, you see it in TV dramas and stuff a lot, right? Without a will, you can't inherit what's owed to you."

"Lucifer, this is serious…"

"Stop acting like I'm always joking around, dude. I *am* serious. Because I never got a will—because no one ever told me about this— I never knew how important this place and its relic were to my life. That's what it is."

Urushihara had no time for Emi right now.

"The ancient Devil Overlord Satan was Satanael Noie, the angel who split from the heavens. He befriended the demons in their realm in order to resist Ignora and her continued research into immortality. But you can see how it's working in here. No one person could lead the demon realms until Maou made Satanas Arc his home base. In other words, Satanael lost."

Gabriel and Laila hadn't spelled it out for him, but he had put everything he knew together, and that was the conclusion he made.

"All the broken robots around here were troops that invaded from heaven. So are the guys we and the Malebranche called the

'Silverarms' ages ago. Those things that caused us so much trouble after we merged with the Malebranche were probably the pawns of Satanael."

"Those, huh? That means the Devil Overlord must've caused all kinds of chaos in the demon realms. But the way Gabriel put it, Satanael didn't really have the time or resources for that. And why did the angels have to wage war against each other anyway? Up on Ente Isla's moon, they didn't have to worry about that killer disease any longer, did they?"

"...You're surprisingly slow sometimes, Maou. Doesn't Camio always chide you about not paying attention to people's feelings?"

"Wh-where did *that* come from?"

"Don't you get how much fear Caiel and Sikeena put into Ignora and everyone else? Gabriel, trained for battle and all, couldn't take them. Neither could Satanael or Sariel, even in a one-on-one match. I guess you forgot this, but without Alas Ramus's and Acieth's power, even you and Emilia couldn't have beaten Gabriel or Sariel—and the Sephirah children from the angels' home planet beat the crap out of them. You know, Maou..."

Urushihara pointed at Amane, frowning as she looked at the Yesod root.

"...If Alas Ramus and Acieth weren't around, could you even beat Amane? Or the landlord?"

"No way," Maou immediately replied.

"You know, as a fetching young lady, I don't really like being sized up like that. I wouldn't lose, no, but..."

Not sure how Amane wanted to be treated, Urushihara soldiered on.

"Satanael thought that if they kept up with their immortality research, it would inspire the anger of the Ente Isla Sephirah. So he stole the root. But the angels freaked out. If the tree wasn't operating right, they thought, who knew what was gonna happen? So they opposed Satanael by accusing him of messing up the Sephirah. If anything *else* happened, after all, there'd be no way for them to escape. Maybe it's unethical, or whatever—but unless you've got an advanced society and order and stuff, that's meaningless. Instead, they prioritized what was endangering their lives. They *all* nearly died once, you know."

"Man, what the hell? That's not very brave of them. It's real ugly."

"Could you say that to Chiho Sasaki?"

"Huh?"

Maou knew the angels only as they existed now. Urushihara rejected his observation out of hand.

"Could you say to Chiho Sasaki, like, 'There are these guys who keep wanting to destroy Sasazuka, and you and your family with it, but you're just gonna have to accept that, okay?'"

Maou winced. Emi gasped a little as well. There was no telling whether Urushihara meant what he'd said, but there was no way Maou or Emi would tell that to Chiho at this point. They couldn't, they both realized at once.

"No, you'd try to do something about it, wouldn't you? Not that I'm one to talk, but..."

Again, Maou and Emi realized that they had once put Chiho in that situation—a girl who knew far less than she did now, and who was nowhere near as strong in heart and body at the time. Back then, they had Urushihara under Maou's control...but could they have really said that Chiho was safe, just because they took care of Olba the traitor? No, they couldn't...and she wasn't, hence why Sariel came along soon after. And until he did, Maou and Emi pretty much left Chiho in the lurch—not revealing anything, not doing anything.

"Most human beings, you know... They'd be terrified. Chiho Sasaki was all alone, and maybe it was hard for her, but it didn't affect her surroundings. But once you get more people involved, that's when consensus sets in. People start agreeing that they don't wanna see that horror again, and that shuts their minds away from exploring other avenues. And if you think it's someone else's problem, you can say whatever you want about it 'cause it's a faraway issue to you. Ignora and Satanael were afraid of Caiel and Sikeena's return, for opposite reasons, so they fought things out in a hurry.

The demons fought with Satanael after gaining his powers and those of the angels on his side, but in the end, they lost. And when their defeat was set in stone, the 'will' was lost, so to speak. This."

Urushihara glanced at the capsules surrounding them. Kinanna was finally crawling out of his capsule, much as Urushihara had. He closed his eyes on all fours, and whether asleep or awake, he lay still thereafter.

"Emilia… Why do you think the relics of the Devil Overlord Satan were bequeathed to me?"

"Huh?"

"Why did they keep them at all? I can't carry a spear *that* big around, and it's not like the Nothung is that great a sword, even. Even if I bothered reading the Sorcery of the False Gold, it's not like it would help me in the demon realms. And the thing in Kinanna's neck… What *is* that anyway?"

"…Well… I don't really know what you demons think of as the treasure of your realms, exactly, but… Wait, why are you asking me?"

"Because you're the most likely out of anyone here to know." Urushihara pointed at Alas Ramus. "Like, if Maou says right now that he'll take in Alas Ramus and raise her himself, what would you do?"

"Huhh? He'd *never* do that."

"You're *that* sure, huh?"

Maou winced at the knee-jerk skepticism, but the thought of paying for her education took the edge off his retort.

"What if he had lots of money and Alas Ramus said she wanted to live with him alone?"

"That'd never happen in a million years."

"It's a hypothetical, okay? Stop dismissing it."

"Even as a theoretical construct, I hate it. There's no possible way the Devil King could be a single dad for Alas Ramus. He can't merge with her, he can't take care of a little kid…and, *ugh*, when I heard he didn't even give her a futon to sleep on when she was at his apartment…"

"Well, Ignora probably thought the exact same thing. So, Maou, disregarding what Emilia thinks, if you were living with Alas Ramus and some unfortunate disaster happened to you, what then?"

Maou looked at Urushihara, Alas Ramus, and then Emi before turning around. He observed the large terrarium holding the Yesod root as he spoke.

"If I was living alone with Alas Ramus and something happened to me… Well, isn't it obvious?"

An impulse drove him to put a hand on Emi's shoulder. She didn't brush it away.

"I'd have her go to her mom. What else?"

"So there you have it."

It wasn't likely meant as a signal. But Maou, Emi, and even Urushihara couldn't help but think that those words were meant to trigger something.

"The sword, the spear, the sorcery, and the gem… They were nothing but a last will and testament, to guide us to the root underneath. Satanael gave them to four demons he trusted in case he lost them—these four 'keys.' He used them to guide me here and get me back to where *my* mother was. But before I could accept his last wishes, I was taken away from Satanas Arc. The demons that took Satanael's relic keys couldn't search for me, and with the exception of Kinanna, they all died. And your dad was among them, Camio."

"*Cheep…* My ancestor…"

The shaking gradually grew stronger.

"…But what's with this rumbling? Don't tell me this whole thing's gonna lift up like Satanas Arc and turn into a spaceship."

"It's nothing as stupid as that. I have a hunch it'll stop real soon."

The voice was the same, but this time it was Copyhara responding instead of Urushihara.

"The root's started to move. So the thing the Devil Overlord took away long ago can be reunited."

"Reunited…? Wait."

Maou looked at Gabriel. He needed to be sure. The "split up" thing that he'd mentioned when discussing the past with him in Nerima could be only one thing—the moon of Ente Isla.

"I guess you can't blame a kid for the sins of his parents, right? But it's too late, dude. How laissez-faire were you with my upbringing anyway?"

The moons, split apart at the end of a "family argument" between God and the Overlord, were now approaching each other once more.

"The whole moon…?"

Amane looked up. "…Hey, Maou? I think you better hurry up and contact Kamazuki or Emeralda soon. They're over in the Central Continent, or whatever you called it, right?"

"Oh, yeah, you're right. If I don't tell them when something happens, they can get scary with me."

Maou hurriedly took out his phone and began tapping out a text.

"But, you know, this really opens up some prospects for us…but at the same time, we got a whole lot more to do, all of a sudden. Um, what should we start with once I contact them? Actually, Ashiya's over in Efzahan now—maybe I should contact him and inform the other summit members. After that…"

"Um, hold on a second, Devil King."

Just as Maou was restlessly considering his future plans, Emi suddenly stopped him cold.

"So we really *have* set up the whole path to finishing this, right? Then isn't there something we ought to do now, while we can?"

Her stern voice made Maou lower the hand holding his phone.

"The things Lucifer made me realize… I think we need to address them, even if we have to start now. I mean…"

Emi frowned.

"At the end of this battle, at least one of us might wind up dead… and then we'll lose that chance forever."

Maou, realizing what Emi was getting at, turned toward Urushihara.

"You're right. Which means we'll have to work out plans with you, Urushihara, and Ashiya and Suzuno, too."

Urushihara, a bit confused by having his name called out, looked back at him.

"Huh? What're you talking about?"

"You just said it, man."

"What?"

"But first we need to quiet down the turmoil across the demon realms. I'm gonna return to Devil's Castle and see how things are over there and in heaven. Given the scale of what we just did, heaven might decide to storm us as soon as they can. We can decide what to do after we gauge the situation. All right?"

"That sounds good to me," Emi agreed.

Maou put the phone back in his pocket.

"Urushihara, Camio, back to the castle."

The resolve in his voice was unmistakable.

"Before the final battle, Emi, Urushihara, and I need to go and make some amends. We gotta let Ashiya and Suzuno know right now."

※

"'There has been no error made in this observation. All observational equipment is in full working order, and all personnel involved with this observation are of sound mind'…is it?"

At the Central Continent, in a camp built on the ruins of Isla Centurum, Suzuno Kamazuki grinned wryly at the message a Church knight brought from headquarters.

"Whatever is the matter, Suzuno, dear?" Emeralda asked.

"Nothing. But, you know, it can be quite nice to see someone who normally acts all stuffy and above it all fly into a panic."

Suzuno, relaxing in her tent, read the parchment scroll over several times.

"This seal marks the document as top secret within the Church. It is sealed by holy magic, so nobody ranked lower than a parish bishop may open it."

"Oh goodness, does that kind of holy magic exist? I've *never* heard of that."

"Though it appears to be a normal red seal, there is a secret contrivance in the production of the wax. The only people who know how to produce it are the Archbishops, some of the cardinals, and the chief astronomer who sent this."

"The chief astronomer sent it?"

"Yes. The moment has come sooner than expected...or, perhaps, at long last. And if the chief astronomer has spotted it, then before very long, every other observatory in the world will pick up on it."

Rising from her work chair, Suzuno invited Emeralda out of the tent.

The sky was blue in the Central Continent; sunny, cloudless skies had persisted over the few days since the Devil's Castle launch. In that short time, people were already telling exaggerated stories about this "miracle," a divine blessing upon the devil-smiting Hero Emilia, the crusader force, and the Federated Order of the Five Continents. Every time she heard these tales, Suzuno had to prevent herself from laughing.

The sky above was beginning to segue into evening, the red moon and the blue moon hazily visible through the air in the atmosphere.

"I thought there was no option but to launch Devil's Castle a second time from the demon realms...but it would appear they've found a far more innovative approach. Would you like to read it?"

Suzuno handed the message over to Emeralda. She read it, a tad puzzled.

"...Huh?"

She blinked several times.

"What? ...Huh? What?"

Her eyes darted between the sky and Suzuno several times, a finger batting the parchment. She could tell this was beyond the realm of imagination—but to her, uneducated in the ways of astronomy, she couldn't come to a ready conclusion about the impact this event would have. So she asked Suzuno.

The message from the chief astronomer on Isla Centurum was as follows:

"The red moon above is about to catch up with the blue moon at an incredible rate of speed. We cannot deny the possibility that the two may make contact very shortly."

"So you mean to tell me the Devil King has moved the demon realm all by himselllllf? Goodness!"

"That appears to be the case."

"And that's going to result in a lot more than 'nooothing,' I imagine?"

Emeralda's question was atypically uncertain.

Suzuno gave her a conflicted smile. "There's not much I can tell you. But it will certainly make the world rather anxious. And after that... This is based merely on what I know from Japanese books and television and such, so please do not take it too seriously... But at worst, it may change the shape of our world's coasts."

"Huh? The coasts? ...Ah!"

Startled, Emeralda looked at the moons in the sky. Suzuno, in a cold sweat, turned away from her face.

"Wait a minute, please! You don't mean it will affect the power of the tides...?"

"Well, yes, I imagine it will..."

"What kind of ridiculous nonsense is *that*?! If you have these two enormous things moving this fast in such a short time, it'll change a lot more than just that, you know!"

"Mmm, well, it *used* to be a single moon, after all..."

"...Bell... Did you think that once I heard the truth behind this world from Gabriel in Nerima, I would just settle down to a normal, boring life in Japan?"

"No. I assumed you would go on a lot of dining excursions."

"*Hmph!*"

"Ow!"

Suzuno inadvertently blurted out exactly what she'd seen from Emeralda during her stay last winter. It was greeted by a swift chop to the crown of her head.

"Y-you did not have to hit me over it!"

"*Hah! Hah!*"

"O-ow! Stop! Not full force!"

"What kind of bad, bad girl bad-mouths other people's eating habits without *firmly* guarding themselves?!"

The catfight continued for a while longer, Emeralda constantly on the attack and Suzuno desperately resisting.

"*Huff…! Huff…!*"

"Hee-hee-hee-hee-heee…"

The pointless bout between two of the strongest people on the planet dragged on. The nearby knights and Church officials silently kept a prudent distance, not knowing what was going on and not wanting to be caught up in it.

After about three minutes' worth of karate chopping, Emeralda brushed away the sweaty hair stuck to her forehead and asked the panting Suzuno a question.

"*Haah, haah*, Bell… Have you ever heard the term 'Roche limit'?"

"What does that mean? Is it Japanese? Rush… Roche limit?"

"More of a general Earth term, my dear. At its simplest, it means that, if a large celestial body is tooooo close to a smaaall celestial body, the tidal effects will cause the smaller one to disintegrate, unable to keep its form. The 'limit' is how close they have to be before it happens."

"And what of it?"

"It means that 'they used to be one moon' is no obstacle, you know? They now exist as two separate bodies, so if they come too close, their gravitational pulls might destroy them both. And even if they somehow came together as one, if they're inside the Roche limit with Ente Isla, there will be collisions and destruction; Ente Isla's environment will be destroyyyed…"

"Oh… It will? Since when did you learn that, Emeralda?"

"During my 'diiining excursions.'"

"…I apologize."

Suzuno regretfully took her previous words back.

"But we'll have to believe they took that Roche limit into account and made sure all was well. There's nothing else we can do down here."

"That's truuue, but dear Bell, do you really think we or 'Emiliaaa and her friends' can defeat a god?"

"Where did *that* come from?"

"Breaking up moons, bringing them back together... No matter how powerful Alas Raaamus is, we're talking about people with enough power to do all that loooong before humans arrived in Ente Isla. I can't imagine we can outmatch them, can you? Heavens no!"

"That's uncommonly timid of you."

"Well, I'm not fighting on the front lines this time. It goes against my will to sit back and wait, naturally."

"Yes, I think I know how you feel. I've always been a frontline person myself. All the desk work I have been faced with as of late bores me."

"...But you don't seem too anxious, dear?"

"No, because I trust my friends."

She blurted it out so fast that it made her laugh at herself.

"Could you not say things like that? It gives me goose bummmps!"

Emeralda winced, visibly concerned.

"My apologies, my apologies. But there is no other way to put it. And, well, to tell the truth, should it come to battle, I have a feeling that it will resolve itself quite easily, in the end. With our victory, of course."

"My, how connnfident of you. Might I ask for the reason, dear?"

Suzuno pointed at the couriered message in Emeralda's hand. "That is Exhibit A. You would think the enemy would start attacking well before something like *that* happens."

"Ahh..."

Even Emeralda could grasp what Suzuno meant now.

"We did exercise our due diligence before and after the day of the summit, certainly. But the fact that the heavens did not initiate any sort of attack until the demons launched their entire realm at it... It's strange no matter how you think about it."

"That it iiis."

"And realistically speaking, the red moon must have set off on this journey several days ago. But neither here nor in the demons' realms have we heard word of an attack. Based on that, I feel the heavens have little to no force left to deploy at this point."

"Doesn't that strike you as a little optimistic, dear?"

"Or do you think the heavens are so confident in their firepower that they can fend off an entire celestial body advancing upon them?"

"...Ahhh, yes, that sure doesn't seem possible..."

It was a very simple matter. In the annals of warfare, it was no exaggeration to say that the stupidest move to make was to invite the enemy right into your stronghold for a single, climactic duel. A fight on one's home turf was nothing more than a final struggle to delay the inevitable. The side with the advantage would never invite the enemy to its own territory, allowing them to damage the homeland—there was no point to it. If there was a surefire way to win, it involved fighting someplace where you couldn't be hurt. Thus, if there had been no attack at all since the red moon began to move, it proved that the heavens lacked any long-ranged methods of assault—or the ability to wage war entirely, maybe.

"So...no ultra-long-range weaponry, then. If they had thaaat, they wouldn't have a problem."

"Indeed. If they did, there would be no reason to kill Archbishop Robertio, or to put any 'revelations' in their dreams. No need for these roundabout 'miracles' to drive a crusader force our way. If there is no way to engineer 'divine judgment,' it proves that the heavens' offense does not work at long distances."

Plus, as Gabriel had made no secret of multiple times, the heavens never had that big of a standing army. In fact, after Camael, Suzuno and her friends hadn't seen another new angel come their way.

"But in that case..."

Emeralda returned the message to Suzuno, her face still dubious and anxious as she looked up at the moon, blue as ever in the daytime.

"What are the people up there doing if things have gotten that bad, I wonder?"

"..."

The angels Suzuno had encountered—no matter what supernatural powers they possessed, no matter how wildly they acted—all seemed to have personalities, characters, and motivations that were recognizably "human" in nature. Even Camael, with his extreme overreaction to the name Satan, didn't deviate from the standard for human beings. So really, if you thought about it, there wasn't a single factor that Suzuno's side lost out to against heaven. Maou and Acieth, in fused form, completely overwhelmed three angels. Even with the guy in the space suit, they had been caught by surprise after Maou's and Camio's power was drained, leaving Emi their only fighter—and Acieth dominated that fight solo.

And even now, even if all their demonic force wielders stepped down, they still had Emi, Alas Ramus, Acieth, Laila, and Urushihara ready to do battle. All of them, plus Amane Ohguro. The Earth Sephirah vowed not to interact with Ente Islans, no matter what the circumstances—but based on previous experience, Alas Ramus and Acieth were exceptions.

Meanwhile, based on what Suzuno and the rest knew, the enemy's deployable force consisted of Ignora, Camael, Raguel, and the requisitioned Heavenly Regiment. In the case of the space suit, Laila's impression was that Ignora was inside, not some new, unseen foe. It was more natural to think that Ignora, having run out of pieces to play, was now coming out herself. Plus, though it had been caught by surprise, even the space suit had tasted defeat already.

"There *should* be nothing to worry about…"

But Suzuno had deliberately avoided thinking about it. The angels were human, too. And if they were, and if they hadn't shown any sign of resistance or surrender yet, Ignora had only two plausible choices to make.

"No… Even if that were the case, something would have happened long ago."

Suzuno tried her hardest to banish the thought. Ignora, too, was human. A human with a mission she had to fulfill, no matter how cornered. To the people of Ente Isla and Earth, and to the family members of the Tree of Sephirot, that mission was unacceptable, but it wasn't a problem they could solve via negotiation. Ente Isla, after all, had nothing to do with why their homeland was attacked.

And so…

"Your face is all tense, darling."

"I haven't been able to eat any udon lately. I must be going through withdrawal."

And so she busily banished the possibility that heaven would detonate itself out of despair.

"Ohh?!"

But the moment she chased that final ray of anxiety from the bottom of her mind, the phone nestled within her Church robes began to vibrate, making her voice ratchet up. Running back to the tent, she crouched in a corner and looked at it. It was a call from Maou. With a contented smile, she answered it.

"Hello? Sorry this is so sudden. You okay right now?"

She heard an unexpectedly low, sunken voice, erasing her smile in an instant.

"No problem. What's wrong? What happened? An attack from heaven?"

She jumped straight to the worst thing she could imagine.

"No, not that. Not that, but...an equally important problem we gotta solve."

"Oh..."

It pleased her to hear that nothing bad had happened to the members in the demon realms, but if it was something as serious as an invasion from heaven, she couldn't breathe a sigh of relief yet.

"Emi told me she texted you about most of what happened here..."

"Yes. We're seeing the red moon approach the blue moon here Ente Isla as well. Also, I find this hard to believe since I haven't seen him, but she said a Sephirah that looks exactly like Lucifer showed up?"

"Yeah. He's completely identical...and unlike Alas Ramus and the others, he didn't come with a name. So I dubbed him Copyhara."

"...Wow. Well. Right. Yes."

Suzuno had only a vague response for this, unsure whether to laugh or yell at him.

"Did she tell you about how he came from Chi's house?"

"She did. He appeared from her fragment."

"Yeah, so about Chi…or Chi's house, more like…"

"What? Wait… Did something happen to Chiho or her family?!"

If danger had befallen either of them, that *would* be more urgent to Maou's team than a heavenly invasion.

"Did someone break through our protection around the Sasaki residence, or Sasazuka overall…? Ah, yes, Amane is with you, so… Oh, we should have contacted Sariel… *Damn* it!"

Why had she never considered the possibility?

"The enemy is not in Ente Isla. They are attacking Earth, attacking Japan, attacking Sasazuka! Was Ms. Shiba unable to do anything?! Ahh, now is no time for this. Emeralda and I must go at once…!"

"No, it's not that. It's not that…"

Maou, compared to the panicking Suzuno, was oddly calm. Frigid, even. There was nothing but remorse in his mind.

"In a way, there's already nothing we can do."

"What…was that…?"

"All we can do right now…to…nothing else."

"Devil King! Devil King? Stay with me! I did not hear you. What are we doing? I will do anything that is required! Do not lose heart! Whatever I can do to help you…"

"…Sorry."

"Sorry? For what? At this point…?"

Something devastating had happened—something that had depressed Maou like nothing before. That alone made Suzuno's heart quiver.

"Devil King…"

"So we need to go and clean up the mess right now. I'm gonna get Emi and Urushihara to join me on the way to Sasazuka. I'm also gonna call Ashiya in from the East, but can you come to Sasazuka as soon as you can, too?"

"Yes… Yes, I understand. Just calm down… Ah, no, I also need to take a step back, but please, explain in detail what is going on. I must know what to prepare for."

"Ah, yeah. Okay. You may wanna sit down for this, Suzuno, but…"

She strained to hear the dejected voice, speaking slowly in fits and starts.

"...........What?"

The words that flew into her ear were, in a wholly different way from before, completely beyond what she had imagined.

".........*Ughh*...... Ah, no, um, that is true... Devil King, why did you put it like *that*...?"

The more she heard, the closer Suzuno came to throwing in the towel on the whole thing.

"Yes... Right... Ahh, all right, all right. So? ...Yes, yes, I understand this is very important. Ah, and it is *meant* for that, certainly... Well, no, not 'meant' per se, but yes, I do have it. All neat and ready. Anything else? No? All right... Right. I will wait for you to contact me, then. Okay. Farewell."

At the end of it, Suzuno's rear end was on the floor of the tent. She had been bowled over.

"...Ughhh."

She looked at her closed flip phone, scowling at it.

"Do not *dare* threaten me!"

"What is it, dear?"

"Wahh?!" Emeralda suddenly came into sight, surprising her anew. Suzuno shot up to her feet.

"E-E-E-Eme..."

"You had quite the *ominous* conversation going, so I cleared out the folks by the entrance, all righty?"

"Oh. Right. Thank you. Yes, I should have been more careful. Thank you for being considerate."

"It's fiiine, but is there a problem with the Devil King, by chance?"

"Yes, a problem, or... Well, yes, an issue, but not exactly a big one. *Serious*, but perhaps in a different sort of nuance."

"You're not making much sense, but it's not bad news? But..." Emeralda grinned a bit as she glared with her eyes—a neat trick to pull off. "You were all *impassioned*, going on desperately, like, 'Ohhh, whatever I can do to help you'..."

"Aghh!"

Suzuno attempted to throw her phone at Emeralda. Instead, she bobbled it. It fell helplessly to the ground.

"You knowww, I have recently been flustered by the strange mysteries of human relationships..."

"Y-yes?"

"And I hardly want to aaask this, but *you* haven't fallen victim to the Devil Kiiing as well, have you?"   ·

"No, no, no, no, no, no, no, no, no, no, no, no!! Such nonsense!!"

"Will you knock that off, please?"

Now she was no longer smiling. Suzuno couldn't tell if she saw through the lie.

"Sooo? Did something happen with Chiho? Will you be back in Sasazuka soon?"

"Ah, um, yes! I must return once I hear from the Devil King again."

"And this can't wait until everything else is over, dear? Aren't you a bit pressed for *time* at the moment?"

"No, it definitely must be addressed right this minute. If any of us lose our lives during the assault on heaven, it will be too late after that."

"Oh, *myyy*, rather serious all of a sudden, no?"

"I *am* serious. This could not be more serious. It could not, but... yes."

Suzuno sighed, head buried in her lap.

"It can only be done *now*, is all I can say, yes."

*

The classic main events of astronomy—solar eclipses, lunar eclipses, meteor showers—are often observable only under certain weather or geographical conditions. But if you have enough will and a decent method of transportation, it's not hard to see whichever you want. That's what Maou and Ashiya were doing right now—sitting atop the roof tiles of Heavensky Castle in Efzahan, over on the Eastern Island, taking in the sights up above.

It was far too distant to see with the naked eye yet, but as Ashiya put it, Efzahan's astrological observers were already in a panic over how the positions of the moons had changed.

"So what do you think's gonna happen?"

"About what?"

"The demon realms are red, and heaven's blue, right?"

Ashiya looked up at the corner of the sky Maou pointed at, toward two particularly bright specks of red and blue. He used his own finger to circle the blue point of light.

"I think it will be far more than a matter of 'red and blue make purple,' my liege. There might be some more purple light in the night sky, but I am not sure the naked eye could detect it... But either way, the color will be little different from how it is now."

"Yeah? Well, that's boring."

"That is the prediction, at least. Depending on the state of the atmosphere, it may not look red *or* blue at all afterward. That, and something called a Roche limit. The angels of the ancient past may have had the technology to move an entire moon, but considering they failed to save their home planet, it's unlikely they were able to cancel out the Roche limit. I doubt we are going to see a single celestial body, when it's all said and done."

"No? What's that Roche limit anyway?"

"It is the minimum range that two objects with mass in space can approach each other without one being torn apart by the gravitational pull."

"Whoa. Where'd you learn about stuff like that?"

"I read about such research in the library once. Although the red and blue moons will come close to each other, they are unlikely to merge into a whole. If they *do*, in fact, it would wreak havoc on this world."

"Ughh... So we're not gonna have a giant purple moon, then?"

Maou looked up at the night sky.

"No, my liege, but things will look different indeed. The minimum and maximum orbital distances from the planet will have to change, in order to reduce the effects on the tides, and thanks to that, they will look fairly different in size from before. Have you ever heard terms like 'supermoon' or 'strawberry moon'?"

"Yeah, they mention those on TV sometimes. But it's, like, I remember stuff like that when I leave for work but forget about 'em by the time I'm off duty. Then I recall it late at night, and I'm not gonna bother going out again to see it."

Maou shrugged, took a flip phone from his pocket, and looked at the calendar.

"So we'll just barely have enough time?"

"I cannot offer guarantees, my liege, but assuming the two moons do not come together, I think we should delay our plans until we are sure they will not come any closer to each other."

Ashiya nodded to himself, looking at his own smartphone.

"I still can't get used to the sight of you using that."

"Oh, I've rather mastered it by now." He flicked around on the screen, bringing up his schedule app. "Alas Ramus came to Villa Rosa in July of last year, in the middle of Tokyo's Obon holiday. It would have been ideal if we'd assaulted heaven before that day, but apart from Acieth and Erone, we all have adult responsibilities, so..."

This whole assault on heaven had gotten its real start because Maou had wanted to give the greatest present ever to Alas Ramus, his beloved daughter. Her birthday was the deadline for this endeavor, but...

"Based on my ballpark calculations, unless we delay our invasion of the heavens by at least a month and a half, launching Devil's Castle and landing it on heaven will both come with some measure of danger."

It was already mid-June. A delay like that would push the mission toward the end of July.

"If we give 'em *that* much time, won't they try to hatch something on us?"

"By this point, that possibility is rather low. We have made a rather bold move, but ever since they tricked the Archbishops before the Crusade began, the heavens have done nothing. I reasoned they may attempt some form of sabotage, but we've heard nothing from any of

the summit participants. I believe the enemy faces personnel short-
ages even worse than what I surmised from Gabriel."

"Yeah, sounds right..."

"And however poor the enemy's detection skills are, even they
must know Devil's Castle was launched toward the demon realms.
And yet, still nothing. I put all of this data together to analyze
every angle I could think of, but I sincerely doubt refusing to act
against us offers any strategic advantage. Essentially, I have concluded that our enemy has no option left but to meet us on their
home territory."

Maou seemed convinced but still attempted to counter: "Do you
think they're waiting with some kind of all-powerful force that
could wipe us out if we all struck at once? Maybe using some other
Sephirah children or whatever to build a massive arsenal? Or a
weapon only heaven can use?"

"I cannot completely disavow that hypothesis, but the probability
is low enough to safely ignore, I believe. Based on their previous
movements, whenever the heavens reached out to Ente Isla, they
have preferred sowing confusion indirectly over staging a direct
attack on mankind. They use little in the way of real force at all, and
it is hard to believe they will begin to just because they are being
cornered."

In the past, they tried having Olba eliminate Emi. They tried
seizing Emi's holy sword. They tried stealing Alas Ramus and her
Yesod fragment. They tried having Ashiya and Emi stage a second
demons-versus-humans war. They messed with the Archbishops'
dreams in order to trigger a Crusade...

"...Yeah. It's all petty like that."

"Right?"

The heavens had tried to create chaos in Ente Isla many times
before. The conspiracy in Efzahan caused heavy damage there, and
in the demon realms—although most of the casualties were caused in
battle by the two sides being tricked into warfare. As far as Maou's
team could tell, the only person to lose his life as a result of a direct
attack from heaven was Robertio Igua Valentia, de facto leader of

the Six Archbishops...and even there, they had no incriminating evidence.

"But enough about that," Ashiya said, suddenly brimming with enmity. "What scares me far more is Emilia, demanding you pay child support in the midst of all this."

"*You're* pretty petty, too."

"If our enemy causes trouble, we may solve it by defeating them. The only way you can solve money problems is to get more money."

"Yeah. And no matter what I tell her, all I'm doing is delaying those payments."

"Reality can be so cruel," Ashiya all but cried out.

"Well, apart from *that* cruel reality, there are some crimes I need to account for, too."

"Mmm..." Now Ashiya looked distressed. "That *is* a thorny issue. Not one caused by the enemy, nor one driven by money. Or perhaps wealth was involved at first, but... What do you think?"

"Not power, not money... Something from the heart, maybe? Trust? That kind of issue. So while I have the chance, I want to settle one more past sin as well."

"Another past sin? ...Ah."

"Yeah. Everybody's coming back to Sasazuka for their own reasons...but for *this* problem, it's just you and me."

Maou looked up at the blue moon.

"We've learned the hard way how tough it is to make money. And what do you think'll happen if we wind up dying in battle?"

"Please, do not speak of such horrid things, my liege."

"Look, it's a possibility, isn't it? And I don't wanna die without apologizing for stealing."

"There is no reason for you to have feelings of guilt toward *any* human..."

The sentence sounded more contrived than anything.

"...is what I would have said a year ago, I imagine."

"Well, right now, I'm a ball of guilt. Especially considering the victim. I mean, really, I just wanna apologize for that, you know?

It doesn't need to be this big 'atonement' thing, but I still feel bad about it."

"That is still much more sincere of you as a person than saying nothing."

"Yeah. As a person."

At that, the two demons exchanged a smile.

"And if I have your approval, that's a shot of confidence for me."

"I am honored, my liege."

"So think of Emi's demands as common sense, too, all right? It'd be supporting Alas Ramus, after all."

"If it was anyone but Emilia demanding it, I wouldn't be so stubborn like this! It is her presence that irks me!"

"Yeah. We both really *have* become human in that way, huh?"

"That is an even *more* horrid thing to say!"

"Hey, what're you planning to do about Rika Suzuki, in the end?"

"Huh?! Why bring *that* up all of a sudden?!"

"Whoa. Rare to see you so flustered like that."

"Of course I am. I never expected *that* topic for a single moment!"

"Tell me. Maybe I'll learn something from it."

"There is nothing at *all* you can learn from that, my liege! Besides, I believe I have fully turned her down by now! And yet, *look* at her!"

"You don't have to shout about it. The Azure Scarves are gonna give you looks."

This was the seat of government for the entire Eastern Island, built over generations by its emperors. Nobody ever climbed up to the roof of Heavensky Castle unless they were there on official roofing-related business. And now two grown demons were lying on it…talking about *this*.

"Ms. Suzuki is merely interpreting things to suit her aims. I have no intention of 'doing' anything about her."

"Yeah. You're probably right."

"What about you, my liege?"

"…Me, huh?"

"Because *that* is a topic you surely don't want to die leaving unaddressed?"

"No, you're right, but..."

"One even less solvable with power or money than your other crimes. *That*, indeed, is a problem of the heart."

"I don't need *you* telling me."

"You're the one who guided me to the question."

He was right. Maou regretted stirring that hornet's nest. But maybe that's what he was aiming for in the first place. Ashiya was correct—if he didn't provide an answer, it'd show a severe lack of faith and sincerity. The moon was already on the move. Things were rapidly coming to an end. He didn't have much time left.

"But do we really need to settle *everything* at this point? That's not too sincere, is it?"

"I would advise you to stop trying to run away, my liege."

The reply came like a whip. Maou had no leg to stand on.

"Ugh... Hey, Ashiya?"

"Yes?"

"It was really stupid of us, wasn't it? Trying to conquer the world when we let these human women have their way with us."

"It is common in history to see absolute rulers act subservient to their family, friends, or benefactors. Those are two different matters."

"If I can't see them as separate, I guess I'm sunk, huh?"

"Please, Your Demonic Highness, pull yourself together! You are a functioning member of society!"

"This is *such* a bummer..."

"My liege! Please, remember your dignity as you led all of us as Devil King!"

"Now I wonder how I even acted like that. It's crazy what your environment can do to you."

"Lord Camio would cry if he heard that."

Maou, hands covering his face, was looking smaller and smaller. Ashiya smiled and patted him on the back.

"It is all right. Apart from the question of Ms. Sasaki, Sadao Maou has earned himself more than enough social standing. There are many who appreciate you. And I am sure...everyone will understand."

"...Yeah," Maou replied, breathing through his hands. "Now I'm sure of it. If you weren't around, the Devil King's Army would've been annihilated long ago."

"You praise me far too much, my liege."

Emi, Suzuno, and Chiho... Everything that everyone besides he and Ashiya had always thought and said—now, for the first time, Maou understood it.

"We really *do* need to settle all this."

"We do."

"Compared to that, waging a war against heaven seems easy."

"It always was, I imagine. Our primary mission was to give Alas Ramus a birthday present."

"Weren't we talking about a Christmas gift at first?"

"Now that you mention it, we were. It's already been half a year, hasn't it? Time flies like an arrow."

"Hell, put it *that* way, and it feels like just yesterday that I was fighting your Iron Scorpions."

Everything was in the past now.

"I will need to make several trips between Ea Quartus and Efzahan. I will be on hand for a conference to discuss rebuilding the eastern Central Continent with the Federated Order and Eight Scarves, and after that, I will arrange it so I can meet with Bell to adjust plans. Are you going home now, my liege?"

"Yeah, I got work tomorrow. I'm heading straight home from here."

"Then, Your Demonic Highness, may I ask you for a favor?"

Ashiya looked at Maou with earnest eyes as he stood up.

"If you could, please take our suits and dress shirts to the dry cleaner as soon as you can. If you can prepare a formal outfit for Urushihara as well, I would appreciate it."

Ashiya normally washed and ironed their dress shirts at home. He rarely let Maou use the dry cleaner, even during his managerial training—but he immediately opted for it here. That was how serious things were.

"All right. I'll send the request once I'm sure when everyone will be there."

"Very well. Then for now, let us have Lord Camio watch over the enemy instead of worrying about it ourselves…and let us decide on a date to settle matters from our lives in Japan, and a date for the final battle."

Maou and Ashiya both recalled that fateful day when they were tossed into Tokyo in the middle of the night. That, and the person who first took them in.

"No matter what, before we attack heaven… I need to apologize to Chi at her house for continually getting her involved in this… and *we* need to apologize for stealing ten thousand yen from her dad right after we fell to Japan!"

◊

It was half past seven in the morning, just a few minutes since opening time, when the first customer entered the door, sending the bell above it chiming. Maou and Kaori looked up, only to find a familiar face. Kaori, who happened to be wiping down a window by the door, went over to their guest first.

"Hello and good morning! You're the first customer today."

"Hey, Shoji. Glad to hear that. I got my members card… Oh?"

They raised an eyebrow after spotting Maou at the register.

"Hey there, regular. The manager's coming in this afternoon. I'm the main guy this morning."

Maou, who was crouched behind the counter flipping through order forms, stood up and lightly waved at Sariel, dressed in a loose polo shirt and chinos.

"Oh, is she? Well, thanks in advance."

"Sure. It's hot out. C'mon in. And good morning to you, too, Yuzuki. Hot, isn't it?"

Maou waved at the small girl cradled in Sariel's right arm as well.

"…Yeh."

The two-year-old who Maou called Yuzuki lightly nodded.

"You've sure grown since last I saw you."

"Oh, has she? I don't think she's changed *that* much in the two months since I brought her in."

"Maybe not to the parent, but to someone who only sees her once a month, there's a *huge* difference, you know? Anyway, you want the breakfast special?"

"Please. And Yuzuki will have a child-sized bowl of udon. She's been eating nothing but noodles lately."

"All right. You can wait upstairs." He motioned toward the staircase deeper in the café. "Hey, Shoji, Mr. Kisaki's having the usual."

"Sure thing! Here, Mr. Kisaki, take this receipt. I'll come up to see you later, okay, Yuzuki?"

With that, Kaori typed "Mitsuki Kisaki"—the first customer of the day—into her tablet. The first floor of Yesodd's Family Café was the main space, but upstairs, they had a special by-the-hour safe section meant for parents going out with young children—and that section just had its first visitor of the morning.

Bringing the morning breakfast special upstairs on a tray, Maou saw Mitsuki Kisaki, better known to him as Sariel, sitting limply on a floor cushion. On a nearby pastel-colored play mat, baby Yuzuki was playing with her favorite blocks.

"You worn out? You got rings around your eyes."

"Yeah, last night was, well, she cried a lot."

"Not even an archangel can beat a crying baby, huh? I made your iced coffee on the strong side for you."

"Thanks. Hey, Yuzuki, time to eat! C'mon, let's eat together."

At Sariel's bidding, she obediently toddled over and sat on a pillow next to Sariel.

"She doesn't need a high chair?"

"She doesn't like them. She kneels on these pillows when she's eating at home, too."

"Precocious kid. What do you want to drink, Yuzuki? No juice for now, right?"

"Barley tea is fine. What do you say, Yuzuki?"

"...'nk you."

Sariel shrugged at the soft whisper of a voice, but his daughter, unfazed, began to eat.

"Well, enjoy," Maou said, watching Yuzuki begin with the mini-tomato as he went downstairs. Kaori met him halfway.

"She showed up downstairs, so I came up to—*ooh*, Yuzuki, you're a good eater, huh? That's great."

"Just tomatoes and udon," Sariel replied. "That's all she eats lately. It's driving me up the wall."

"Oh, right, Mr. Kisaki! I have some news."

"What is it?"

"You're on the clock, Shoji."

"Aw, but I can't keep this to myself! Did you hear about Chiho Sasaki?"

The moment the name came up, Maou shivered a little. It didn't escape Sariel's attention.

"Of course. What's up with her? I heard she went on a little study-abroad trip a while ago."

"That's right! She had a homestay in the UK for three months, and she's coming home from it today...but *despite* that, the president here made other plans instead of picking her up at the airport."

"Oh? Well, *that's* hard to excuse."

"Right? Totally!"

Sariel, playing along with Kaori, looked up at Maou.

"When *my* wife comes off work, I *always* drive over to pick her up, you know."

"Aww, how nice! You could learn from that, president!"

"Well, I get to be a stay-at-home dad, thanks to her job. It's nothing to praise me for."

"Enough, Shoji. Get back to work. Go check the self-serve drink machine for me! And don't encourage my staff to goof off, either, okay?"

"Okaaay."

Once he had chased off his overbearing employee, Maou turned to Sariel.

"But you pick her up *every* day? Isn't she a manager in the customer support department now? That *has* to keep her late sometimes. What do you do with Yuzuki?"

"I don't remember telling you about her promotion…but yeah, if it's past ten, I don't bother. On days when she gets off on time, I brush my kid's teeth so she can doze off in the car while I go pick her up. It's just hard otherwise. If she can't see her mom before she goes to sleep, the crying gets three times worse at night."

Then Sariel hushed his voice, ensuring Kaori in the upstairs staff kitchen couldn't overhear him.

"I tell you, I really respect Emilia now. I'm shocked she could handle that baby by herself back then—"

"I know," Maou interjected. "I had a small army of people lecturing me about it."

"But Chiho's studying English abroad, huh? I've heard people talk about doing it, but I never knew anyone who went through with it."

"Yeah, her university arranged with a sister school so she could do it during summer break."

"I see. I only heard about it from my wife, but she said it was one month, not three."

"One month in London."

"Oh! Well, that must've been a valuable experience. So where did she go the other two months?"

"You *know* that, don't you?" Maou winced, still keeping a careful eye out for Kaori. "Well, she didn't give me any details, either. She'd dodge the question whenever I asked."

"So she's completely lost her trust in you, huh? But I guess Chiho's a junior in college now, isn't she? Once she's back, she'll have to plunge right in to the job search. But not only were you unaware of her return date, you even put other plans first… It won't be long before she abandons you entirely, I think."

"Will you stop that? Like *you* know anything."

"Hmm? But hang on. Wasn't Shoji high school classmates with Chiho? Has she found a job yet?"

"I took a gap year, sorry! I'm still a sophomore, so I'm workin' here instead!"

"Oh, pardon me."

Kaori blurted it out as she passed by on her business, not looking none too concerned about it.

"We don't have any extra toilet paper left, prez."

"We don't? Okay, can you buy some at the drugstore across the street? You can use our petty cash."

"All right. The usual brand? I'll be right back."

Kaori took up the wallet they used for incidental purchases like this then lightly strolled out of the café. After she had disappeared into the summer sunlight, Sariel let out a small sigh.

"Three years... Well, *five*, from the very beginning. Compared to the rest of my life, it went by faster than the blink of an eye, but the days were certainly packed, I think."

"I firmly agree. I didn't even imagine any of this would happen at first...and you actually marrying Ms. Kisaki was completely beyond the realm of possibility. The news flipped out the whole Sasahata Shopping Arcade."

It was three years ago when the archangel Sariel and Mayumi Kisaki, Maou's former boss and benefactor, made the shocking announcement. Those who knew Sariel's true nature, and the relationship "Mitsuki Sarue" had maintained with Kisaki originally, all treated it as some kind of tasteless joke. Once they had learned it was the truth, though, they all felt a shotput tossed by an Olympic athlete into the air in the middle of an earthquake. This was *Kisaki* they were talking about, after all, alongside Sariel, aka Mitsuki Sarue. Anyone who knew them both didn't need any further information to see why this was such an impossible couple.

But now they had a child, Yuzuki Kisaki—and as Sariel said, he'd quit his job at Sentucky Fried Chicken to raise her. Mayumi Kisaki, meanwhile, was still working her way up the ranks at Japan MgRonald Holdings, demonstrating her shrewdness on a daily basis.

(When asked why she married Sariel, Mayumi always had the same answer: "For *my* life, he's the most convenient partner in the universe.")

"Hee-hee-hee... Honestly, I still feel like I'm living in a dream right now. Every night, when I see my wife and child before going to bed, I say a little prayer, begging to not wake up from this dream. Even though there's no 'God' in my life at all."

I can't believe this happened. He had thought it, stated it, and shared it with others more times than he could count. It was a complete shift from his life up to that point, and he felt like he *had* to put it into words, lest it proved to be an illusion all along.

"Yeah... And if anything, I value the time I spent here *far* more than you do. I wouldn't trade my time in Japan for anything."

"But you didn't know that Chiho Sasaki was coming home today."

"Look," Maou spat out, "customer or not, you gotta watch your mouth, all right?"

Sariel gave this a smile as he bit into his breakfast sandwich. "Well, it's what you get for holding back at the end. I wish I could give you even a tiny slice of the happiness I'm feeling right now."

"No thanks. I got enough."

"So what's this appointment that's so much more important than Chiho?"

"Man, lay off. I don't wanna say. If I do, Shoji's gonna start yellin' at me again."

Maou almost seemed to despair at the thought.

"But it's a work meeting. And along with *that*, my ol' ball and chain's coming back with our daughter. They made a couple stops on the way and have a lot of baggage to carry, so I agreed to meet them at Tokyo Station."

"Ball and chain? That's a pretty old-fashioned term. I don't think young people these days would understand it." Sariel grinned as he pictured the "ball and chain" in question. "If you're making metaphors, why don't you call her your 'gal Friday' or something?"

"Shut *up.*"

Maou let the joke slide.

"As your friend, let me give you some advice: Watch your step if you're out on a moonless night. If you get stabbed and this place shuts down, that'd be a crisis for the entire Kisaki family. We'll lose our favorite rest stop."

"You're not my friend. And I ride a scooter to and from work, so I'm fine. Anyway, I got work downstairs, so enjoy your breakfast."

Kaori had just brought up her bag from the drugstore, so Maou passed by her on the staircase.

"Eesh. Don't even *remind* me of moonless nights."

The mumbling was overheard by Yoshiya Kohmura, the other part-timer at this café; he had already changed into his uniform and had just taken an order from another customer downstairs.

"Good morning, president. Did you say something?"

As he began grinding the coffee beans prepared in advance for him, Maou groggily recalled the events of three years ago. The end of the "assault on heaven," as he and his friends called it. The conclusive event that eventually led him here, right to this moment.

"Oh, good morning, Yoshiya. No, nothing."

Waving the question away, Maou set off to prepare for the lunch hour...

"Prez, we have a special coffee for the customer on bar seat three."

But for now, he had a new order that had come in at some point.

Turning the handle of his coffee mill, Maou found himself rubbing his back with his left hand.

"When I'm fatigued, these old wounds flare up, I think."

After a quick rub or two, he looked into the empty kitchen, then saw Yoshiya, polishing utensils by the customer seating. He gritted his teeth and tensed up a bit.

"If I'm like this in the morning, it's gonna get even worse later. Gotta pull it together."

He continued muttering to himself as he adjusted the speed of his grinding. These were strong, full-bodied beans he got from Guatemala via his usual wholesaler; a coarse grind resulted in a smooth, perfume-like fragrance...or so he thought.

"All right, today's special coffee... Huh?"

As he brought the expertly made cup back to the bar, he found:

"Ooh, I'm in luck. You're running breakfast today?"

A person who'd just showed up in conversation earlier was seated there, her eyes as sharp as ever.

"Whoa, don't surprise me like that! Hey, Yoshiya!"

Surprised, Maou turned toward Yoshiya. He sheepishly waved back.

"I told Kohmura to keep quiet about it. I didn't want you all weirdly nervous over me."

"Well, *this* startled me a lot more. Your husband and child are upstairs, you know."

"I know. That's why I'm here."

After she had her child, Mayumi Kisaki cut short her long hair, which had been the envy of many. Her old shoulder bag by her side, though, was still overstuffed with a backbreaking amount of weight.

"But what are you doing here at a time like this? That's rare. Are you reporting to work late?"

"Nah, well, I had this big job fall apart on me in the early morning. It was so sudden that I didn't have anything else to allocate the time to, so I just said 'screw it' and took the day off from the department."

That was certainly unusual to hear from her. She took a sip of her coffee.

"This is good. Guatemala shade-dried?"

"Would you mind not holding taste tests in here, please?"

"What? Just spying on my rivals."

"I have a feeling MgRonald would blow us away."

Kisaki gave him a mischievous grin as she looked around the café. "Hee-hee-hee! Every time I come here, I try to find holes I can bring up with you, but you patch them up whenever I come back. It's boring."

"Well, a good restaurant grows with its clientele."

"You're able to say that now, huh?" Kisaki eagerly eyed Maou. "Not only did you not wait for me to leave; you even leaped way ahead of me. Now I missed my chance to get out, and I wound up promoted again. What're you gonna do about that, huh?"

"Congratulations on becoming a section director. I heard from one of your former staff."

"Ugh. I can't believe someone at my old haunt is just giving out internal company information."

"Well, don't yell at him too much. Want me to call him down?"

"They only just came in, didn't they? I'll head up once Yuzuki is done eating. If I'm next to her, she'll start playing games and begging for attention, and she'll lose focus. I hate to admit it, but Mitsuki's a lot better at that kind of thing than I am."

When they heard about Kisaki and Sariel's marriage, the most preposterous pairing in all of creation, most people irresponsibly assumed it'd end in a quick divorce. But her old friends Yuki Mizushima and Himeko Tanaka, whom Maou met at the small but tasteful wedding reception he'd attended, both predicted that they would be just fine, as long as Sariel didn't fall too far out of line.

"But how are things going with yours?"

"She's growing up just fine. Getting a little sassy lately."

"Oh?"

Kisaki, freely tossing the subject Maou's way, smiled at the response.

"Ah, and isn't Chi returning from her study abroad today? You going to go meet her?"

"Ms. Kisaki..."

"Hmm?"

"If my own former 'staff' keeps leaking stuff about the army to you, make him cry for me, all right? Why does *he* know, of all people...?"

"He'll be joining me on the next group training session, actually. I'm looking forward to it."

With a smile, Kisaki finished her coffee and stood.

"Well, I've got the day off. Time to go enjoy a little family time... Can you combine my tab with the one upstairs, President Maou?"

Maou, called that by his former boss, courteously bowed his head.

"Right away."

In a few more moments, he heard "Yuuuzuuukiiii! Mommy got

off from work today! Are you done with breakfast? Let's go out with Daddy somewhere!!" shrilly shouted from upstairs. He shared a smirk with Yoshiya over it.

"Good morning!"

The manager of the Eifukucho location of Yesodd's Family Café stepped in, despite being scheduled to replace Maou in the afternoon.

"Oh, good morning, manager." Yoshiya looked at the clock. "You're in early."

Maou, meanwhile, shot her a look of surprise. "You're super early, Aki. Was your mom all right?"

"Yeah. Thanks for covering me this morning, president! It wound up being no big deal..."

Akiko Ohki—a former frontline coworker of Maou's at the Hatagaya Station MgRonald and current manager of this Yesodd's location—cheerfully reported to her job like always. Maou had been pitching in this morning because Akiko's mother had a medical emergency that required a trip to the hospital for surgery, but...

"Well, I heard she was being admitted at first, so I was super freaking out, but it wound up just being appendicitis. She's absolutely fine now—fine enough that she kicked me out so I don't cause trouble for my boss."

"Really? I mean, I don't think appendicitis is anything to joke about..."

"Yeah, but they wrapped up the operation last night, and the doctor said she'd be good to leave in two or three days. But you have an important business meeting today, don't you, president? As hot as it is, I figured you'd wanna go home to change first, so I came in early."

"Oh. Well, I'm glad your mom won't be there for long. But I thought you might not be able to come in, so I asked for some help early this morning. We were just about out of to-go ice coffee bottles, too."

"Really? Did I not order any?"

"There was nothing in the ledger system."

"Oof... I'm sorry about that. I thought I did...but that was a close one. It's a hot one outside, so we're gonna sell a bunch."

"It's fine! You were worried about your mom. Just double-check next time, okay? Also..." Maou grinned. "You can use the company wallet to treat Kawacchi to something when he makes the delivery."

"Aww... He's *so* gonna whine about it again!"

"We got customers, manager, so try not to carry on too much about silly stuff. Go get changed, okay?"

"Ugh, yeah, if Yoshi gets on me, I'm done for..."

"Oh, and Ms. Kisaki's upstairs with her family."

"Eep!"

Akiko let out a half-shriek as she gritted her teeth at Maou.

"P-president... I promise I'll work hard for you, so *please* don't tell Ms. Kisaki about my ordering mess-up..."

"Why do you think Ms. Kisaki has firing power around here? Just go get changed!"

"All right."

Akiko briskly sailed to the staff room, dodging Kisaki's aura pouring from above. Her occasional bouts of airheadedness hadn't disappeared much over the past three years.

Back when he was figuring out how The Maou Company, Ltd., and Yesodd's Family Café would work businesswise, he tapped his old coworker Takefumi Kawata as an external observer. Much as Kisaki was agonizing over how she'd go about starting an independent operation, Maou pondered over how different business types would attract customers in the saturated, fiercely competitive café industry. At the end of it, he decided to try for a place that prioritized parents with young children first—and it was Kawata, who had studied regional business management, who guided him toward that idea.

Kawata himself had taken over his family's restaurant after graduating from college, but his parents were still in good working health, so as a model for expanding his family business in the future, he agreed to help launch The Maou Company on a paid basis. He was still in this "observer" role, but sometimes he'd pitch in when they needed to plug a gap, like today.

As for Akiko, despite all her voiced concerns about finding a career during her time at MgRonald, the shaky employment nightmare came true for her when she began her job search. Her inbox was flooded with rejections, plunging her into a pit of despair. Between that and requiring an extra year to get into college, her parents were really putting the screws to her, apparently—so when she heard Maou was launching his own firm, she all but tearfully begged him for a job. He knew her Kisaki-trained frontline skills were worth relying on, and between that and a certain someone's *very* authoritative recommendation, Maou brought her on. Judging by how the Kisaki family were regulars at the café she managed, there was no doubting Akiko's skills in the post.

"Okay, if we're all good here, I guess I'll head out. Yoshiya, hold down the fort for me."

"Yep. Have a good one, president. Oh, and also..."

Just as Maou prepared to leave, Yoshiya spoke up in a bright, unreserved voice.

"Say hello to Sasaki for me, too! She's coming back from the UK today, isn't she?"

"...You too?"

Please, guys, Maou sincerely thought to himself, *stop worrying about other stuff and just focus on your work!*

✳

In the midday sun, with the heat seeming to work its way into his nostrils with each breath, Maou puttered down the side of the Koshu-Kaido road. He felt like a little more speed would help him cool down, but the old habits from his MgRonald delivery days made it impossible for him to go above 20 miles an hour. Speed limits on the street, after all, didn't always match up with the law—but ever since he'd obtained the MgScooto, he swore never to break 20 mph on his way to and from work.

The Maou Company was a small business through and through, but he never fudged his staff's work hours or other regulations, the way that was all too common with outfits its size. The way he ran the company, if a labor inspector came in five minutes from now for an inspection, he wanted to be sure they would uncover nothing untoward.

Unfortunately, this also meant that the company wasn't as flexible as it could have been. So, despite the improbability of it all, Maou didn't want to suffer an illness, injury, or any other setback. That, and if he wanted to retain this healthy organizational structure as the company grew, he had to exhibit model behavior as its first leader, even in places where people weren't looking.

Fortunately, the Koshu-Kaido road was a wide one packed with stores and office buildings, along with parked cars doing this or that business. Even going 20 mph didn't mean other cars were buzzing by him on the passing lanes.

"Man. The Devil King would *never* accept that."

Noticing a truck parked by the curb—no parking space allotted, no cones put in place as the crew unloaded the back—Maou marveled at how the world carried on with its own business, regardless of what people thought was okay. But keep working that way, and you never knew when it'd come crashing down. Maou constantly reminded himself that he was a business manager, whether he liked it or not.

Making a right at the intersection in front of Sasazuka Station, he rode under the railroad overpass. By the time he'd passed the Bosatsu Street Shopping Center, he could faintly see his apartment building in the distance.

Villa Rosa Sasazuka had changed a lot as well. Every apartment was now equipped with an air conditioner—and, shockingly, the second-floor rooms now had expanded windows overlooking the backyard, opening up to small but functional balconies. There wasn't room for private baths in each apartment, but compared to when he first started living here, the conditions had grown unimaginably better. By now, he couldn't even remember how three men could live in one of these tiny rooms without any air conditioning. That, and despite the sea change in environment, the rent was still unchanged, at 45,000 yen.

"But then, Emi's apartment is still 50,000, so I can't be *that* thankful..."

Turning off the engine, Maou pushed the MgScooto to its parking space, removed his sweaty helmet, and let out a shallow sigh.

"Phew... Wish I could stop by the public bath before I leave."

The local Sasanoyu public bathhouse used to be open early in the afternoon, but due to the proprietor getting on in age, it had recently moved its opening time back to three PM. His plans for today forbade him from lolling around his apartment that long just to take a bath.

"Well, I'll change, anyway," he said, making excuses to no one in particular as he carried his helmet up the stairs.

"Oh?"

Just as he opened the door to his apartment, he spotted something in the corridor that hadn't been there when he'd left. It was a small used dish and cup, placed atop a plastic tray—the remains of somebody's meal.

"...Well, I'm glad she's eating...but this is from yesterday and there's still some left. In this heat, you keep leaving it out like this, it's gonna attract flies. Eesh."

He picked up the tray as he grumbled, taking it inside Room 201. The air conditioner timer worked just like he set it, so the sweet nectar of cool air permeated the space.

Feeling the sweat evaporate from his skin, Maou opened the fridge and scanned its contents.

"I got onions and sausage left. Maybe I could make some kinda spaghetti..."

Working fast before the cool air could make him sluggish, he put the dirty dishes in the sink and washed them alongside the stuff he'd used for breakfast. Once everything was in the rinsing rack, he took a bag of precooked pasta from the fridge, along with some loose veggies, cut-up sausage, ketchup, and black soy sauce. A quick trip to the pot later, and he had a nice pasta meal plated out. There were more veggies than he'd thought at first, making for a hearty dish.

Letting it cool down a bit under the ventilation fan before delivering it, Maou changed out of his sweaty clothes and tossed them into the laundry basket. Then, grabbing a midsize tote bag, he put his wallet, tissues, a handkerchief, a small towel for wiping sweat off, and an antibacterial sheet for his hands inside. After that, he wrapped the plate of spaghetti he'd made and ferried it to the door of Room 202.

"Hey! I might be late tonight, so I put your food at the door. Try to eat your meals in order, okay? Even if you chill them. See you later!"

He knew there wouldn't be a response. With a sigh, he placed the tray on the floor, checked that Room 201 was locked, and closed the door to the corridor.

"There you go."

As he looked through the door's window, he saw a pale, wispy arm reach out from behind the door of Room 202, grab the tray of pasta, and roughly shut the door again.

"What a pain. I *really* wish I could swap places with someone."

Scowling, even though he wasn't all that worked up about it, Maou walked down the stairs then set off for Sasazuka Station on foot. He checked his watch; it was a little past eleven.

"Crap. Maybe I was too slow again. It was twelve twenty, right?"

Checking his phone's messages one more time, he stepped up his pace a bit, not letting the oppressive heat get to him.

THE
DEVIL
ADDRESSES
PAST
SINS

It was a day in mid-July, exactly one month after the red moon of the demon realms had begun to accelerate. The summer was already starting to get harsh, but Maou was sweating for other reasons. His focus narrowed as he faced up to the warm machine in front of him. It spat out a checking account statement. Staring at the cold, hard numbers printed on it, he froze a bit in front of the ATM, unable to move.

For Maou, a self-styled contributing member of society, the numbers printed on the receipt didn't exactly promise a smooth future ahead. But they were the result of a lot of hard work. He couldn't lament that, and there was no reason to.

"Are we really gonna be okay?"

"Yes. I have checked everything carefully, my liege. There is no need for you to worry about finances until we complete our battle."

"You're really sure about that?"

Maou and Ashiya stared closely at the receipt, virtually boring holes into it.

"Yes. Extremely sure. As a rule, all of your utilities are being paid for through your credit card. That includes the water, gas, electricity, phone, internet, and everything else! So once we make it through the day of your card payment, you will see *no* more inappropriate withdrawals from your account!"

"Well, it's not 'inappropriate' if I'm withdrawing from my own account..."

"I... Yes, I know. And Urushihara has mostly been in Ente Isla the past two or three months, so we've had no unexpected online shopping to deal with. I suppose I have come to see all purchases made via credit card as 'inappropriate,' you see..."

"Yeah, sorry we put you through all that trouble. And I guess we'll have more for you shortly..."

"Please, Your Demonic Highness, enough with that nonsense! This is my just punishment, as leader of the Devil King's Army... Or karma, I should say. But still...I am heartbroken, it is true. Right now, of all times...I cannot help but feel that we have been betrayed!"

"Whoa there."

As the two demons lamented to each other in broad daylight, an exasperated Emi brought a hand to her hip.

"You just said something I think I better not ignore."

"What?!"

"*Who* betrayed *whom* here?"

Ashiya raised a fist high into the air then pointed straight at Emi. "Emilia! You were fully aware of the poverty endemic to the Devil King's Army, and yet you choose *this* moment to demand child support from my liege! What *could* I call it other than a betrayal?!"

"Hey, if I could ask you, Alciel—since *when*...did I *ever*...have to consider your stupid army's *budget* in what I do?! You're the top *chef* in Devil's Castle! D'you *know* how much it *costs* to raise a kid these days!"

"Y-you dare say such things at *this* point?! You dare place a child and money on the scales of heaven? You should be *ashamed* of your selfishness!"

"Look, it's a fact that finances are part of a loving family! In fact, I'm surprised you haven't thanked me for not mentioning your king's support obligations even *once* before now!"

"Man, this stereo presentation really brings me back..."

From the side, Maou exhaled at Emi's and Ashiya's arguing.

"It *is* nostalgic, yes. But from the outside, this is such an embarrassing argument to endure…" Suzuno put a hand to her forehead, blushing.

"Well," Urushihara nonchalantly added, "whether you're ashamed of it or not, you'd better pay out what you can right now, huh? Emilia and Ashiya may be going on like that 'n' all, but at least in our *future* plans, all five of us need to act as equals, y'know?"

"Mmm… Yes, that is true…but what has gotten into you lately, Lucifer? You have been acting unusually sensible."

"I've always been sensible with you guys, dude. It's just that you never listen."

"You should know that in this world, *what* you say does not matter as much as *who* is saying it."

"Y'see, this is why humans are so stupid," Urushihara continued. "They make no effort to grasp the *essence* of things, y'know?"

Suzuno rolled her eyes even farther back.

"So in *this* situation, who's gonna speak up first, if it's that important?"

"That'll be me. It's up to me to get the ball rolling." Maou nodded to himself, face more solemn than anyone else's here. "The battle awaiting us is one that none of us are guaranteed to emerge from alive. That's why we have a duty to wrap up everything now."

Maou's words made the bickering Emi and Ashiya silently nod.

"Our battle against heaven has finally reached its climax. The future of Ente Isla and Earth… Well, not just that. The future of Alas Ramus and the other Sephirah as well…and the Sephirah who'll be born in however many planets in the universe from now on… We owe it to all of them. We need to atone for our past sins today."

"…Yes, you're right."

"Indeed."

"Yeah, pretty much."

"Mmm."

Emi, Ashiya, Urushihara, and Suzuno—all four of them meekly accepted Maou's resolution.

"It's not about humanity, or the Devil King's Army. We represent *all* life in Ente Isla, and we need to stand up to our past, or we'll never move on. So please, Emi. I'm barely gonna be scraping by for a while after this, so if you can go easy on the child support thing until after the battle's over..."

"Stop babbling. I told you a hundred times." Emilia—Emi Yusa—grinned a bit. "I know full well what takes priority here. So...you take the lead for us."

"...Thanks."

"Also, just to be sure, *they* understand what kind of business we're visiting them about, right?"

"Of course they do. I explained everything to Chi and her mom in advance. That's why *all* of us are here today. And the timing's right, too. It was around this time of the year when we *really* started getting Chi wrapped up in this."

The words "all of us" made all of them brace themselves a bit more.

"All right. Let's go."

Maou took out his phone and called the number he already had up on the screen. The other side picked up after one ring; he explained that everything was ready, and once that was acknowledged, he hung up. The call didn't last more than about ten seconds.

His resolve renewed, Maou let out a deep breath and spoke to the four people around him.

"Sounds like they're ready, too."

The air grew heavier. But no one said anything. There, at the Sasazuka Station intersection with summer in full swing, the five figures steeled themselves as they began walking toward the 100 Trees Shopping Arcade.

✳

This was a well-trodden street to everyone but Urushihara. It was a quiet part of town, children's laughter and shouting occasionally heard from afar. A classic Sunday afternoon scene like you'd see anywhere in Japan—but the quintet walking down this street was a poor match for it, with how gloomy and downtrodden they looked.

Once they'd reached their destination, Maou stepped up to push the intercom button.

"Ah! Um… I-I'll be right there!"

A familiar voice sounded surprised as it greeted them. The intercom shut off before Maou could reply, and then they heard pattering footsteps up to the door.

"Umm…"

Chiho Sasaki greeted them there, unable to hide her ambivalence.

"Are we a bit early?"

Maou looked down at his watch. They were exactly five minutes ahead of schedule.

"Th-that's okay, but… Wow. I'm surprised you have suits on. Even Urushihara…"

"Yeah," Urushihara bluntly replied as he wriggled around in his brand-new suit. "I know we don't exactly look natural, but this is important, y'know?"

"Politeness demands at least this much," Ashiya said, tense and uncomfortably tugging at his necktie.

"It'd be too off-putting if we arrived in Ente Islan formal wear, right?"

Emi, dressed in formal black business attire, glanced at the rest of her party.

"Yes. That's why we arrived in the Japanese norm instead, as unusual as it may make us look."

Suzuno, for her part, was in a silken kimono of light purple, meant for visiting other families. She bowed lightly.

"Chi… Um, I mean Sasaki, are your parents at home?"

Finally Maou—Satan, King of all Demons in Ente Isla, but who still preferred to go by Sadao Maou around here—looked straight at Chiho Sasaki. To her credit, Chiho didn't turn away, standing tall and nodding at him.

"They are, Maou. They've been waiting for you, actually. Come right in."

"Thanks. Let's go, guys."

"Thank you," Emi said as they all somberly went through the

Sasakis' front door. For her, Maou, and Suzuno, this was not their first visit. The familiar front foyer was still there, and their living room was down the corridor and past the door.

"You can come in."

Chiho opened the door for them.

"Oh, hello there, Mr. Maou! And everyone else... My, how *dashing* you all look!"

Beyond the doorway, they saw Riho Sasaki, Chiho's mother and a familiar sight to them...

"...Hello."

...and another middle-aged man, his rigid face not hiding his confusion at all.

This was Sen'ichi Sasaki—Chiho's father, a career police officer, and the most important person out of everyone they needed to conduct today's events. He had a loose polo shirt on, looking every bit a dad enjoying his day off, and seeing Maou's group only clouded his face further.

"Thanks for letting us in. I appreciate you taking the time out of your busy schedules to see us."

"C-certainly," Sen'ichi replied, slurring it a bit as he reacted to Maou's polite address. "Come on in."

Once everyone was in the living room, Maou promptly walked up to Sen'ichi and put his hands and knees on the floor.

"Maou?!"

And not just him. Behind him came Ashiya, Urushihara, Emi, and Suzuno, all following his lead—kneeling before Sen'ichi and Riho and bowing their heads.

"We sincerely apologize for all of this."

"Maou..."

"I am aware that Chiho and Ms. Sasaki informed you about everything. What I did to Chiho...I'm not sure we can ever make up for. We've constantly betrayed your trust in us as her parents."

"Ah? ...Ahh, well... Umm..."

"We convinced ourselves," Emi continued after Maou had fallen silent, "that we were taking ample consideration of your daughter's feelings. So we procrastinated on explaining everything as we should have, and we continually lied to you instead. And I know we could never apologize enough for that."

"Hmm? No, uh…"

"Yusa…"

"I promise you that we never proactively sought to place your daughter in the path of danger. However, in the end, we failed. In fact, we have been saved by her hand on multiple occasions."

"Yeah. And this…like, I know we can never properly make up for it, but…"

Ashiya apologizing in a business suit seemed natural enough, but Urushihara's attempts at polite remorse were a wonder to see.

"I want it to be clear that Chiho never had any intention of deceiving you. It was entirely through our own wishful thinking that we placed this excessive burden on her, forcing her hand in our deceits. I know this is asking much from you, but I sincerely hope you will allow us a chance to atone for these acts." It was Suzuno who wrapped up their appeal, quietly but with a palpable force.

"Ashiya… Urushihara… Suzuno…"

"Ahh… Mmmm…"

Sen'ichi hemmed and hawed. That was to be expected. So Maou lifted his head, looking at the man they needed to apologize to the most.

"Chiho, what's going on here? What's this all about?"

The voice, settling over Maou's head, was filled not with anger, but with sheer confusion.

"Um…?"

Their eyes met for the first time. Maou had seen his face twice before, and it looked bewildered.

"I mean… All I heard was that Mr. Maou was coming here today."

"Huh? Um, Chiho and your wife didn't…?"

"No, they didn't say anything. But they were both weirdly smiling at me all day, and, um, you're dressed to the nines, so… I thought, you know, perhaps…"

The still-bewildered Sen'ichi looked at his daughter, then at the man kowtowing in front of him.

"I was prepared to have you asking permission to see my daughter, but..."

"To see... What?!"

This was more than Maou could take.

"But if it was *that*, you wouldn't have these other people with you, and you're sure not *talking* that way, either... Honey? Chiho? You mind explaining to me what kinda thing this is?"

Riho, picking up the hot potato, grinned a bit as she surveyed the room. Then she extended a slightly sorrowful hand to Maou.

"Sorry about that, Maou."

"No, um, but... Today..."

"I understand, of course. But I've been thinking a little. And I figured that no matter what we told him, it'd just be too confusing. So we didn't tell him anything."

Chiho, the attention now directed her way, bashfully turned away a bit.

"Sorry, Dad."

"That's fine, but about *what*?"

"Well, um, I didn't think he and his friends would be this tormented about it, so... But, yeah, they would be. I guess I've been kind of numb to it, in a lot of ways."

Sen'ichi, faced with his wife's and daughter's elusive behavior, grew more and more perplexed.

"But if I could say, Maou," Riho began, "I'm perfectly fine. I've talked with Chiho about it numerous times, asking her questions about what I didn't understand, and I've come to accept it. And yes, maybe you were hiding a thing or two from us, but it's clear to me that you've always put Chiho first."

"Y-yes... Thank you very much."

Riho's true intentions were still a mystery, but hearing that from her was at least a slight comfort to Maou.

Then, as if suddenly having a new idea, Riho turned to Emi. "By the way, Ms. Yusa, is Alas Ramus around? I haven't seen her lately."

"Alas Ramus? She, um, yes, she's around, but I didn't feel right bringing a toddler in for our apology...so..."

"Is she…*inside*?"

"Yes…"

"Well, while we're all here, would you mind introducing her to my husband? I think that'll be the quickest way to get started."

"Are you…sure?"

"It's the easiest thing to understand, isn't it? Out of it all. Besides, I've only heard about her, so I'd like to see what she's like for myself."

"All right, well, if you don't mind… Alas Ramus, be a good girl, okay?"

Emi stood up and put her hands forward. The next moment, with a light *pop*, and a glint of purple softer than a camera flash…

"Chi-sis! Hiii!"

"Hmm?!"

"Ooh! Is *that* how she looks?"

From out of nowhere, a small child appeared, taking Sen'ichi visibly aback while Riho clapped her hands.

"Wh-what was that?! H-how did you…?!"

"And I believe that Mr. Maou has a similar child…?"

"Huh?! Whoa, whoa, she's *definitely* not suitable for this meeting! And she's actually napping right now!"

"Oh, that's all right! Show us!"

"Wha…? But…"

"Do you mind showing her, please, Maou?" Chiho asked, pushing the reluctant Maou along. "With Acieth's size, nobody will be able to explain it away as a magic trick."

"…Well… Hey, Acieth? …Um, I don't think it'll be that easy to wake her up…"

Maou stepped back a bit. Then, in the space between him and Sen'ichi:

"Agghh!"

A young woman appeared.

"Whooaahhh?!"

Even the quiet father had to let out a surprised holler.

"Oww… Maou! What is meaning of this? You be the mean to me, I shoot more of the things from my face, buster!"

"Sorry, Acieth! Not here, okay? Now's not the time or place for it! Once I get paid, I'll treat you to whatever you want, so hold back for now! You're in Chi's house!"

"Ooh, now you say it! …Wait, Chiho's house? Ahhh, yes, then I better be on top behavior."

"Wha-wha-wha…"

"Huh? This man, he smell like Chiho, is he the father?"

"Yep. I told you yesterday, didn't I? We were going to her place to apologize."

"Yes, but you did not say I show up, too… Oh, but I must give my greetings! Hello, Mr. Chiho Dad! I'm Acieth!"

"Y-yes…"

"Ah, you're Acieth? Well, I'm Chiho's mother!"

"Her mother?! Wow! Is this the big party or something? But bringing me and my big sister out, is that okay? Too late now, but…"

"…Yeah, so that's why I didn't think she'd be a good fit for this moment…"

"Wh-wh… Where did those two come from…?!"

Sen'ichi stammered to himself as the two oblivious Yesod children looked around the Sasaki residence. Maou had no idea where they'd take the conversation from here.

"All right, she should be here any moment now…"

The moment Riho copped to it, they heard the sound of a scooter screeching to a halt outside. The intercom rang out.

"Hello! MgRonald delivery!"

"Whoa!"

The voice was intimately familiar to Maou, Emi, and Chiho.

"Ah, um, long time no see, Ms. Iwaki…"

Fresh from the Hatagaya Station location of MgRonald, a place that had indirectly connected these visitors from another planet to Chiho Sasaki, was manager Kotomi Iwaki, here with a delivery.

"Ooh, I *thought* it was your place, Sasaki! The phone number seemed familiar, so… What's going on?"

Iwaki was at the foyer with two large, insulated bags. The sight of the living room, seen through the still-open front door, made her eyes bug out behind her glasses. Anyone would be surprised, after all, if they saw two of their employees kneeling on the floor in business attire at someone's house.

Then, realizing something, she gasped a little.

"Oh... Are you in the middle of something? Does it have to do with Ente Isla? Did you not tell your father before now?"

Iwaki hadn't been acquainted with Maou and Emi for that long, but she knew the truth about them, finding out the same way Chiho's mother did.

"Sort of, yes. Things are still kind of going in all directions for the moment, but..."

When Chiho had told her mother that Maou and his friends wanted to visit the Sasakis to apologize for lying to them, Riho didn't react the way Chiho thought she would. In fact, she took the news pretty casually. When Chiho asked why, she had replied that, yes, they may have lied about their origins, and they may have exposed her to danger unbeknownst to her.

But...

"Did Maou or Yusa *force* you into any of that Ente Isla stuff, Chiho?"

That was the question Riho had asked her yesterday, eyes pointed straight at her.

Chiho, of course, denied it with all her might. The only times she'd *really* been put in danger against her will were when the underground mall collapsed in Shinjuku and during the Shuto Expressway rampage that Urushihara and Olba had carried out. Even those two experiences were cherished memories to her now—and in every other case, Chiho had actively volunteered to be by the side of Maou and his friends. In fact, whenever they tried to push her away, she'd use this or that tactic to stay close by and involved.

When Chiho explained all this, Riho smiled, trying to calm her down.

"Do you remember when Maou and Ashiya and Urushihara took

that summer job over in Choshi? You wanted to go with them, but I stopped you then."

"Yeah..."

"I wound up thinking better of it, but when I asked Yusa and Kamazuki to take you over, Yusa was actually against it at first."

"Huh?"

"Yes, I think Yusa understood that you wanted to go, too. And she didn't phrase it this strongly, but basically she said that Maou had work to do, she couldn't let a teenage girl be by herself that long, and they couldn't take responsibility for you at all times if something of the otherworldly sort happened. So she couldn't agree to it. It's pretty funny now that I look back at it."

"Funny? Why?"

"I mean, aren't those perfectly *normal* reasons?"

Chiho had wanted to join Maou on that job purely out of her own selfishness. And the fact Riho had wanted to push her on him—if you saw him and Emi as regular people—had to have been nothing but an annoyance. Thus, to a typical resident of Japan like Riho, Emi's reaction was common sense.

"So I think it's because of that. Even after I knew everything, I could tell this wasn't Maou and Yusa getting you involved—it was you consciously getting *yourself* involved. I know I didn't raise a dummy who's clueless about what she's doing. So even if you ran into danger, it's not my job as a parent to be mad at you for that."

"...Is that how you think of it?"

"Well, if you'd wound up dead or permanently disabled, that'd be a *much* different story. But getting angry about *that*... I don't know. I just don't feel like *that's* what I should direct my frustration at."

Riho was searching for words, a little unsure of her own feelings.

"But anyway, if they feel they have to apologize, I'm sure that's something they see as necessary for themselves. So why not have them come over?"

"O-okay..."

Riho had already been given the chance to meet all of them, after all. To Chiho, this was enough to convince her that, well, that's how it was.

Now that everyone was here, and Chiho realized that her father not only didn't know about Ente Isla, but also wasn't even expecting a massive crowd and magic show, she was having a lot of trouble dealing. Despite that, though—as she took in Alas Ramus's and Acieth's appearances, and all the fallout from that—she began to think her mother had made the right choice after all.

"Well, if you need another clued-in third party to comment on anything, let me know, all right? And…if Acieth's there, we'll be ready to take any extra orders you may have, okay?"

Iwaki left them with those words, but having her daughter's boss from work walk into this mess did nothing to soothe the mind of Chiho's father.

"Will this…be enough? It won't, will it?"

Looking at the receipt and knowing that Acieth's voracious appetite still hadn't settled down, Chiho assumed with a sigh that nobody else was likely to get a chance at this food order.

*

"Soooo………………………what do I do?"

After they'd finished explaining everything that had happened, Maou and his four companions each taking turns, those were the first words from Sen'ichi Sasaki. He was thoroughly flummoxed.

"Well, why don't you say whatever's on your mind?"

His wife, meanwhile, was almost blunt by comparison.

"What's on my *mind*?"

Sen'ichi gave her a look like a lost puppy. Then he turned toward Maou, Ashiya, and Urushihara, seated on the sofa opposite him. Emi and Suzuno stood behind them. He stared at them all—plus the two girls packing away the MgRonald order, oblivious to everything else—then his eyes settled on his feet.

"For now… Yeah. For now, I…understand. Yes."

He didn't actually mean this. He was just mumbling to himself as he organized his thoughts. Maou and the rest got that, so they didn't move an inch as they waited for his next statement.

"I understand why my wife didn't say anything to me. Certainly, I wouldn't have taken her word for it alone…but also, unlike her, you know, I've hardly met any of Chiho's friends. If I came in expecting an apology from all of you, I probably would've been all tensed up, with my preconceptions and so on, so… Yeah."

He took a deep breath then finally looked at Maou.

"The last time we met, I figured that if there was ever a next time, it'd probably wind up being this big, shocking incident. So I was prepared for that…but never for *this*, sort of."

"Oh?"

Maou raised an eyebrow, unsure how to take this roundabout observation.

He had last met Sen'ichi in the summer of the previous year, in the town of Komagame, Nagano prefecture. Maou and his friends had come to Sen'ichi's family home to help out with farm work. Riho had pointed them over there, after the Choshi job ended early and they had a free summer on their hands, and Maou had met up with Sen'ichi once to thank him. They simply chatted a bit over tea before parting ways, and in Maou's eyes, nothing had happened that would've put Sen'ichi on edge.

Now Sen'ichi looked from Maou to his daughter before letting out another deep sigh. "Well, you know… It's not like I've fully digested all of this yet, but yes, I understand the long and short of it. What all of you are doing and everything. But this… What did you call it? The assault on heaven?"

"That's right. Our term for it anyway."

"And you say that's the only thing left; you guys fighting against your enemy. But Chiho's not gonna be part of that, right?"

"Of course not. We would never take her there. We can't, for that matter."

"And is the war gonna reach here at all? Through your...warp Gates or whatever?"

"No, sir. If they catch even the slightest sign of that, the Sephirah here on Earth will block it with all their might. I think they'd cut off all connections between Ente Isla and Earth at once."

"All right. Also, one other important thing..."

"Yes?"

Sen'ichi took a deep breath, a few beads of sweat on his brow.

"...You, Maou, and Chiho... You aren't a couple or anything right now, are you?"

"Ah... Huh?"

Unlike Chiho, Riho, or even the absent Rika Suzuki, Sen'ichi had learned of Ente Isla strictly through verbal discussion. Maou was ready to give sincere answers to any questions he might have, but nothing could've prepared him for this.

"Are you two romantically involved?"

"D-Dad!"

Chiho blushed instantly.

"Um... I'm sorry, what do you mean by that?"

"Well, I mean it pretty plainly," Sen'ichi replied, his pace accelerating. "I'm asking whether you and my daughter are in a romantic relationship with each other!"

"Huh?! No?! No, um, we haven't... Not *that*, no!"

For a single moment, the memory of what had happened with Chiho after the summit flashed in Maou's mind. But that didn't *quite* seem to connect to what Sen'ichi meant, so he ignored it. Regardless of how Sen'ichi took that hesitation, he spent a few moments leering doubtfully at Maou. Then he turned away.

"Fine, then."

"Y-yes...?"

"Because if you were like that with my daughter, I'd have a few things to say about it, but if not, then I don't. I can talk it over personally with her later. You don't have to say sorry about anything."

"N-no, but..."

"If you *really* need me to," said Sen'ichi, talking louder to stop his guest, "I'll accept your apology for this." He picked up the envelope Maou had placed on the living room table early on in their discussion. "I don't remember the incident at all, but I *do* recall doing some shopping on the way home and having less cash in my wallet than I thought... Or, at least, I was pretty sure."

The envelope contained a 10,000 yen note.

Right after Maou and Ashiya came to Japan, they were caught wandering the streets of Harajuku late at night and taken to the police station by none other than Sen'ichi Sasaki. Maou then used what little demonic force he had left to steal a 10,000 yen bill from him, to cover expenses for the time being. It was a crime, one that Maou and Ashiya deserved to be judged for, but until they came here today, nobody apart from Maou and Ashiya had been aware of it. Even Urushihara was a little surprised.

But even after he learned about it, Sen'ichi exhibited nothing but confusion and puzzlement. There were no signs of anger or disappointment.

"You know, when your beat has an entertainment district in it, you run into drunks passed out on the street, people screaming unintelligible nonsense at you... It's not uncommon for me to take in foreign people with no passport and nothing to prove their real name with. Honestly, even if you told me exactly which night it was, I don't know if I'd find any records of your time with us. I didn't even feel victimized at all. This is kind of like opening an old book and finding money you forgot about inside. Nothing to really get angry about."

"...Thank you very much."

"And when it comes to lying about who you were, well, if my wife and daughter don't mind it, I don't see any need to, either. We're not the type of parents to pry into our child's acquaintances and decide who's right and wrong for her. With the career I have, I keep telling her she can't get involved with antisocials, but you don't exactly count as that."

"Antisocials?" Acieth asked, unfamiliar with the term.

"Sorry. That's police shorthand for people who're a threat to law-abiding individuals. The 'bad guys' sort of thing."

"Oh. But in that case, Maou and friends, they are the worst bad guys, no? They are anti-*human*, not antisocial."

Please stop, Maou thought—but she was telling the truth, so he didn't fight back. But Sen'ichi seemed to take a liking to the unreserved girl, so he gave her a sincere response.

"Well, that's the thing. That's part of the reason Maou and his friends stick out, of course. But this is all so far beyond common sense. There's so much that I can't measure by our standards, and in a way, I don't think it matters."

"Aww, you do not say that! You are the dad! You must yell strongly at them, for Chiho's sake!"

"Acieth..."

"Daddy! Don't be mean to Chi-sis!"

Alas Ramus, despite not understanding any of this, took advantage of Acieth's momentum to lord it over Maou, distracting him and Sen'ichi from the topic.

"Ah, girls, can you be a little more quiet...?"

He was still here to apologize, and he didn't want them derailing everything before Sen'ichi was done talking. But, unexpectedly, Sen'ichi flashed his first smile of the day.

"Alas Ramus?"

"Yeh!"

"Do you love your daddy?"

"I'unno!"

"...!"

Maou had expected an emphatic yes in response. He didn't get it, which floored him—a fact Sen'ichi picked up on.

"You must wonder why I'm not angry at all, don't you? Well, Alas Ramus right now is one reason."

Maou was thrown a bit by the riddle-like response.

"Girls unconditionally love their fathers only until about the age of four or five. But it's important that they don't after that, and lately, I'm finally seeing it as a good thing."

"Oh, *really*?" Riho interjected.

"Don't distract me," Sen'ichi said, looking aside at his wife.

Maou mulled over this statement, the words of a man with seventeen years of fathering experience. Alas Ramus certainly didn't always do what he or Emi wanted her to do. When they'd all lived at Emi's place, he could tell that she acted a fair bit less well-behaved than when she lived with Maou alone. Nothing drastic—she just sometimes sassed back or rebelled a bit in order to bother Emi. She expressed herself in a lot of ways, which she never did when she was just an occasional visitor to Emi's apartment.

"My daughter's made a lot of choices for herself. She's learned, and experienced, so much in her life—and your powers, and your presence, were an indispensable part of that. And if they are, then as her dad, I don't deserve any kind of apology from you."

"…Father…"

"Not to stop you, but it's a *little* too early to start calling me 'Father.'"

"Oh, um, yes. Sorry about that. B-but still…we're demons, and we caused a lot of damage to Ente Isla…"

"Well, look, when you're a cop, you learn pretty quickly that there's no such thing as superheroes, or absolutes, in this world. And I'm definitely not someone high up enough that I'm going to judge a war taking place in some faraway world. Don't you think that'd be irresponsible?"

"…I can't really say."

"Now, if all of you were on one side, maybe I'd take pity on you and get angry at the other side. But you, the Devil King, and you, the Hero, are raising a kid together, and so I can't feel *that* way at all. It'd be like trying to evaluate who was 'right' in the Hundred Years' War from our modern perspective. It's pointless."

Sen'ichi looked at Alas Ramus, currently stealing some fries from Acieth, and reached over toward her.

"Right now, all I want from you guys is to keep being good friends to Chiho."

Everyone there—Maou, of course, as well as Emi, Ashiya,

Urushihara, and Suzuno—knew what he meant when he said that, gesturing at Maou's own "daughter." Alas Ramus was beloved by many people, and so was Chiho Sasaki. What he meant, spoken in the plainest of terms, was "never do anything that would sadden those who love her so much." He wasn't speaking to the Devil King of another world. He was speaking to his daughter's friend.

"...All right. I will."

The answer, too, was just as simple.

$$*$$

The white moon was floating in a blue sky, amid the relatively tranquil summer sunlight. It was two in the afternoon, and after leaving the Sasaki house, Maou was walking through the Sasazuka neighborhood with Chiho (pushing her bike), Emi, Alas Ramus, and Acieth. Ashiya, Urushihara, and Suzuno opened up a Gate right in the Sasaki living room, off to Efzahan, the demon realms, and the Central Continent, respectively. That was their ace in the hole for convincing Sen'ichi they weren't lying, but it seemed like he had accepted their extraordinary story without it.

Once Maou, Emi, Alas Ramus, and Acieth had stepped out the front door, they all gave a deep bow to the family before going away. Chiho was on her way to her test prep center, and they were all chatting with each other, as if there were no assault on heaven to think of at all. Their conversation was mostly about how Acieth was feeling and Alas Ramus's likes and dislikes.

They wound up talking all the way to Sasazuka Station, where they split up—as if tomorrow would be just as normal and humdrum as yesterday.

"You have the work, yes, Maou? I promise Erone I have snack with him, so I go to Mikitty's. Bye, big sis!"

Acieth gave Alas Ramus a friendly pinch on the cheek before running off.

"I don't have any business in Ente Isla today, so I'll head home. I want to do some of Alas Ramus's laundry."

"And I have test prep to go to, but are you going back home to change, Maou?"

"Nah, I got nothing to do at home, so I'll just head over. It ain't a crime to report to work lookin' snappy, huh?"

In just over a week and a half from now, they'd have to stage an all-out attack on the heavens—and yet, this. Or maybe "this" was what everyone wanted the most right now. So Emi and Chiho kept discussing the same old everyday things, as if nothing were amiss.

"You don't think you should change? If you get any grease on that, Alciel's gonna yell at you, isn't he?"

"She's right. And you're gonna slip all over the kitchen in those leather shoes."

"True... Good point."

Maou's reaction seemed to indicate he expected as much from these two.

"But I put this suit on and everything..."

Despite that, though, he seemed intent on reporting to work dressed to the nines.

"Will you be late if you go back to change?" Chiho asked.

"No, nothing like that," he answered airily.

This confused her a bit. She assumed they'd all split up at this point, like they usually did—and Maou wasn't the sort to care how he looked in public anyway. As long as he didn't look disgusting or break any laws, any outfit was fine to him. If this suit wasn't important to him, like it was during managerial training or during this apology today...

"!"

After reaching that thought, it finally dawned on Emi.

The biggest reason why all five of them had gone out of their way to visit the Sasakis was because they weren't certain they would all survive the assault on heaven. To put it another way, all of them coming together helped a lot to quell their pre-battle anxiety. And right now, Maou was dressed as formally as he could picture, attempting to banish any lingering concerns from his mind.

"Ughh..."

She hated it—how simple he was to understand. This obvious, tactless man.

"Well, stop dragging this on and just go home and change!"

"Huh?"

"Yusa?"

This, too, was Emi's usual tone of voice.

"Hey, Alas Ramus?"

"Yeh, Mommy?"

"What do you think of Daddy's suit? Does he look good?"

"Huh? Hey, Emi…"

"I hate it."

"Alas Ramus?!"

This was, without a doubt, the harshest thing she had ever said to them. It took both Maou and Chiho off guard.

"It smells weird."

"A-Alas Ramus?!"

"Daddy should smell like fries."

"Huh?! I—I smell weird? But I took it to the dry cleaner for this and everything…! And I've been using this towel to keep the sweat off!"

"But she smells French fries on your hands on your days off. If you smell like detergent or bug spray, she might not like that as much."

"Aww…"

The sight of Maou acting all pathetic made Emi giggle.

"She's saying it doesn't seem right on you. So go change, okay? Your usual UniClo outfits look a lot better, and plus…"

Then Emi looked at Chiho, still unsure how to address Maou after this scathing appraisal from Alas Ramus. Her grin instantly turned into a heartfelt, affectionate smile.

"…I think you'll get your feelings across better that way."

"…Ah! E-Emi, you…!"

"Anyway, we're heading home. Oh, and I've been in Ente Isla too long to remember, but if you're staying in Villa Rosa, you mind picking up your stuff from my place whenever?"

Maou stayed frozen to the spot, Chiho's eyes darting between them as she tried to ascertain what was going on. Emi just waved instead of giving an answer.

"See you guys later. Thanks for today, Chiho."

"S-sure..."

"Daddy! Chi-sis! Bye-bye! Study hard!"

Emi, with Alas Ramus waving behind her shoulder, quickly disappeared beyond the station turnstile.

"Um, Maou?"

"...I'm sorry, Chi, can you give me just ten minutes? I'm gonna go change after all."

"O-okay. I can wait that long, but..."

"I'll be right back!"

Chiho stood there, listening to the sharp clack of Maou's shoes as he darted back home. She was worried about how much he'd be sweating at that pace, but she didn't have to wait long.

"Sorry! I'm back!"

The same old Sadao Maou, in his same old UniClo shirt and pants, was pedaling the same old Dullahan II over to her. Exactly ten minutes had passed.

✳

Pushing their respective bikes, Maou and Chiho walked from Sasazuka Station toward the neighborhood of Hatagaya. Even though they were walking down the same street, even though they were both headed to the same area, they had different destinations—Maou to work, Chiho to the test prep center.

Emi had been acting unusual when they'd split up. Maou was acting a bit odd himself. And based on that, Chiho felt strangely tense as they walked along silently for a bit.

"Hey..."

"Y-yes?"

"Ms. Iwaki came to make that delivery, didn't she?"

"Um, yeah. I think she picked up on a lot of it."

"Ah… Really? Well, unlike Ms. Kisaki, she's probably not gonna wheedle us about it later, so that's fine."

"Y-yeah."

Then a bit more silence. Things were clearly different from usual, so every beat of the conversation wound her up more.

"Speaking of which, not to change the subject, but you own a bicycle, Chi?"

"I do. It's been a while since I took it out, but…"

"Why use it all of a sudden?"

It wasn't strange or anything, but he had never seen it before, and it wasn't like her test prep was located far from her workplace. Maou couldn't help but wonder why she had it.

"Didn't Libicocco tell you? Some guys approached me after test prep the other day."

"What? Some guys?!"

Maou's eyes opened up in shock.

"Yeah. They were kind of pushy with me, but Libicocco chased them off."

"H-he did?"

"But I can't rely on Libicocco all the time, you know? So I decided to take my bike back and forth instead."

"Oh… The test prep center isn't that far from MgRonald, is it? Why didn't you use it before now?"

"You're asking me *that* now?"

"Huh?"

He thought it was a normal question to ask. But Chiho frowned, slightly peeved.

"It's because I don't have to worry if I'm going to test prep."

"Worry? Worry about what?"

Chiho pointed straight at Maou's face—or to be exact, she pointed two fingers at his eyes.

"If I'm riding a bike, my bangs get all messed up, all right?"

Not even Maou was dull enough to say "Yeah, so?" to that. The wind messed up anyone's hair on a bike. Of course, she'd be going into the changing room at work and making herself as bland-looking as possible in a moment. But for just that minute—for just those few seconds—between dismounting and going through the door...

"Look, don't you think it's about time you realized how hard I've been working?"

Naturally, there were some shifts where everything was so busy that Maou and Chiho wouldn't even have a single second to take a look at each other. If anything, her efforts were probably fruitless more often than not. But still:

"I've been trying to make my bangs cute so maybe you'd see them, Maou."

"...I'm sorry?"

"And I never rode to your apartment because I didn't want the food I bring to get mixed up in the basket, and someone always walked me home afterward anyway."

Chiho was no longer in the same place as him. Not in their jobs, and not on the battlefield. Maou had lingered too long, and now they had drifted away.

"You know, Maou..."

"Hmm?"

The more they walked, the closer they'd get to their destination. So Chiho laid out her approach.

"Why did you keep my memories intact for me?"

"Ack..."

That yelp might have sounded like a half-hearted reply—but between him stopping and where his eyes were pointed, Chiho could tell it wasn't.

They were at a large intersection now, and to their left, one cross street away, was the Koshu-Kaido road, the Shuto Expressway spanning above it.

"Chi, did I ever tell you about when I founded the Devil King's Army in the demon realms?"

"No. I've never heard about it from you."

"So from Ashiya or Urushihara, then?"

"From Ashiya, a little."

"Really? Did he say anything weird about it?"

Maou winced, like a teen whose mother was showing off an old family album to one of his friends.

"I don't think anything about it was *that* strange. He told me up to when you and he became friends. The Malebranche hadn't shown up yet."

"Oh, up to that point? So did he tell you that the first guy I recruited was Urushihara?"

"Wasn't it Camio and his Pájaro-something tribe?"

"Ahh, they... They weren't 'friends' exactly."

Chiho didn't ask what the difference was, but if what she knew about Maou's past was correct, it seemed fair to assume Maou thought of Camio like a member of his family.

"Well, maybe it didn't come up, but the clan I come from doesn't have any survivors left besides me. Laila saved me, that old guy raised me...and once I grew up and became the Devil King, I looked for other members of my clan, but there was nobody left exactly like me."

"Exactly like you?"

"Like, you know how Libicocco and Ciriatto look pretty different, even though they're both Malebranche? That sort of thing. Our mob, they were called the Blacksheep clan, but whenever I thought I'd found someone like me, the horns or the fur would be all different, and stuff."

"Oh... Really?"

"So first I convinced Urushihara and Adramelech to join me. Then, a while later, I took in Ashiya and the Iron Scorpions...and a lot of other stuff happened, but the point is, I always selected my companions of my own free will."

That generally lined up with what Chiho had heard.

"Now, there was a lot of infighting between us and the Malebranche, Malacoda in particular. There'd occasionally be offshoot forces we had to put back in line. In the end, they stormed Ente Isla and lost to Emi's forces, but..."

"Right."

"And I'm sure you know my history after I came to Japan, but after a lot of twists and turns, I got a job at MgRonald, and then you applied there, too, right?"

That was the highly abridged version, but to Maou, those two facts were at the crux of his story.

"I was the guy handling most of your training…and, you know, that was the first time I ever trained someone."

"Oh, was it?"

Maou didn't tell her at the time. And quite a bit of the crew around Chiho had learned at least a thing or two from him as well.

"Like, training someone solo, I mean. Man to man. I did it together with Mae a few times, or I'd just teach a few things to someone I shared a shift with, but that was my first one-on-one experience. Right after your interview, Ms. Kisaki came up to me and said, like, 'Okay, she's all yours.'"

That made Chiho a little happy to hear. She thought she had blown the interview pretty badly—so much so that she didn't even remember much of it. But learning that Kisaki approved of her immediately afterward, despite it being so long ago, gave her an ever-so-slight sense of pride.

"So I was glad for that. You know, having Ms. Kisaki leave a new hire in my hands. I always had a lot of respect for her, and I figured I'd never be brought on full-time if I never trained anyone. So…"

Maou looked at Chiho and smiled warmly.

"I'm wanna, I—I mean, I'm gonna be working here starting today! My name's Chiho Sasaki! Good to meet you!"

"So I was really into this assignment. Like, 'I'm gonna *totally* make a great crewmember out of this girl.'"

"Mmm…" This sounded a bit odd to Chiho. "You mean you wanted to score points with Ms. Kisaki?"

"Well, at the time, yeah, I'm sure there was some of that."

Maou didn't recall his exact feelings back then. But putting words to his memory like this, it likely wasn't far from the truth.

"But in all my life, that was the first time a superior believed in me enough to entrust someone else to me."

"You're making me sound like I was a preschooler or something."

"Well, I meant to treat you as carefully as one anyway."

"You *meant* to?"

"Ahh, stop pressing me," Maou said, lifting up his hands in surrender. "But to me, Chi, you were the first human being I viewed as precious."

"Is that something I should be happy about?" she asked, knowing the answer.

"I'm not the judge of that. I'm a demon, despite it all."

"That's true. Despite it all."

She decided to let go. To be frank, it was all in the past.

"And I know I've been going on for a while, but my point is, I didn't want the people I held dear to forget about me. If I let that happen, and they just gave me this blasé look starting the next day... Well, I didn't want to imagine that. I had a few coincidences happen in my life, and then I started thinking about things that way."

"If I can take the opportunity to ask what kind of coincidences...?"

"Having Emi there."

"Ah, it was her, huh?"

"Yeah. I put you through all kinds of hell, and part of me was, like—just because I don't want you to forget about me, should I really leave you be? But if I did that, the only human who'd know everything I did was Emi."

Maou winced—an emotion from the bottom of his heart.

"And it was, like, *anything* but that. So..."

He stared straight at Chiho.

"Not wanting someone you hold dear to forget about you... I guess that's part of loving someone, isn't it?"

"...Huh?"

This was unexpected. She'd already concluded this would be like any other chat—that he'd try talking his way into another deadline extension. For a moment, she forgot to breathe.

"I've been thinking about a lot of things. I'm a demon, but over the past year or two, I've come to realize that my feelings—my spirituality—they aren't that different from any other human being's. But when it comes to loving the opposite sex, I really *do* know nothing about that. I didn't have any parents or friends to show me the ropes, and physically speaking, I'm not sure if demons even have the capacity. But..."

Maou didn't take his eyes off her. Chiho, feeling her palpitations grow stronger, couldn't reply.

"And to be honest, I've been kind of sick lately, and...after a series of improbable events, Sariel visited to take care of me."

"What? You've been sick?! Huh? And Sariel took care of you? What?!"

It was shock on top of shock. Chiho exclaimed far more loudly than she'd intended.

"And I didn't have anyone else to ask, so I asked him. Like, what does 'love' feel like? He's had the hots for Ms. Kisaki since forever, y'know—but if things go naturally, Ms. Kisaki's absolutely gonna reach her natural lifespan before him. Same with Laila and Nord. They're destined to leave the people they love in the past. So it's, like, how can they *have* those kinds of emotions?"

✻

"So let me get this straight. After all this, you *still* don't know what kind of feelings Chiho Sasaki has for you?"

"It's not that I don't know. It's just... You see how I am."

Chiho's kiss after the summit—that explosive bolt of energy that had built up for so long, following Maou's delayed answer—was such a straight expression of her feelings, it trampled all over Maou's nature as a demon. It wrecked his health, after years of never suffering any illness apart from malnutrition at a very young age. He could almost feel his body going out of control, like all the demonic force was leaking out of it. It struck him so hard that Sariel could've stuck a whole onion in the rice porridge he'd made for him out of spite, and he would've eaten it, not noticing.

"I want to cherish Chi. But if you're asking me whether I care about her so much I can withstand this level of passion..."

"What are you, a preteen?"

"Huh?"

"No, maybe not that. *You're* thinking like a man in his forties or fifties. The kind who, despite having actual feelings, pretends he's not suitable for his partner, like some dried-up tumbleweed."

"...My mind's a little bleary, but I can tell you're bashing me."

"Not that there's much point reasoning with someone willing to eat *that* kind of rice porridge..."

Sariel turned from the pot he was washing in the sink and sighed.

"I said this to one of your men before, but there's no way to tell what the other person *really* feels in their heart. There are a lot of loving couples in the world, but how can you quantitatively measure that from the outside?"

"...Stop using all these hard words. My head hurts."

"A perfect ten in Chiho Sasaki's heart is different from a perfect ten in yours. You're not duty-bound to give back exactly what your partner gives you, and besides, that's not even possible."

"Chiho's ten is different from my ten...?"

"Lemme try to put it this way: Never once have I ever wanted Ms. Kisaki to reward my love poetry with some of her own."

"Ha-ha...! I get it. If she asked for *that*, I'd take a step back, too."

"Ms. Kisaki cares far more for work than for the trappings of love...and I'm fine with that. But if her exhaustion reaches its peak at some moment, I want to be wherever she returns to. I've always felt that."

Sariel and Kisaki were not at all a couple. It was entirely a crush on Sariel's part. Based on Kisaki as of late, their relationship wasn't as stormy as when they'd first met, but if asked whether she had romantic feelings for Sariel, a hundred people out of a hundred would shake their heads. He was aware of that, of course, but that didn't stop him from waxing on about this stuff. Truly an amazing case.

"So is Emilia's father the type of person to sing love songs every time he sees Laila?"

"...I heard he's pretty lovey-dovey with her, but nothing like that, no."

"Is Chiho the type of person who'd weigh her private life against work and choose work every time?"

"...No. That's not her style."

Chiho didn't have the sort of work-first, everything-else-second credo that Kisaki basked in. At least, she didn't in Maou's eyes.

"What, so you're saying there's no answer, then?" he asked.

"Not in terms of love having a particular shape, I mean. It all comes down to what *you* want Chiho Sasaki to mean to you. That, only you can say. Not even she can tell you. But if you ask why Laila and I can find it within ourselves to love human beings, well, it just comes down to how we want to be thought about."

＊

"I hate to say it, but the talk we had definitely helped me work out my feelings."

"*I'd* hate to say that, too."

Sariel was their enemy. Everyone who knew the archangel could tell that he'd never find the ideal future he dreamed of. But put that aside, and here was a man unafraid to discuss his most intimate hopes in detail—and in a way, thanks to Maou and Chiho, he no longer hid any of that from Kisaki.

"He's *so* happy, isn't he?" Maou said, chuckling.

"As someone who put me in a lot of danger," Chiho said, smiling back, "I can't say I like it very much."

"So, yeah, Chiho..."

"Yes?"

"I don't want you to forget about me."

"Yes!"

"Why didn't I erase your memories back then? I know I've said a lot, but in the end, it all boils down to that. I didn't want you to forget about me. And now that's even more true. If you forgot about me now, I know that'd leave a hole in my heart."

"...Yes...!"

"So...give me just a little more time to answer your feelings. I've got one other thing now; one more thing I need to solve before I can answer you. Nothing to do with the assault on heaven. It's a problem strictly about me…or between me and you."

"…Yes!"

Tears were forming in Chiho's eyes, tears she couldn't hold back. She was trying her hardest to keep them in, but she was rapidly approaching her limit.

"That…and we have a certain order to think about. You remember what I told you, Chi."

"Yes… Yes… Right."

Chiho knew that Suzuno had confessed her love to Maou. It was different from the romance-driven love Chiho felt for him, but Maou had postponed his answer to those feelings as well. And no matter what he decided, Chiho made him promise that he'd save his answer to her for the very end. Considering Maou's behavior up to now, that wasn't too much to ask. That's why Maou was so preoccupied with the "order" of things.

"…Um… Like, I'm sorry. You had yourself all ready, and I'm giving you this half-assed response."

"That's all right. I'm totally fine with it. But, um, I don't think I, um, will be able to focus on *studying* too much today…"

Wiping away the tears she could no longer contain, she revealed a beaming smile beneath the streams.

"It's certainly not done yet, after all."

"No. If we can solve a few other things before then, it'll be easier to think about more stuff."

"…Thank you very much."

"Don't thank me. Really, I'm sorry I've made you wait so long."

He put both hands against his cheeks. They were blushing—something very unusual for him.

"…!"

"Maou?!"

"…No, um, I—I feel so ashamed right now. I totally get why you ran from me that one time now. I, um, I'm gonna go on ahead a little! Good luck with your test prep, Chi! See you!"

Before he even took another breath, Maou was on his Dullahan II and pedaling away at a furious speed. Chiho watched him zoom away. It was all so unexpected.

"Oh, come on..."

She stood there until she could no longer see him. Then she shrank down, trying to shut in all the unbearable heat coming from within her chest. Despite her efforts, the love and happiness kept streaming out.

And that was why.

"But Maou..."

She wanted to release her feelings, like fireworks into the summer daylight. She knew everything there was to know about Maou—about Satan, the Devil King—but she still loved him. She wanted to shout it to the world.

And that was why...

"*Haaahhh...!!*"

Those feelings were exhaled, even hotter than the summer air.

Restraining the tears threatening to shoot out anew, Chiho took out her phone and called a very familiar number to her.

"Hello?"

She thought she was cutting it close timewise, but when she heard the noise in the background, she realized she was just in time. Or maybe the person she was calling was expecting Chiho to call her at this exact moment. The recipient of the call sounded like she was in a rail station—in front of Meidaimae Station, perhaps—and that made it natural for her to be able to answer Chiho's call. And from that moment, until this one, the world that she saw had moved itself. Chiho wasn't aware of this. But *she* was.

"*Call? From Chi-sis?*"

"*Don't take the phone, Alas Ramus.*"

Through the speaker came the drama of a mother keeping a smartphone away from her child.

"*Hello? Chiho?*"

"...Yusa?"

Emi's voice sounded as normal as ever. The same Emi Yusa that Chiho had known ever since she'd met and befriended her.

"Chiho? What's up?"

Emi, picking up on Chiho's erratic behavior, lowered the tone of her voice. She was worried for her, from the heart.

So Chiho drummed up the willpower to ask. She could no longer look at the path Maou had disappeared down.

"Yusa... Why... How... Did you know this would happen?"

✳

"Hello, Your Demonic Highness. Did your apology at Lord Chiho's residence go well? ...Your Demonic Highness?"

It must have been the middle of his afternoon break. Libicocco, entering the staff room next to the changing area, removed his crewmember cap and sat on a folding chair, munching on a bag of something from the nearby convenience store and reading a magazine.

"Everything okay? You look kind of pale."

Maou all but fell into the staff room, his breathing ragged. Feeling the AC breeze on his face, he dragged himself inside.

"You're sweating a whole lot. Is it that hot outside?"

"...No......... It...... It's nothing..."

"My liege?"

Maou was acting off. His panting was more of a wheeze, and despite all the sweating, his skin was a paler shade than usual.

"Urr...p... Libby... Sorry, that, that bag..."

Before Libicocco could respond, Maou grabbed the plastic bag from the convenience store...

"Nn...oo...*gghhh*..."

"M-my liege?!"

...and expelled the contents of his stomach into it.

"Wh-what has happened to you?! Did—did you get food poisoning...?!"

"D-don't say that...in here... It's not that... I'm sorry about, about the bag..."

"It's fine, it's fine! But you have a fever, too, don't you? What happened?!"

"Don't raise your voice. I feel a little better now. I can push myself to calm down. Ngh... *Haah...*"

His skin tone went from white to blue as he stood up, bracing his arm against the wall.

"Are you really all right? You should ask Ms. Iwaki to give you the day off..."

"I'm fine. Really. Unlike last time...there was no contact, so probably..."

The warm feeling came back to the pit of his stomach. He could feel himself recovering.

"Or is it the other way around...?"

Maou shook his head as he changed clothes, still catching his breath.

A kiss is a way to express your love, strongly, via physical contact. If his body had a negative reaction to love, the opposite of fear, he could understand that. But back there, he hadn't even held hands with her, much less shared a kiss. Despite that, though, he immediately felt the demonic force inside him being rent apart.

He had touched Chiho several times before. They held hands all day during their date in Shinjuku. She had even held him in her arms once. If his body was going to physically recoil over a little affection, it should have happened well before now.

Was it because her feelings up until now had been more of a childlike puppy love? Or a blind sort of romance that hadn't quite matured into full-on love? That couldn't be the case, either. Rika Suzuki had told Ashiya she had a thing for him; Suzuno had told Maou she loved him. They were adult women, and their love was backed with supreme confidence. Even when Chiho grabbed his hand as they went upstairs to Laila's apartment, her feelings couldn't have been much different from now. She had even demonstrated her loyalty to him as a Great Demon General, and he physically picked her up during the *zirga* after obtaining the Spear of Adramelechinus.

So why only now?

"Ahh, this is..." he groaned.

◊

"Why is Japan so *hot?!*"

That was the first thing Chiho shouted as she jammed the button on her AC's remote. It was a familiar unit in a familiar space, and once it detected the temperature in the dank, humid room, it let out a whine and began blowing cold air in. At almost the same time, the door swung open.

"Chiho! You're back?!"

Riho, her mother, was standing there, holding a back scratcher for some reason.

"Oh, hi, Mom. Why the back scratcher?"

"I heard a strange noise, so I was scared. When you come home, can come through the living room or front door? It's bad for my heart."

"The last time I did that, you spilled curry all over the carpet, remember? I can't open a Gate in places where I could run into someone."

"Honestly... Then at least text me when you're coming back or something. I know you have ways to. Because when you open a Gate, it causes a lot of noise and shaking, you know."

She lightly shook the back scratcher in her hand as she let out her complaints.

"Well?" she went on. "Tell me, which one was better?"

"Hmm... If I had to pick, Ente Isla."

"It wasn't cheap, you know, having you study abroad in London."

Riho hung her head, although she'd half expected that answer.

"As your mother, you know, I'm happy with any job you think is your calling, but...you know, having you tilt *this* much toward another world..."

She sized up Chiho, head to toe.

"I mean, what kind of country were you even in?"

Her baggage was the usual wheeled sort, but Chiho was sporting the traditional wear of somewhere or other, featuring a rainbow of colors woven into shiny, silk-like fabric.

"Well, the design comes from the Wurs clan, but the fabric's made by the Welland clan."

"Yes, yes... You're a lot more impressionable than I thought. You purchased that picture book with the cute British characters in London, too."

"You could at least call it being broad-minded."

"Well, look at it from my perspective, too, won't you? My broad-minded daughter, going off to a whole other world..."

Riho smiled, a mix of emotions behind it.

"So how's your stomach?"

"Hungry!"

It was a routine Chiho had played out with her mother thousands of times since childhood.

"Great. Your father's been in Kyoto since last week, helping with security at this international conference. When I'm alone, I always wind up cooking too much..."

"I'll eat anything if you made it, Mom."

"Oh? Well, that'd help a lot. Eat it all, for all I care... But before that, go take a shower, will you? You're smelling pretty dusty."

"What? Oh! Sorry!"

Realizing this, Chiho blushed then left her baggage behind and made a beeline for the bathroom.

"Don't put that outfit in the washer! I'd hate for all those colors to fade!"

"Okay!"

"Oof..."

The way she stormed around the house hadn't changed one bit since her early childhood. It hadn't...but now she was a college junior. She was past twenty, a grown woman. Riho sighed as she used the back scratcher on her spine, even though it didn't itch at all.

"Maou's perfectly happy working in Japan, so why is *she* so eager to work in Ente Isla...?"

Chiho had gone through two bowls of chicken and vegetable stew, left simmering for over a day to seal the flavor in, alongside some rice cooked up the day before and on the dry side as a result. She put both hands together, her face revealing her joy.

"Thank you *so* much!"

"You sure ate a lot."

"I did." She nodded, grinning wildly. "Honestly, if I'm gonna try to make it in Ente Isla, *this* is the biggest hurdle."

"Oh?"

"There's lots of good food over there, and by their standards I'm enjoying some pretty haute cuisine every day…but it gets so boring."

"Oh, does it?"

"When I was in London, they had this place called the Japan Store off Piccadilly Circus, where they sold snacks and instant noodles from Japan."

When her host family told her about this store, located on a side street off one of London's busiest neighborhoods, Chiho didn't see it as anything important at first. Her college friends and advisors told her a million times that once she spent a week overseas, she'd be aching for white rice and miso soup—but her three weeks in London were so busy and exciting, she didn't have enough time to miss Japanese food.

Everyone also told her that British food was awful, but given this was the other side of the Northern Hemisphere, she assumed it wouldn't agree with her at first, and either way, it wasn't as bad as they all said. A lot of the soups and stews were better than in Japan, and most of the sushi places had actual Japanese soy sauce, as opposed to the "sushi" joints run by outfits from every Asian nation except Japan you often saw overseas. As long as the soy sauce was good, she knew, any sushi would be great, no matter how crazy it was—although either way, food was never a concern of hers.

But:

"Old Lidem, you know… I think she must've heard from Albert, but she tried to make some more Japanese-style food for me. She even opened up a restaurant serving Japanese-ish stuff. But…like, it's all kind of off…"

"People like her don't take half-measures, do they? And why are *you* being so fancy?"

Hearing about Lidem opening a restaurant must've shocked Riho. Chiho's Ente Isla study began right after her time in London ended, during her school's summer break. She spent it on the Northern Island, in the "Goat Pasture" city of Phiyenci, the area she came to grow fondest of. Her mission: Do an internship.

"So what did you do in Ente Isla?"

"Well, I dunno... To sum up, I guess I mostly just did miscellaneous stuff for Lidem...but to put it another way, I was a politician's secretary, a cabinet secretary... That kind of thing. I met a lot of Northern Island people, collected their demands and petitions, built a schedule for Lidem, and sometimes I'd step in and create resolutions for Lidem's or the Wurs clan's decisions..."

"Oh...?"

"Well, you said Lidem would be best because she goes around to a lot of Ente Isla, so that's what I did, is all."

Chiho, realizing her mother was sounding a little put off, hastily tacked on that addendum. It didn't have much effect.

"So in the final week, I had Emeralda and Rumack guide me around Saint Aile. The imperial palace was *so* pretty. I took a lot of photos, so I'll show them to you later."

She made it sound so casual, but this wasn't like checking out Japan's Imperial Palace, or the changing of the guard over at Buckingham Palace in London. She was going inside a palace ruled by a real, living absolute monarch, and the fact she saw that as normal was nothing short of ominous.

"And you know, Lidem told me to bring my parents next time. You could check it out, too, Mom."

"Well... Well, certainly, someday. But after this, Chiho..."

"...Oh, right! I gotta go out again after this."

"What? But you just got here...!"

"Yeah, but it was just a forty-minute trip. I'm not all jet-lagged like after the UK, so once I change clothes, I gotta go. Thanks for the stew!"

"...Sure, sure. Just tell me if you need dinner or not later, all right?"

"Okay!"

Flinging some new clothes on (along with some quick makeup), she flew out the front door. Riho watched her go, then sank back into the living room sofa.

"If she's like this before she even finds a job," she muttered, "I *hate* to think what'll happen once she's married. I'll need a new hobby to pass the time, I suppose. *Siiiigh...*"

Chiho hurried toward Sasazuka Station, feeling just a little bad for her dejected-looking mother and promising herself that she'd make up for it later. Today, at least, she had something even more important than her mother to handle.

"She should arrive in the afternoon... When was it again...?"

Chiho checked her messages then the train schedule on her phone.

"Great. I'll be on time. Ten minutes early to Tokyo Station!"

Running through the cityscape—both familiar and fresh after three months away from it—Chiho jogged through the 100 Trees Shopping Arcade, crossed the Koshu-Kaido road, and arrived at Sasazuka Station.

There, right in front of the turnstile:

"Oh!"

"Ah!"

She ran right into Maou, who was traveling to Tokyo Station at the same time.

"Hey. Welcome back. We'll be on time, right?"

"Thanks. We'll be ten minutes early if all goes well."

Maou and Chiho both waved and greeted each other. Then they went through the turnstile—Maou pressing his wallet against the card reader, Chiho using her phone.

"Y'know, everyone at work knew you were coming home from 'study abroad' today. They slammed me for not meeting you at the airport. I think that bastard Libicocco told them."

"Ahh... Did he? Sorry. I'll explain things to everyone later..."

"Nah, it's fine... I think that'd hurt my rep even worse. But how was it? Did you get a lot to think about?"

"There's still a lot troubling me, but I think it gave me a lot of material to work out my future with."

"Yeah?"

"For now, I intend to find a job in Japan. But when choosing the firms to apply to, I have one condition I'm not gonna waver on."

"What's that?"

"A workplace where I don't have to be in Japan during summer!"

"Yeah, that doesn't even sound like a joke any longer. This is definitely the worst summer I've seen since coming to Japan. I've even started willingly buying sunblock."

"Sunblock? …Hmmm?"

As they waited at the platform for the next train to Shinjuku, Chiho took a closer look at Maou's face.

"Are you applying it all the way down your neck?"

"…No."

"Well, your neck's got weird tan lines on it. Like, your shirt collar, and probably your helmet visor, too."

"…Oh. Well, you know, I don't wanna waste it…"

Watching Maou awkwardly grope at his neck, Chiho let out a hearty laugh. The sight of him finding a chin hair he'd missed and wincing with the same awkwardness was even funnier to her.

"Seriously…"

The next train to Shinjuku slid into the station just then, blocking Chiho's muttered observation.

"That part of you hasn't changed at all."

THE
HERO
FINDS AN
ANSWER
AND CHOOSES
HER WAY

It was the afternoon after their visit to the Sasaki residence, about four PM—two hours into the shift.

"Maou, if you could?"

Thanks to it not being very busy, Maou was somehow able to overcome his illness enough to carry on—until Iwaki came along, Libicocco in tow. The MgRonald upstairs café space had only a few customers dotted around.

"I'll let Libby handle upstairs."

"All right. But...did my headset batteries run out? Did a delivery order come in or something?"

He had heard nothing on his headset, so he thought at first that he'd missed an order or the like.

"No, nothing like that. Can you just come with me for a moment?"

"S-sure. Thanks, Libicocco."

"...Yep."

The taciturn Libicocco, taking Maou's place, gave him a worried look as he toddled down the stairs. Once he was pulled into the staff room:

"This is a managerial order, all right? Maou, I want you to take off early today."

"Right... Wait, wait?"

"Kawata agreed to come in just for the dinner rush, so we'll be fine here. So go home and get yourself better, okay?"

"Oh, um, manager, no..."

"That's a managerial order."

Iwaki was being unusually strict.

"Maou, I know this is a very important time for you. That's why you were at Ms. Sasaki's house, right?"

Ah, yes. Iwaki *did* see him on all fours at Chiho's place.

"You said you'd be better in a little bit, so I kept an eye on you, but... Maybe you don't realize it, but you've been going paler and paler. People are gonna think you caught a cold, and I can't have you handling food like that."

"...All right. I'm sorry."

Being told that, Maou had nothing to counter with.

"Can you get home by yourself?"

"Yeah, I can do that... It's real close on a bike."

He staggered his way toward the changing room, but:

"Agh?!"

Iwaki, waiting outside, flew in after hearing some kind of loud crashing sound.

"Are you all right?"

"Y-yes, I'm fine," a panicked-sounding Maou said from a rather low position on the ground.

After a little while, he successfully changed out of his uniform. His face looked even worse, though—being freed of the tension of work must've done that to him.

"Why don't you take a little break before heading home?"

"No... Um, I really don't think it's a cold, but if it is, I don't want to spread it... I'm sorry. Say thanks to Kawacchi for me."

"...All right. Be careful."

Iwaki said nothing else as Maou left, making sure every step was a sure one before he took it. Watching him stagger his way through the town in twilight, Iwaki returned to Libicocco.

"So can demons even *catch* colds?"

"No, I sure haven't heard of that. But my liege has been living here for a while now... If it's anything like before, he'll get *real* bad quick, then he'll recover just as quick. He doesn't have a fever or anything; he just gets drained of energy, kind of."

"No fever?"

"No. Well, I can't say, really, but last time, he was all better once he returned to the demon realms, so I think he'll recover pretty fast this time, too."

"I hope so," Iwaki said, slightly anxious. "If it's just him not feeling well...maybe demons *can* catch colds. Try not to catch it, Libby."

"Aw, quit making it sound like I'll catch the stupid from him or something."

"You're getting pretty used to life in Japan, aren't you?"

For someone who'd only recently learned about Maou and Libicocco, she already seemed to have a lot of insight into what made them tick.

"But I don't think my liege or Alciel has ever gone to the doctor... Can this body get sick after all?"

It made Libicocco worry, just a bit—enough that he resolved to at least buy a mask at the convenience store on the way home.

But the King of all Demons hadn't moved one bit from the MgRonald bicycle parking area. He was crouched by his Dullahan II, unable to get up, because he couldn't work his knees at all. His left hand groped at thin air, failing to grasp the handlebar.

"Boy... I'm done for."

The nausea was acting up again, but no matter what he did, he had to avoid throwing up behind the MgRonald. At this point, though, it was only a matter of time.

"This is so pathetic... Come on... Do it, King...of all Demons..."

Having a near-death experience just because you were trying to answer the feelings of a human girl was beyond pathetic.

"...You really *are* pathetic. You call yourself Devil King?"

But someone picked up on his self-utterances.

"Here, grab hold of me. Come on. Can you stand up? You can leave the bike here tonight."

"Ah... Yeah..."

Someone took Maou's hand and lent him a shoulder to lean on. His hazy vision turned upward, and he was laid down on something soft.

"Hey. Sorry, I know it's real close, but if you could drive us toward Sasazuka Station..."

His nose told him he had been placed inside a car. Taking a relieved breath, he fell into a deep sleep, all but losing consciousness.

＊

When he awoke, it was already dark.

Maou had been laid down on his back, the orange light from the miniature lamp blinding him.

"Oogh..."

His breath felt tepid as he came to. He was still unwell, but not as scarily limp as he was outside the MgRonald.

"What...time is it...?"

He tried to look at his wristwatch...then realized it wasn't on him.

"Huh? Ah... Wait... When did I take it off? Where's my phone...?"

His foggy mind ordered him to twist around, seeking the phone in its usual position by his bed.

"Mmh..."

Hearing a light groan, he realized that someone was lying next to him. He blinked, his eyes finally getting used to his surroundings.

"...Huhh?!"

Realizing it was Emi next to him, he gasped. The sudden intake of dry air made him choke. He coughed a few times.

"Mmm..."

Emi scowled a bit at the noise but quickly took a deep breath, turned over, and faced away from him.

"...Wha...?"

Maou had been placed on a futon, with Emi sleeping directly on the tatami-mat floor, using a seat cushion as a pillow.

Thinking hard with his addled brain, he moved his heavy head around. No matter how hard he squinted, it looked like nothing but Room 201 of Villa Rosa Sasazuka—with Emi sleeping next to him. Then, finally, he spotted his phone plugged into the wall, as well as the clock hanging above it.

"Ah… Seven…"

Not that much time had passed since he'd left his shift early. If *this* was how he was, Iwaki was right to order him off duty—but he still had no idea how he got here. Vaguely, he could recall leaving the restaurant, becoming incapacitated outside, then someone helping him out. It was probably Emi, but he had no idea why Emi would be there, and even if she was, she had no reason to be sleeping in the same room with him.

"…"

They had shared an apartment not long ago, if only for a little bit, so he could tell whether Emi was in a deep sleep or not. He also knew that Emi had a knack for waking up and falling asleep almost instantly. She told him about this at some point—being raised on a farm meant lots of early mornings, and during their Devil King–slaying quest, there was a lot of camping out and accommodations in rough regions. If you couldn't get yourself awake fast, it could cost you your life.

What's more, life with Alas Ramus, dealing with her crying at night and so on, meant her sleep was shallower than most people's. Whenever Alas Ramus was involved, Maou usually couldn't protest too loudly, so he hesitated to bother her about the noises she made while asleep, but…

"…I gotta go to the bathroom."

He had a sudden urge—probably why he woke up from this nap—but he knew Emi didn't have much chance to sleep soundly like this, so he couldn't help but stop himself. The toilets at Villa Rosa Sasazuka were ancient; when he flushed his, it was loud enough that he feared waking the neighbors. Still, if he held it in, his tank was gonna be beyond full later if he went back to sleep. Should he stay, or should he go?

Just as Maou began waging that lonely war against himself, he felt a vibration from somewhere.

"Hmm…?!"

He thought his phone was ringing at first, but the vibration pattern didn't sound right.

"Mmm…"

It must have been Emi's smartphone. With a light yawn, she sat up.

"Oh, you're up? How are you feeling?"

She turned toward Maou, as if it was the most natural thing in the world.

"…Ah…um…"

The response was so thin and pathetic that his unnaturally tense reaction to Emi's natural greeting was brutally obvious. Unable to respond, Maou watched as Emi stretched out, rubbing her sleepy eyes as she naturally brought a hand to his forehead.

"Ah, what…?"

Her fingers pushed his hair away, her palm resting on his head.

"No, there's no fever. In fact, you seem kind of cool. Is your blood pressure going down?"

"Ah, ah, um…"

"Why're you so nervous?"

Emi smiled a little under the mini-light. The sight of Maou acting so perturbed must've struck her as funny. A little while ago, he would've eagerly spewed vitriol at Emi, no matter how afraid he was that she might harm him—but by the look of things, she'd definitely helped him out after he collapsed outside the MgRonald, and his mind was still too befuddled to come up with anything snappy.

"I'll turn on the light."

Emi stood up and pulled the string twice. Light filled the room.

"I put Alas Ramus in my body. If that really *is* a cold, I don't want her catching it, so don't worry about that."

"Ah, yeah… *Urp…*"

Even the fluorescent light beat down powerfully upon Maou. It made him feel nauseated all over again.

"The light's too painful?"

"…No, um, if you could turn it down a notch…"

"Right, right."

Emi pulled the string again. Out of the two circular bulbs in the socket, the larger one shut off.

"…Why…?" he bluntly asked.

"Chiho contacted me," Emi quickly replied. "She said you were acting weird."

"…I couldn't have been…"

"You were just barely all right when you left her, weren't you? But it still looked unnatural to Chiho. You had your mind all made up, but you still fled right at the last minute."

"No, that…"

"So you gave Chiho an answer, then?"

"…Stop badgering me. You knew, didn't you?"

It was Emi, after all, who had gone on about Maou's suit at Sasazuka Station.

"I didn't *know* anything. I just couldn't imagine you'd do anything else."

Outside of apologizing to the Sasakis, Emi could think of only one thing Maou would feel obliged to address while he was here tying up loose ends. It was the only scenario that made sense to her—and she was right. And since Emi's take made perfect sense from Maou's perspective, he very quickly changed clothes, so he and Chiho would feel as natural as possible around each other.

"You know, I've thought this a few times before, actually, but you like *looking* the part before you dive into something, don't you?"

"…"

"I'm not saying that's a bad thing. Once you're grown up, it's hard to really put your mind to something unless you do. I'm like that in some ways, too."

"Stop acting so grown-up. You're only one year older than Chiho."

"Yes, but I spent my time differently. I was in a different culture." Emi, unruffled by Maou's jab, put a hand to her hip and sighed. "So the way Chiho put it, you were all dressed up and ready to go. You gave her an answer, and the moment you did, you made a disgraceful exit."

"Chi wouldn't have phrased it so *nastily*..."

"Well, what do you want? That's basically what happened. Also..."

Even the soft fluorescent light was a bit strong for Maou. The glare made Emi's face hard to discern.

"...She seemed pretty shocked that I knew you'd reply to her feelings."

"...Huh?"

He thought hard with his woozy mind. Why would that be a shock to Chiho? Emi must have known something that Maou didn't.

"So thanks to that, right after you replied to her and ran off... Before she could be happy about it, she brought up Alas Ramus first."

"...Sorry, I don't understand yet. Why would Alas Ramus come up?"

"I'm impressed you still don't know after everything I said," Emi replied, honestly exasperated. She sat back down by Maou's pillow, elbow on one knee as she peered into Maou's face. "Now I'm getting a bit angry. At you, and at Chiho, too."

"Huh...?"

"She said she thought that if you chose her, it'd be removing Alas Ramus from her father."

"...What was that?"

"Chiho can *really* be a handful to deal with sometimes, can't she? She reads too much into things, I guess, or thinks about them too much. It's almost rude, in a way."

This surprised Maou, hearing Emi criticize Chiho at this point.

"But *I* understand you a lot more than she does. And to me, it sounds like you all but gave her an answer, but now she's lost all her confidence. Like, 'What if this destroys the family you and he and Alas Ramus have?' and so on."

"That..."

"That was the gist of it anyway. And along those lines, the way you ran off on her, she was worried that you were still hiding something."

Emi, smiling above him, was a scary sight to behold. He was unable to respond as she went on, the look persisting on her face.

"And if you're like *this* after running away, your illness must have something to do with Chiho, doesn't it? And I get it if you don't want Chiho to worry over you, but me, I don't want her to have the wrong idea about us forever. If you ask me who I'm gonna care about more, you or Chiho, it's gonna be Chiho every time. You understand that?"

"Y-yeah…"

"I mean… You realize that, in just a few days, you and I are gonna be leading the army in the assault on heaven? Think about the timing a little. If you knew it would turn out like this, why didn't you take action sooner, or maybe give your answer some other time so it didn't come to this? 'Cause whether I want to or not, we're gonna be partners up in heaven, trusting each other with our lives. Do you know how it makes me feel if my partner's bedridden and he's hiding why for some stupid reason? You realize that we're fighting a battle where children's lives are at stake, right?"

She smiled the whole time, unrelentingly. That was what was so scary.

"Come to think of it, weren't you under the weather before we launched Devil's Castle, too? I'm not gonna give you the right to remain silent here. Tell me what's causing all of this."

"…All right."

Maou tried to take his eyes off Emi's stretched-out smile. But he had no choice except to relent.

"Hmmmmmmmmmmmmm…"

Pushing back his fatigue, Maou did his best to explain his Chiho-adjacent illness, from when it first began post-summit to the present day. He received a kiss from Chiho. When he gave her feelings serious thought and attempted to reciprocate them, he felt ill like never before in his life. He even revealed his convalescence with Sariel, leaving nothing unsaid.

The response was just that flat, emotionless "hmmm."

"Look, I'm baring everything I have for you here…"

"No, I mean, it sounds like nothing but you talking about how much you love her to me. Not even my father goes on at *that* much length."

Emi's serious exasperation seemed to make a laughingstock of all the resolve Maou had drummed up for so many things.

"And you treated me like a child earlier, didn't you, saying I'm only one year older than Chiho?"

"…What about that?"

"Well, I don't need you lording it over me if you're laid up because you kissed a cute girl and replied to her love confession."

"…Ngh…"

He had no response. The debate was completely one-sided.

"But all right. So in the end, all you have to do is stop hiding things from Chiho. Just talk to her. Face up to her. Right?"

"Stop hiding things? I can't really do much about that right now."

"It doesn't matter whether you can or not. What's important is that you make yourself face up to her… Why do I even need to tell you all these things?"

"Is that how it is?"

"Go ahead and doubt me if you want. It's your and Chiho's problem; do whatever you want. We're gonna have to beat Ignora before things start to calm down anyway. Why don't you just take your time, let it simmer, and get dumped in the end, regardless?"

"Hey…"

"Wow. Now I feel really dumb worrying for you. I wish Chiho could understand how spineless you really are."

"Hey…*urgh*…!"

Maou got up to complain, unable to weather this tirade any longer. But his elbows and shoulders still didn't work the way he wanted. He collapsed back onto his futon. Emi didn't turn around.

"Did you eat anything, by the way? There's not really anything in the fridge that's good for a convalescent. It's all just fried stuff."

"………………Lately…Libicocco's done all the cooking."

Frustrated, Maou had his head buried in his pillow, no longer caring how he sounded to Emi as she nagged him.

"Oh, but you've got some frozen rice. I could make some porridge for you, but can you eat that?"

"I don't need any."

"Why are you sulking?"

Emi turned toward Maou, who was mumbling into his pillow after his valiant attempts to sit up had failed. Despite her harsh words, her face had an oddly gentle look to it.

"Well, once you get your appetite back, if you eat something greasy that's been sitting in the fridge for a while, you'll wreck your stomach. I'll make sure this is okay to heat up later, so let me make it, all right?"

"Nnh..."

Maou replied with a groan as Emi took out some miso and chopped vegetables and prepared a simple rice porridge.

"Eat this once you feel better. And stay hydrated, too, please. I put a few sports drinks in the fridge. I'll leave one bedside for you, all right?"

"...Mmh."

Maou remained facedown on the futon, whether he couldn't get up or just didn't want to.

"You're gonna asphyxiate."

"..."

"If you lag behind in battle because you're dragging all this Chiho stuff, I'm not gonna help you out."

"...Like that'll happen."

"I don't know..."

Despite the bravado, Emi kept her breezy smile on. Maou never stood a chance.

"But if you're sulking that much, I'm sure you're all right. I'm going home, so take care."

Double-checking to make sure she'd turned the gas stove off, Emi picked up her shoulder bag from a corner of the room.

"Ugh, my hair's a mess…"

She used a comb to smooth out her bed head as she walked toward the front door.

"…Hey."

"What?"

"…Why were you sleeping?"

"Huh?"

Emi, in the midst of putting her shoes on, turned back around. Maou was on his back again, looking up at her.

"Why were you sleeping next to me?"

"It wasn't me originally. It was Alas Ramus."

"Huh?"

"She saw you were sick and wanted to make you feel better, so she latched right on to you. I told her to stop because she might catch it, but she wouldn't listen to me."

"…Oh… Really…?"

"So I lay down so she was between you and me, and when she fell asleep, I put her back into my body. But you still weren't waking up and I was a little tired myself, so I just took a nap, is all. I set an alarm because even if you didn't wake up, I wanted to leave before eight. I have to feed Alas Ramus and take a bath and stuff."

It was a perfectly sensible reply. It still took Maou aback. He sighed.

"…Oh. That's fine, then. Sorry."

"It wasn't because I wanted to sleep beside you or anything."

"Did anybody even say that?"

"You asked me because you were anxious that was it, didn't you?"

She saw right through his mind.

"Well, *sorry*. I've really got no idea what women are thinking lately."

"Do you act that way around Bell, too?"

That stabbed Maou once more where it hurt. But he didn't have it in him to resist the tsunami any longer.

"I don't know. Suzuno and I have talked a few times but never alone. And even with Chi, you saw how we interacted normally with each other until just before we talked today."

That made Emi stop tying her shoes.

"So as long as you're not alone with her, conscious about *that* sort of thing, you're all right?"

"...Maybe. I can't say for sure yet, but..."

Emi took her shoes off and sat back down next to Maou, placing a hand on his forehead, then his chest. Maou had no idea what to make of this mysterious behavior, worrying that his heart palpitations would be interpreted the wrong way.

"Mmm... I bet Bell could see it with one touch, but not me, I guess. This is going to sting a bit."

"Huh? *Gaghh?!*"

Suddenly, a shock ran up and down Maou's body. The hair on his head stood up, as if loaded with static electricity, and he could virtually feel the shock in his fingers. It was a familiar feeling to him.

"Wh-what are you doing?! You trying to kill me?! 'Cause I could really die right now!"

Emi had injected a sonar blast of holy energy into his body.

"I thought so," she said flatly, ignoring his protests. "Devil King, does it feel like the demonic force inside you is being upset? That force makes us sick as it is, but it's sloshing around in the weirdest way in there."

"I think that's what's happening. That's why, after I took Copyhara to the demon realms, I began feeling better pretty quickly. Like, if you were gonna scan me for *that*, then *say* something first."

"Like you'd say yes to it. But in that case, no matter how bad off you are, if you can fill up your demonic force, you're fine, huh?"

"That's what I thought, too. But I'm not completely out of demonic force like last time. I had a decent amount stored up, but this is *still* happening. I guess if I don't have enough to put me in demon form when I go back to that realm, then probably..."

"Hmm... I see." Emi removed her hands and fished through her shoulder bag. "Then it's simple, isn't it? It's not gonna solve your problem with Chiho at the root, but if you have enough power to become the Devil King, that'll fix you up, right?"

"What're you talking about? I can't *do* that in Japan, and that's the problem—"

Maou couldn't finish the sentence. Too weak to even turn over in bed, he had no way of resisting it. A warm, soft sensation stopped him cold, a sweet liquid flowing into his mouth. Emi's low mutter came into his ears from a position closer to him than she had ever been before. Even if he wanted to escape, his head was held down, his mouth kept shut; there was no way to stop the flow.

"Nhh... Ooh..."

It lasted just a few seconds, Emi's face occupying his entire vision, but to Maou, it lasted long enough to have his life flash before his eyes.

"*Pahh!* Wha-ah..."

When his view opened up again, Emi was holding what looked like an opened energy shot in her right hand. Then he felt the liquid—forced into him mouth to mouth—burn like a searing flame inside him. But it wasn't strictly the 5-Holy Energy β causing his throat, stomach, and intestines to writhe in agony. Emi's own powerful holy energy, filled to the brim by her recent stay in Ente Isla, had gone along for the ride. The already agitated demonic power was blown away. He could feel it being crushed, eradicated from every cell in his body.

"Don't worry. I put up a barrier."

By the time Emi leaned back and wiped his lips with her handkerchief...

"...Come on, Emi..."

...Maou was in Devil King form, brimming with demonic force from head to toe, and already sitting up on his futon.

"Hey, we already proved it works, right?"

She was right. If a human body was flooded with more holy energy than it could process, it sustained an inversion and transformed into amplified demonic force. Everyone around Maou knew about that; he'd had Emi and Suzuno help him pull off that exact trick to turn demonic before.

"I—I don't mean that…"

But that wasn't really the issue. The issue was Emi's position.

"Why are you still stammering, as big as you are? You feel fine now, right?"

"Huh? Ah, no, um, yeah. I'm great."

He nodded, in a daze—and as he did, the demon's stomach growled prodigiously.

"Okay, I'm going for real this time."

Despite the mind-boggling events, Emi was serene as she tossed the empty bottle of 5-Holy Energy β into the Devil's Castle recycling bag and put her shoes on.

"N-no, Emi, you…!"

"You've been suffering under a lot of wrong ideas, so I'm just gonna say it—I have *no* intention of playing the same games with you as with Chiho and Bell, so don't get me wrong on *that* count."

"Ah, uh, I, b… But just now…"

"But just now what? You thought I was gonna climb on the band-wagon, too? Even if I did, what's the big deal? You wouldn't even have to acknowledge it."

"N-no…um…"

"Who besides me right now has enough holy force to crush your demonic power and flip it over to max? No offense to Bell, but she sure can't, and neither can Eme. And with the battle coming right up, there's no easier way to do this than that. So that's why."

The dumbfounded Devil King Satan balled himself up, exhausted. The next moment, he reverted back to Sadao Maou, looking as healthy as he ever was.

"Now, it doesn't benefit any of us if someone finds out about this, so *please* find a solution, all right? So I never need to do it again?"

This man, back from his demon form, cowered before the resolute woman in front of him. He sat on the futon, looking pathetic with his clothes ripped up beyond repair.

"Otherwise," Emi said as she gave him a sideways glance, "you're gonna make Chiho real unhappy."

With that parting line, she left Room 201 without waiting for Maou's reaction.

"…"

Maou, left alone, tried to ease his chaotic mind. The more he did, however, the less able he was to find a clear response to what had just happened. So he decided instead to throw out his ripped clothing, change into sweats, eat the rice porridge, and go back to sleep. He didn't say anything; he didn't think anything. That was what Emi wanted—demanded, really—from him.

For now, at least, he thanked her. He didn't think about it, didn't want it in his memory—but he thanked her for helping him when he was sick and for making dinner for him. Nothing more.

"…It's good."

No harm in that reaction, at least. He said no more as he finished up the porridge, washed the pot, and lay back down…

"…Oh, right, I had to piss."

The succession of shocking events had deadened his senses, but now they were back up and running. Once he was done in the bathroom, he turned out the light and lay back down on his futon.

"Maybe I better cut down on my shifts until it's all over… I'm not gonna be able to keep up otherwise."

He looked to his side. The cushion Emi used as a pillow was still there.

"What am I even gonna *do* about the child support? Ugh…"

✳

Going down the stairs outside, Emi found Erone standing there.

"Did something happen? I saw the barrier."

"Oh, just a little thing. The Devil King's been sick, and he wound up turning into a demon up there. So I put that up on an emergency basis."

"Oh. Is he okay?"

"Yeah. He's almost never been under the weather, so I'm sure his body didn't know what to do with itself."

"Ah. Well, that's good...but you should be careful, too, Emi. I'm glad you're trying to help my brothers and sisters, but I wouldn't like it very much if something happened to all of you."

Emi tousled the hair of the oddly concerned Erone to help him feel better. Erone always was a *lot* more considerate than Maou.

"We're fine. I'm not fighting for you. I'm only fighting for Alas Ramus."

"Eesh. Really?"

Erone smiled at Emi's own consideration.

"I know how warm your hands are, Emi. You must really love Alas Ramus. I'm not a Yesod, but I can tell."

"Of course. I'm ready to do anything for Alas Ramus. And today... I think I've decided what I should do after it's all over. Erone..."

Emi looked down at the innocent boy.

"When you grow up, don't wind up like the Devil King, all right?"

"Why not? I think he's a fine person."

"He's a good guy...but someone who makes girls worry and cry over him... That's never a good thing."

"...I don't think Satan does *that* kind of thing..."

"You'll understand when you're older."

Erone, despite his honest misgivings, still nodded and accepted that classic grown-up cop-out.

"Anyway, I have to get going. Try not to catch any colds, Erone."

"Um... Okay. See you later."

After that unexpected counterpunch, Emi hurriedly talked her way out of there and headed off. She focused a bit, making sure Alas Ramus was still sleeping inside. Then, for just a moment, she touched a finger against her lips, shoulders drooping.

"This really can't go on... I'm acting so stupid."

Her legs stopped.

"When it all comes to a head, I gotta be sure I can settle things..."

The hand that touched her lips clenched into a fist as she made a promise within her heart.

"Even...if I have to go against Chiho's wishes when it happens..."

Only the dark Sasazuka night sky could listen in on her resolution.

◊

Just as Mayumi Kisaki was enjoying her day off with her family at the freshly opened Yesodd's Family Café, Emi Yusa was having a busy morning. She was in Kobe, Hyogo prefecture, a city far to the west of Sasazuka, and she had just climbed from the back seat of a car parked at the Shin-Kobe Station roundabout, her long hair tied back. She was accompanied by Alas Ramus, sporting a small Relax-a-Bear purse around her shoulder.

"Stay there, okay, Alas Ramus? I gotta get our luggage from the trunk."

"Mommy, let's go in the station! It's too hot out here!"

"Not yet. Just wait a little bit, all right? And did you say thank you to Rika yet?"

"Yeah, when we got out of the car!"

"No, say it for real, all right? No mumbling it out the door."

"Aww, Emi, don't be such a fuddy-duddy! She *did* say thank you to me. Didn't ya, kid?"

"See? Rika says so, too!"

"Eesh…"

With a wry grin, Emi took a wheeled suitcase from the back of the car, checked for anything she might have missed, and closed the door.

"I was kinda worried when we hit that traffic jam on the highway, but it's never anything serious around this time of day. But anyway! Have a nice trip back, okay, Emi?"

Rika Suzuki, stepping from the driver's seat, lifted her driving sunglasses and gave Emi a wink.

"Sure thing. Thanks a lot for the ride, Rika."

"Oh, don't mention it! Anything for a friend, y'know? But don't just make it two nights next time, okay? Stay as long as ya want! And I hope I see *you* later, too, okay, Alas Ramus? I'll be waiting for ya!"

"Okay! I'll see you tomorrow!"

The very childlike response made Rika smile. "Ooh, I dunno if Mommy can do tomorrow. But I'm glad you want to come back so soon!"

"Aww, Mommy, when can we come back?"

"We'll have to plan it out, okay? Boy, you've sure grown to be a good talker, haven't you?"

"Hey, it shows how far she's gotten, right? I know it's been a year and a half and everything, but I can't believe how big she is! She's a real cutie! This must be what it's like to have a niece, huh? I'm sure it is..."

Rika squinted, as if the light was too much for her eyes, and looked down at Alas Ramus's feet.

"By the time I see you again, you'll probably have outgrown those shoes, huh?"

Alas Ramus had some summer kids' sneakers on. Rika's family ran a factory that manufactured parts for shoes, and although they were still small-scale, they had introduced their own brand of footwear over the past few years. That was what Alas Ramus was sporting.

"You really couldn't have been kinder to her. I appreciate your family, so tell them I said hi. These soles are so comfortable."

Emi wore her own choice of shoe brand, but the inner soles were a special order, contoured for her own feet by the Suzuki family.

"Aw, I'm happy to hear that! Grandpa will be glad to hear it, too. But, you know, I'll be back in Tokyo soon for work, and I'll probably do another sales run over to The Maou Company, so let's hang out if you're free."

"Of course! Contact me when you do!"

Two years ago, Rika had moved out of her apartment in Tokyo's Takadanobaba neighborhood and returned to her family's house in the Suma district of Kobe. There, she was learning the family trade from her grandfather and parents, mastering the basics of shoe design.

She wasn't going to college or looking for a career, but Rika had still spent a long time in Tokyo, away from her family—and Emi didn't know why until she came to visit her in Kobe just now. When a large earthquake hit the city of Kobe in 1995, the family's property and machinery were all safe, but a large number of their regular clients went out of business in the aftermath. Between that and the recession that hit in the mid-nineties, by the time Rika graduated from high school, the family firm was teetering on the brink of bankruptcy.

The whole family was anxious about this, but Rika's grandmother—her dad's mom—had a pretty anachronistic solution for it. Basically Rika, as the eldest daughter, would get herself married to the son and heir of a relatively powerful midsize firm, in an attempt to save their company. Having your grandma pick a husband for you right in one of the most sensitive times of your life would be traumatic enough, but even worse, the candidate she had in mind was a good twenty-five years older than Rika. It was nothing short of abuse, really—and while her grandmother had a firm grip on the reins in her family, Rika's grandpa and parents were staunchly against it. So after graduation, they had her evacuate to Tokyo for safety's sake. It was her grandfather who chose the Takadanobaba apartment for her; it was a neighborhood synonymous with cheap college student housing, and he figured that if Grandma tried tracking her down, she'd have a hard time over there.

By the time Rika came to know Emi, old age and infirmity kept her grandmother from being involved with the business, but she still had major clout over the family behind the scenes, and she apparently still hadn't given up on marrying her granddaughter into a richer industrial family. They never did come to terms with each other, in the end, before she passed away two years ago—and after the funeral service, Rika went straight back home to Kobe. Not long afterward, Rika began working with The Maou Company, providing accessories and industrial shoes for restaurant workers. It really was a small world.

Emi, who saw Rika as a friend and confidant without ever asking why she was staying in Tokyo, was warmly welcomed by the Suzuki family, now that the old matriarch was no longer in the picture. Rika's younger sister, Rina, in particular, loved Alas Ramus as much as her own kin, endlessly spoiling her.

"You gave me so much stuff, too. I'll have to repay you sometime."

"It's fine! If you really insist, you should show my sister around Tokyo when she visits. She said she wants to find a job there when she's done with school."

"Oh, right. She's still a freshman in college, right? But she's already thinking about her career?"

"Well, given our family, we know what it's like to live in tough times. If I hadn't come back, she might've really wound up inheriting the company, after all."

Rika, for her part, felt guilty about running off to Tokyo and leaving her sister to face up to her grandmother. But as Rina put it: "If you weren't around, I figured, 'Oh well, I guess I'll inherit it,' but I have bigger dreams than that. If you weren't gonna take it over, I wanted to get our firm out into the world more, so we could make lots more money! Like, if we keep it small-scale like Grandma did, it would've gone bankrupt sooner or later, you know?"

"I tell you, she's got even more vitality than I do. She's gonna hit it big, mark my words."

"I'll make sure not to tell Rina about Ente Isla, then."

"Yeah, you better not. With *her* personality, she really *would* wanna use it for her business."

Rika laughed hard at that for a bit then picked up Alas Ramus. "Ahh, but enough grown-up chitchat! It's super-hot out here, so time to say bye-bye, okay? Come back soon, Alas Ramus! And listen to what your mommy tells you."

"Okay! See you later, Rika-sis!"

She handed the child over to Emi.

"Have a good one."

"Yep! Have a safe trip back."

Emi waved, took up the handle of her suitcase, and held Alas Ramus with the other as she went into Shin-Kobe Station. As she did, she heard that familiar, chirpy voice booming behind her.

"Oh, right! Say hello to that henpecked 'husband' of yours, too, for me!"

"Shut *up!!*"

They might've been all smiles a moment ago, but that remark

made Emi scowl back at her. Rika, in the sun, smiled broadly and waved, as if that was the face she wanted to see all day, before hopping in the car and driving off.

"Ugh... *You're* the one who missed your chance to marry after doing that 'will-she, won't-she' thing for ages."

"Mommy, I'm hot! I want juice!"

"Oh, right, I should buy something for myself, too. We have some time until the bullet train... Let's go up to that kiosk."

"Ice cream! I want ice cream!"

"You just said juice, didn't you? No ice cream. It's gonna melt all over you."

"Awww! I want ice cream! Juice and ice cream!"

"This order's getting bigger by the minute... Oh?"

Emi felt the smartphone in her shoulder bag vibrate a little. Reading the screen, she recalled her previous conversation with Rika and frowned a bit.

"What is it, Mommy?"

She showed the screen to Alas Ramus. "I got a note from Chiho. I'll answer it once I buy some juice, so wait a minute, okay?"

Successfully shooting down the ice cream demand, Emi purchased a bottle of pulp-in orange juice (a favorite of Alas Ramus's as of late), leaned against the wall by the turnstile, and fired off a reply.

"What's Chi up to?"

As she grew, Alas Ramus had naturally come to call Chiho "Chi." Emi took a moment to figure out her reply but couldn't find a simple explanation that her child would understand, so she winged it instead.

"Well, Chiho's coming back to Tokyo today, too."

"She was out?"

"That's right. We saw her off in that building with all the planes, remember? Before it got hot out."

"Mmm, I dunno."

Whether she really didn't know or was just being silly, Emi couldn't tell. The child had a way of vividly recalling things Emi had completely forgotten about—but events that left a deep impression on grown-ups passed in one ear and out the other with her. Emi had trouble figuring out how her tiny memory worked.

"Yeah, well, thanks to that…"

Past the turnstile, Emi looked at the electronic train schedule and smiled to herself.

"…Daddy might start feeling a little ashamed of himself."

THE
DEVIL
RELIES
ON
OTHERS
FOR THE
FUTURE

West of Phiyenci, main city of the Northern Island, there was a
sacred mountain known as Mt. Figo. Phiyenci itself was built on
high land, but Mt. Figo towered over it, looking down upon the city.
When Chiho and Ashiya invited Kisaki and the MgRonald hourly
crew over to Ente Isla, they chose a flat plain about halfway up this
hallowed peak.

Three days had passed since the night Maou had found himself
utterly flummoxed by Emi's "deceitful" act. Albert Ende and Dhin
Dhem Wurs were outside together, looking up at the night sky. The
two moons were already far closer to each other than anyone in
Ente Isla would ever believe—and the satellites themselves were also
starting to look smaller.

"Son of Ranga, have the moons ever struck fear into your heart?"

"What kinda question is that? I'm not sure what you mean."

"Well, when I was young, there was a bit of a drought in my clan's
pastures. We had to move our stock out, and we didn't have enough
people, so young me was asked to chase sheep and goats around as
well…and, you know, I noticed something. It felt like, during the
daytime, the moons were chasing me the whole time."

"Oh, that sort of thing? Yeah, I can understand that."

It was something any youngster might have experienced—the sun and moon in the sky constantly staying a set distance away from you, no matter how much you ran away from them.

"And now that Devil King's gone and moved the moon, hasn't he? Boy, am I glad I stuck around long enough to see *this!*"

"I can't say I agree with you on that."

"So what do you think, then? Is this gonna have any impact on us?"

"*Man*, it's freezing. Do we really need to talk about that here?"

"Who's to say how much time I have left in this world, eh, boy? Be a good lad and humor an old woman during her camping trip."

"I'd be shocked if you ever *did* die, you know. *Siiiigh...*"

They were on opposite sides of a campfire, the old woman clad in thick layers. Albert eyed her as he listened to their transport goats bleating.

"Well, apparently, we're seeing almost none of the tide changes that Eme and Alciel were afraid of. I'm hearing stories here and there about how the sea currents are clearly changing around the Central Continent, though."

"Hmm. Scary. Simple enough to put into words, but if it's changing ocean currents, that's some serious stuff."

"That it is. The work of God and all that."

"And that 'God' still isn't doing anything? You don't think she's dead already, do ya?"

"Gods dying, huh?" Albert laughed as he prodded the fire. "Yeah, well, the world's been pretty quiet since the red moon went on the move. Y'know how they've been planning the rebuilding of Wezu Quartus alongside the Crusade, to help commemorate Bell's ordination? Thanks to that, the Central Continent's got enough people and resources to handle most of the crises they run into. You just never know what life's gonna serve up to ya, is what I keep hearing from people."

"No, in my life, I've had that thought countless times. But it still makes no sense to me. Why would the enemy do absolutely nothing up to now?"

"Yeah, no matter how strong we might be, holding out this long is nothing but bad news for the other side. That's what they're all worried about—the Devil King, Bell, Eme, Alciel..."

"Well, don't let your guard down. Whether we're fighting a god or not, we're gonna be faced with constant surprises, I'm sure. Tell the Devil King that for me."

"Oh, I think he's already aware of that..."

"Maybe, but make sure you say it out loud and it goes into his ears, all right?"

"Do I really need to?"

"Look, even if you think it's pointless, it's important you say it out loud to him. If he doesn't listen to you and tells you to shut up, well, we all know how long fools like that survive, don't we?"

To Albert, the voice of the wrinkly old woman, mixed in with the crackling fire, seemed to be reflecting on all the "fools" she had seen go by in life.

"Well, I'm sure they'll all listen, except for Lucifer. You think I should tell Eme, too?"

"Tell anyone traveling to the demon realms. Tell 'em you're speaking for me. Make 'em think that if they ignore this gabby old woman's advice, they'll regret it later on. And also..."

The woman, small but burning just as passionately as the fire, stared at the large frame of Albert.

"Once it's all over, let 'em sit back and say, 'Oh, that old coot was all worked up about nothing.' Then, when they're all old men and women like me, they'll do the same thing to the younger folk. Then the cycle's complete."

"...All right. Man, the elderly are *such* a pain to deal with."

"Watch out, you! You're gonna *be* one of us in time. You, and Emilia, and that little Devil King, and I'm sure Chiho as well. You're no spring chicken yourself. Startin' to experience the kinds of things your mom and dad whined about when you were small, aren't you?"

"No doubt. I've been fillin' my stomach with good drink more than good food lately."

"Hah! Sad thing for the head of the Mountain Corps to say."

Albert laughed at the old woman suddenly turning against him.

Being able to laugh at her griping and snapping probably meant he had matured a fair bit as well.

"Do you need me to escort you back home like the old lady you are?"

"Nah, I'm gonna stargaze for a while longer. You should go back as soon as you can."

"Oh, what, am I gonna have to come back to pick you up? Well, I'll see what I can do, then. I'm not that well-known among demon folk, y'know."

He smiled as he lodged the complaint and took his angel's feather pen out from his pocket. Thrusting it into the air, he opened up a Gate and disappeared—likely headed for the Central Continent, where he'd meet up with Emeralda and Suzuno.

Once he was gone, Wurs let out a hefty sigh, breath visible in the cold air, and looked up at the blue moon.

"We're all behaving illogically, are we…? Well, even ignoring the fact that God might be human, for all I know…."

The old woman watched the purple fragment in her monocle glint in the moonlight as she looked through the lens toward the moon.

"Assuming she's not tired of livin' yet, she might have some hidden desperate move she'll break out when the youngsters least expect it. What d'you think of *that*, eh?"

But the astral monocle, capable of telling truth from lies, failed to find the answer in the blue light overhead.

✳

"So you came here just so we could play a game of telephone with that cranky old woman?"

"What is the issue with that? I would never have a chance to visit the demon realms otherwise. I must say, though, this view is astounding. A far cry from the surface down below."

Suzuno was showing some curious wonderment at the view as she stood there with Maou, who had all but evacuated to the demon realms two days ago to flee from his memory of Emi. She had a message from Dhin Dhem Wurs, relayed to her via Albert in the Central Continent, and she had already given it to Emi and Emeralda before coming here to tell a third Ente Islan about it.

From the terrace at Devil's Castle, they could see a gigantic object in the sky. It was night out, and despite usually being covered in storms of red dust, the sky above the realm was filled with twinkling stars and a large blue moon.

Even though they both knew what this moon was, it was hard for a person to describe this dignified sight as a "moon." No matter how large you knew Earth's moon to be, it still looked like little more than a disc in the night sky, able to be fit through a circled thumb and forefinger. *This* moon was a massive presence, taking up over half of one's vision. It was simple in shape, yet went against any human being's impression of what a moon should look like—really, it was just a big *thing* in the air, one that conjured feelings of despair and reminded a person of just how small they really were.

"It is hard to explain, but if I was in the ocean and suddenly ran into a blue whale, I imagine it would be like this."

"Ah...uh...yeah."

Maou smiled at the understandable-but-not-really comparison.

"So? If we are *this* close, can we make it over? And despite being this close, they *still* have not attacked?"

"Yeah, Ashiya was curious about that, too—and so was Gabriel, for that matter. And Gabriel can't tell any lies around Amane at this point, y'know. Maybe Raguel, Camael, and Ignora really *are* all that's left over there."

Maou, personally, didn't think that. This was just conversation. The heavens had free control over Erone at one point, and whoever was inside the space suit that took Alas Ramus from Emi likely had some kind of Sephirah power as well.

"Y'know, though, it's not like Erone ever acted all that hostile with us. Looking at how Acieth and the angels got along with each other, would they really want to take on a combo like Emi and Alas Ramus?"

"So no matter how one looks at it, none of us can picture the enemy having any decisive advantage here, then? Right. And by the way..."

"Hmm?"

"Why are you so far away?"

"...Oh."

Maou and Suzuno were watching the night sky from a corridor about halfway up Devil's Castle, but Maou was using a completely different window from Suzuno. When Suzuno adjusted her position to view the demon realm landscape, Maou jumped even farther away from her.

"The Devil King himself, after all, cleared everyone out because he had a personal conversation to conduct," she said with a wry smile. "I was expecting some kind of happy news."

"*Please* don't get started with that. I'm serious."

Maou shifted to another window down, half-panicked. Suzuno, perhaps expecting that, didn't act offended, her smile growing more genuine.

"Did something happen with Chiho? Or did you have a fight with Emilia?"

"Why do you..."

"Oh, I can surmise. I imagine you cannot even tell Alciel about it, am I right? If I were him, and you started talking about trouble with Chiho or Emilia at this point, I would spend all day upbraiding you about it."

Suzuno stopped Maou's would-be defenses cold.

"How to put it? Once I pick up on how you act, you are so easy to read. It impressed me you could serve as the Devil King despite that."

"Oh, like *you* have any idea."

"No? If I am wrong, my apologies. So what did you want? This matter you could not ask anyone else about except me?"

"..."

Suzuno watched Maou, silent and pouting, and she sighed a bit.

"How about we do this, then?"

Maou turned toward Suzuno as she turned her back to him.

"You find it easier to talk when you cannot see my face, right?"

"...Right."

Maou, understanding what Suzuno wanted to say, turned his own back to her. This, they found, was the best way they had to address each other.

"...But I'm sorry. It's just, you know, I'm not sure what I should be doing any longer. I'm breaking up."

"You are?"

"It's kind of... I must look so pathetic to all you guys lately."

"To us, you demons have never *not* looked pathetic."

"Ah. It all depends on how you put it, huh?"

"And that is the person I love, despite it all."

Maybe it was the conventional wisdom of human society driving him into guilt, but Suzuno's words made Maou's heart fly into action, his blood pressure plummeting.

"So?"

"...I want your opinion, Suzuno. Why do you think demons can convert the fear in human beings into demonic force? All of us, no matter what species we are."

"How sudden. Well, if Ms. Shiba is correct, that is a by-product of demonic force, holy force, and how they interact with the planet, no?"

"How they interact? So you think it's some inscrutable thing we'll never know?"

"I am sure there is some valid physiological reason we have not discovered yet. Think about it. Why are we able to stand on the surfaces of moons and planets? It is thanks to gravity, and while we know what gravity is, how many understand how gravity works between objects, outside of some equations in a book?"

"...Yeah."

"Many people have heard of terms like 'brain cell' and 'synapse.' They might have seen schematic diagrams of the brain, and some scientists have even observed the processes that happen when we remember something. But nobody has impartially observed what 'memory' *looks* like, exactly."

"…Did you see a TV program or something?"

She kept on bringing up examples she must have learned about in Japan, so he couldn't help but say that.

"So perhaps there is an organ all demons share that detects brain cell activity in humans and absorbs some manner of energy from it. I see no harm in theorizing along those lines."

"You don't think?"

"If we can observe and replicate that phenomenon, then even if we cannot determine the cause, we can research and discuss the process and its results. Did you know that, technically speaking, we still can't fully explain how aircraft are able to fly with Bernoulli's principle alone?"

"Really? Well, not that it matters now."

He wasn't sure how convincing that argument was, but either way, they were getting nowhere, and Maou had to take this somewhere. So he accepted Suzuno's argument and resolved to make one of his own.

"Anyway, I've been through a lot of stuff, and thanks to that, I can't really come physically near Chiho right now…or you, for that matter."

"What about Emilia?"

"I… I'm fine with her."

He caught himself before he added "for now" to the end. Suzuno didn't comment, noticing it but perhaps deciding Maou was just trying to act strong around Emi as usual.

"And, honestly, even at *this* distance, I'm not feeling too good. In a way, I objectively understand that, and I really hate it, but…"

"Mmm. I see… Hmm."

Suzuno suddenly turned back toward Maou, addressing him normally.

"If I were to surprise you with an embrace or the like, what would happen?"

"Huh?!"

"I mean, with the final battle so close at hand, I would never want your health to suffer. If we did not have to think about the future, I would be less willing to hold back."

"Whoa............ Uh, Suzuno?"

"Hmm?"

"Um, how did you know that? Like, that's the reason why I haven't been feeling well?"

"Hmm...?"

Maou was thrown, his words ever so slightly shaky. Suzuno didn't miss it this time.

"If you are asking me a question like that... Ahh, I see. And that was why you were hesitant talking about Emilia before?"

"Huh?"

"...Hmm."

"Agh!"

Maou, having his back turned, reacted a beat late. With a light shock, Suzuno's hand came around behind his back, sending his blood pressure tumbling.

"I simply thought that it maybe was the case. It was a possibility I noticed quite soon after I realized I loved you. If you are a demon who grows more powerful from our fear, I thought, what would happen if we *loved* you instead?"

"N-no, uh... Suzuno!"

"You asked me why I knew? Well, let me tell you. I am always looking at you, always thinking about you, always together with you, and under *those* conditions, well near *anyone* would realize it! Just as I am sure Emilia did."

Her voice seemed angry, but she released Maou nonetheless, giving him a little kick from behind for effect. It pushed him forward, bringing the distance between them back to how it was when they were turned away from each other.

"So I assume you acted brave around Chiho and said nothing to her, and it caused trouble for Emilia afterward, or the like."

"H-how do you know that...?"

"Because it is all too familiar to me! You constantly drag your feet

with Chiho, and thanks to that, she asks to speak with me so she can dump all her emotional baggage, among other things!"

Maou refused to frankly address Chiho, and thanks to that, she never truly felt that she had his attention. No matter how mentally strong she might have been, that would make any teenage girl anxious, deep down. And despite never addressing that anxiety at the root, he tried to care for it on the surface—only to obliviously make things worse. Looking back, Suzuno had first picked up on Chiho's anxieties on that day in winter.

"Chiho has had feelings for you for a very long time now, both when your demonic force was gone *and* when it was back in your possession. So I assumed things would be all right…but I had a nagging concern. It was back when Farfarello kidnapped Chiho, when you used holy force from me and Emilia to create demonic force."

As Suzuno put it, anyone intimately familiar with Maou would have picked up on this. But given how her thoughts were based around the same things as Emi's, everyone who was there for that scene would've been able to ascertain the cause of the changes befalling Maou.

"We are both closely involved with you, but we, as human beings, infused you with an opposing force that you converted within you. So I wondered—does that only work when you are *feared* by mankind? Would nothing happen if you were loved?"

"…"

"And that is exactly what happened."

Suzuno fell silent for a while.

"Of course, based on what I see, I think that…"

Her mouth was about to make the "Chi" sound when Maou exploded. "Wait! Wait, Suzuno."

He asked her to stop. A person had to be watching carefully to see it, but Suzuno's eyebrows went down a bit, lips frowning slightly.

"Just…let me finish that thought for you, okay?"

"Okay." Suzuno nodded, waiting for him.

"…I don't know if I should lob this back to you after asking you to wait, but…um, ahh, Suzu, uh, Crestia Bell, I…"

"Suzuno is fine."

"Huh?"

"Suzuno is fine," she repeated, a little more strongly.

"Ahh, Suzuno," he began again, respecting her wishes. "You are a Great Demon General in the Devil King's Army. You are a good neighbor, a companion I can rely on…but back on that day, I simply had no answer for your feelings."

"And not just because you are a demon and I am human?"

"Right. I couldn't answer up to the love you confessed to me that day."

Suzuno looked up a bit at Maou as he declared the truth. She smiled, and the smile threw Maou for a loop. He wasn't expecting that reaction at all.

"Thank you."

"What?"

"I am happy to see you act sincere with me," she said, her smile widening. "To you, I am just one of many people who descended upon your life. In fact, I *aimed* for that life at one point."

"That was forever ago."

"It was only a year ago. To a demon as long-lived as you, I am sure it seems like yesterday."

"Have you ever thought about how *eventful* this past year's been to me? It seems like the ancient past to me now."

"Ha-ha… Yes, indeed."

She nodded and looked up at him again, that soft smile still plain on her face.

"I'm sorry."

"Nothing to be sorry about. Looking at you, I can tell. When you first heard my confession of love, you were perfectly healthy—and now, you cannot come near me. That alone makes me feel rewarded. After all…"

Suzuno lifted a hand, pointing at Maou's chest.

"At the very least, I now have a place on the scales in your heart. Am I right?"

She took a step closer. Maou didn't retreat.

"But this *is* a problem. If someone like *me* is causing this to you, it must be even harder to work with Chiho, no?"

A clammy sweat appeared on Maou's forehead. Suzuno's sharp eyes spotted it, and that was what made her see the problem he faced.

"I feel so pathetic saying it, but yes. In a few ways."

His reply to Chiho's feelings affected him so badly that Libicocco immediately noticed it. He had turned down Suzuno, but not only had she spotted the problem, she worried about him because of it. That may have been the most pathetic thing.

"It *is* pathetic, but this is not simply a matter about you saying no to me. The fate of Ente Isla is heavily involved in it."

"...Yeah, it is. That's why I had to talk to you alone about this. No matter how embarrassing it is."

Maou had spent many hours being exposed to Chiho and Suzuno's feelings for him without any problem. Things had suddenly changed, however, and there could be only one reason for it. And that was: For all the feelings those two human beings gave him, his own body was generating feelings of deep affection just as powerful as theirs.

It was enough to gravely incapacitate even the Devil King. If this had been a normal demon and a normal human, the demon might very well have died from it. And as they planned to help large numbers of demons immigrate to spots across Ente Isla, they might interact with humans, just as Maou and Ashiya did—and over decades and centuries, maybe love between demons and humans would become perfectly normal. But if they were incompatible on a molecular level like this, not only would they not interact—they would be living separately again, hating each other at the root and perhaps waging war once more.

"This is not an issue we can immediately address. We have too little sample data to divine a cause, and for all we know, it might be something related to your own personal nature. But either way... without Chiho's help, you are not going to get anywhere."

"Yeah..."

"Is Chiho aware of this?"

"I don't know. I want to tell her about it once I give her my real reply."

"I see. Well, all right. We cannot address this issue right now, but let us file it as a concern we need to solve going forward. So…"

"Hmm?"

"What kind of reward should I expect for tackling this issue?"

"…What?"

"Because otherwise, why would I bend over backward to help my romantic rival establish true love with the man who dumped me?"

"I, no, um…"

"They say you should not step into lovers' spats, but what kind of work should I do, and who should I work with, to make your relationship work? It makes my head hurt."

"No, that, uhhm…"

"…Pffft." Suzuno laughed a bit at the sight of Maou flailing in front of her. "I promise you that I will seriously address the issue, for the sake of future peace in our world, but I do expect a commensurate reward for it…my beloved Devil King."

"Ooh, ahh, all… All right…"

Maou stepped back, unable to take any more of this. Suzuno watched him, still a bit amused.

"Well, I need to go back. I am a busy woman, despite appearances. With Alciel joining the assault on heaven, I need to give the Central Continent and Efzahan the care it needs."

"…Oh… Oh."

"We got somewhat sidetracked, but I *did* come here to relay that message from Lady Wurs. It seems to me that our victory is assured, regardless of what Ignora is preparing for us, but still, you must stay on high alert."

On this topic, at least, Suzuno put her smile away, dead serious as she watched Maou.

"And do not do anything that will bring regret to Chiho's life afterward."

"…I know. I promised her dad as much."

"Good. Farewell, then."

With that, Suzuno walked past Maou and down the corridor. As Maou turned to watch her:

"…!"

He felt a slight heaviness on his back, preventing him from turning at all.

"Devil King?"

The voice of Suzuno emerged from behind him. He couldn't see her face.

"Whatever you do, *please* return safely. We are all awaiting you."

It was just a single moment of contact. And when Maou tried to respond, the weight was gone—and by the time he finally turned around, Suzuno was through the feather pen–driven Gate and away.

"…That was bad of me, wasn't it?"

Left alone, Maou crouched on the floor for a bit, groaning to himself. But then, with that voiced regret, he toddled off ("toddled" is the only way to put it) to his throne room.

And someone was watching him go.

"Wow, that's how it's going with him?"

It was the classic face Urushihara made—curious, to put it nicely; to put it not so nicely, grinning like a rubbernecker. But Urushihara was never particularly mindful of other people's subtle emotions.

"It's weird, though. Is that the nature of demons, or is the Tree itself affecting him…? Maybe I should keep a closer eye on him."

Copyhara kept muttering to himself as he went in the opposite direction from Maou, heading down to the castle's lower levels. Along the way:

"Ah!"

"Oop. Sorry. I wasn't paying attention."

He almost ran into Emi in the hallway.

"You're Copyhara, right? Not Lucifer?"

"Right. But what's up? Satan went that way, and Crestia Bell's back in Ente Isla."

"Oh. Well, good, then. I have a favor to ask of you. You mind coming with me real quick, before the Devil King finds us?"

"Me? What do you need?"

"I want you to join me in Ente Isla. You said Bell just went back there? If we hurry, we oughtta be able to catch her."

"And you're not gonna tell Satan about this, dudette?"

"No, I want to keep it a secret. I'll explain things to Bell and Eme once we're back in Ente Isla...but before that, I want to confirm something with you. For the sake of peace in Ente Isla, after the assault on heaven."

"Sounds pretty grandiose."

"So you appeared from the Yesod fragment in Chiho's possession, right? How far back does your memory of us go?"

"Anything that happened after Chiho Sasaki took possession of my fragment, I have pretty much the same memory of as you."

Emi gave this a satisfied nod as she took out her angel's feather pen, opened a Gate, grabbed Copyhara's hand, and flew in, as if every second counted.

"In that case, you remember right after the ring with your fragment was put on Chiho's finger..."

The next moment, the Gate disappeared, and they were on their way to Suzuno.

"...Was someone here?"

And by the time Maou staggered by, sensing the residual energy, no trace of Emi and Copyhara was left.

✳

Suzuno let her body flow through the Gate's torrent, as if floating in water. Unlike the trip to Japan, the other side of this Gate to Ente Isla was less than five minutes away.

In the meantime, she frantically tried to organize the feelings in her heart. Her eyes were closed, and behind those eyelids, she could see the flickering campfire she had gazed at with Maou, over in Efzahan. The warmth of his back against hers might have been exactly when her current feelings for him began to bud.

"A good thing my role does not put me in enemy territory."

There was no concept of top or bottom in a Gate linking planet to planet. But the lone droplet that fell from Suzuno's eye, like the remains of an emotion she had shut herself away from, flowed back toward the demon realms she had just left behind before disappearing.

"Ughh! When this is over, I am going to Kagawa, the home of Japan's best udon, and I am going to *stuff* myself!"

◊

It was a typical weekday afternoon at Tokyo Station, and outside the crowded turnstile leading to the Tokaido Shinkansen bullet train, Emi spotted a very unusual-looking sight.

"Where on earth have you been…?"

She eyed Suzuno Kamazuki partly with wonderment, partly with abject scorn.

"Oh, here and there."

"Yeah, I can tell. You've definitely been having a lot of fun, haven't you?"

"Good to see you again, Alas Ramus. You are quite a big girl now."

"Suzu-sis, what's that?"

"This is a *kasa.*"

"A *casa*? But it's not a house!"

"No, a *kasa.* A traditional Asian conical hat."

To be exact, it was a *suge-gasa*, made of bamboo. It matched the white she was decked out in from head to toe, a purple cloth draped around her shoulders. Noticing the target of Emi's attention, she proudly grabbed a piece of the purple fabric.

"Yes, this is my monk's stole. I found a rather nice one. Very eye-catching, is it not?"

"If you say so…but why are you back to the level of religious fervor you had when you first came to Japan?"

Suzuno was dressed in the classical outfit of a Buddhist pilgrim, perhaps on her way to visit the eighty-eight holy temples of Shikoku in southern Japan. But there was nothing particularly holy about Tokyo Station—nor the bullet train both of them had just gotten off.

"I get it if we happened to be on the same train...but were you dressed like that all the way from Shikoku?"

"I always *did* want to take a bullet train once, you see."

That didn't answer the question.

As Suzuno explained, she had gone on a tour geared for beginners looking for a taste of the classic Shikoku pilgrimage. It departed from Tokushima Airport and covered only the first twenty-three temple stops, from Ryozen-ji to Yakuo-ji.

"Back when I visited Kagawa to go on a foodie tour of their best udon noodles, I learned about this tour, and the fact that Okayama is quite close to Shikoku. So my plan was to take a flight to Tokushima, go to Okayama after the tour, and return by bullet train from there...but I had no idea we took the same train, Emilia."

"Yeah. *We* got on at Shin-Kobe, but..."

Emi was glad, in a way, she ran into Suzuno here. If they had bumped into each other on the train, she wasn't sure how she would have reacted.

"And, you know, the pilgrimage has always had an element of traveling for pleasure, but it is still a holy ritual—one where you consider your path in life, learn of the depths of the Buddha's heart, and find enlightenment. Thus, I decided that from the moment I left home until the moment I came back, I would dress in these acolyte's robes. There is nothing improper about that."

"...The Church faithful back home would have a fit if they saw this."

Even now, three years on, Suzuno was still one of the Six Archbishops, among the most powerful government figures on Ente Isla's Western Island. Despite that, here she was going on about Buddha's kindness—and she had a wheeled suitcase with a bag of souvenirs perched on top, suggesting the trip was a lot more secular than she let on.

"Ah, yes! I thought I would give this to you the next time I saw Alas Ramus. This is for Mommy, okay, Alas Ramus? You can have some later."

"Oooh! Okay!"

"I will have a more proper souvenir for you once I return home, but..."

As Alas Ramus did an excited little dance, Suzuno handed Emi a box of caramels—"Sanuki Udon Flavor," it read. It unnerved Emi.

"...Well... I had some Mongolian hot pot caramels once, and if you didn't *know* that, they actually tasted pretty good..."

A bit concerned that the "more proper souvenir" wasn't too proper at all, either, Emi shoved the small box of caramels into the deepest, darkest crevice of her shoulder bag.

Just then:

"Ah! *There* you are! Hey, over here!"

Emi turned toward the familiar voice. Maou and Chiho were approaching them.

"Hey, guys. Sorry to bring you out into this heat."

"Hello, Yusa! And hi, Alas Ramus! Boy, have you grown!"

"Chi! Hello!"

Alas Ramus stood up as tall as she could, hugging Chiho as she kneeled down to greet her. Only then did Chiho recognize Suzuno from beneath her hat and robes.

"Huh? Whoa! Suzuno, is that you?!"

"Suzuno?! What are you doing here? And why are you dressed like that? You got a lot of explaining to do."

She paid little mind to Emi's criticism, but the moment Maou started unloading on her pilgrim's outfit, she suddenly grew resentful.

"This," she plainly stated, "is nothing but a coincidence."

"...Did you take a trip to Shikoku again? And then you took the train from Okayama and happened to share it with Yusa?"

"There, you see? Chiho got it on the first try."

"Yes, and I think it's pretty crazy that Chiho could, frankly."

"Quit being silly. Why are you so proud of that? And what do you mean 'again'? I had no idea you had gone to Shikoku multiple times!"

"Indeed, Devil King, I never told you. And I have no souvenirs for you, either."

She made it sound so casual as she grabbed the handle of her suitcase.

"So what sort of gathering was this? I assumed you were still in Ente Isla, Chiho, but you have returned?"

"Yeah, just a little bit ago." Chiho turned toward Maou and Emi. "But can I tell her what we're here for, guys? I'm technically an outside party, so…"

"It's basically for work," replied Maou, "but really, I'm just gonna be Emi and Alas Ramus's bag carrier."

"Oh? Well, I had best take my leave, then. I would hardly want to get in the way."

Suzuno didn't want to get involved with Maou's "work," but Emi stopped her from departing.

"No, you're fine. We're not meeting with anyone you don't know. If you have the time, why don't we all have a meal together for a change? If he's on time, he should be here before too long."

"Is that so?"

Suzuno still seemed reluctant, but Maou nodded his agreement. "Yeah, stick around if you're able. We reserved the tatami room at this soba noodle restaurant, so as long as you're okay with it not being udon, we can fit one more in easy."

"In that case, perhaps you will let me tag along? Is this other person coming by train as well?"

"No, he should already be here in Tokyo on business. I haven't seen him in a while, either, so as long as it didn't interfere with his work, I figured we could all say hello…"

So it was a work acquaintance of Maou's, one he was willing to have Chiho meet, despite her just arriving back in Japan. Suzuno raised an eyebrow, unsure who this person could be, but the answer arrived very shortly.

"Oh, there you are. Hey, Yusa! Chiho! Maou! And…"

Suzuno turned toward the voice, not recognizing it at first, only to find one of the last people she'd expected.

"Um, Ms. Kamazuki, wasn't it? Why are you dressed like a pilgrim?"

"Heavens! It's *you*, Kazuma?!"

It was Kazuma Sasaki, Chiho's cousin from Komagane in Nagano prefecture. Maou, Ashiya, and Urushihara first met him when Chiho's parents invited them to work at the Sasaki family farm; he later met Emi and Suzuno after they ran up there to join the demons.

"It has been quite a while," Suzuno said. "Thanks again for your help then. So you are working with Sadao here?"

"Pretty much. Plus those two."

Kazuma pointed at two other people coming up to the group— two other faces Suzuno didn't expect at all.

"...Nord and Laila? Hmm? What kind of gathering *is* this?"

"Hello there, Chiho. And hi, Bell. It's sure been a while!"

"Oh? Bell? Why are you all dressed like a Buddhist pilgrim?"

Emi's parents had come here with Kazuma Sasaki—a very unusual combination. Suzuno didn't know what to make of it, and she couldn't imagine what would be happening next.

"Well, we can settle down and chat later, but now that we're all here, let's get going. I had my wholesaler introduce this soba restaurant to me, but it's *really* good. I can take your stuff, Kazuma."

"Oh, really? Well, can you take this? It's pretty light."

"Sure. Ready for some soba, Alas Ramus? What do you want to eat?"

"Ramen!"

Her total dismissal of the idea made all the grown-ups laugh.

"Well," Emi said, "Daddy made a reservation at a soba place, so you'll have to make do with that. Maybe we can have ramen for dinner later, though. You can order whatever juice you want, too."

"Aww... Mommy, ramen!"

Emi tried to placate her with a smile, but Alas Ramus still looked a tad miffed.

✳

The restaurant, inside a building a short way from Tokyo Station, was calm and serene. Suzuno couldn't help but fall back into her old habits with Maou.

"Are you sure you can afford such a fancy place?"

"Hey, I run a company these days, y'know. I'd be useless if I couldn't take my clients somewhere *this* nice, at least. You can order whatever you want to."

"A-all right..."

Maou brimmed with confidence, but Suzuno was still anxious.

"It's all right. He can cover this."

Emi whispered it to her, as if she knew what Maou's finances were like, so Suzuno nodded and decided to see how things unfolded.

Once they were all in the tatami room and had made their drink orders, Kazuma began to explain to Suzuno why he was with Nord and Laila.

"Ahh... I see. You are raising Nord's wheat at the Komagane farm?"

"That's right. I moved to Nagano half a year ago, and the Sasakis have been treating me very well there."

"Oh, no, you treat *us* very well. We're just getting started with wheat, but under Nord's management, it's going really great."

Ever since Maou and his friends had come to help out, Kazuma's wife, Hinako, had fostered a strong desire to get into wheat planting. They had a successful, high-quality crop the first year, and Nord had been managing production ever since as they maintained the business.

"I see... So you have found a place for yourself in Japan, Nord?"

It made perfect sense to Suzuno, until something occurred to her. She whispered into Maou's ear.

"Huh? Then what is Laila doing here? Because she's based in Villa Rosa Sasazuka, no? You know..."

Then she brought up the biggest concern for Maou and Laila at the moment, making sure Kazuma couldn't hear her as she brought it up.

"Laila," a slightly weary-looking Maou replied, "is splitting her time between Sasazuka and Komagane. She's got a part-time job at a hospital here. Plus, with that *other* going concern, we kind of rotate shifts around anyway. Libicocco and I are on duty right now."

"Yeah," Emi added, overhearing them across the table, "it's kind of a seasonal remote job for Father. There's an express bus from Shinjuku to Komagane that gets you there pretty fast, actually."

"Oh... Talk about a sea change... Ah, yes, how is Hitoshi doing? He must be pretty big by now."

Suzuno brought up the name of Kazuma's son. Kazuma gleefully took out his phone and brought up some photos.

"Well, old enough to sass back at me anyway! When we visit Nord's place, the kid plays with Alas Ramus a lot."

"Oh, how nice........................... Um. Ah?"

Then a sudden thought made Suzuno's face pale. To Kazuma and the rest of the Sasakis up in Nagano, Alas Ramus was a "relative" of Maou's. If she was being treated as part of Emi and Nord's immediate family, that would have to spark questions in Kazuma's mind. But Kazuma quickly cleared the air.

"Oh, don't worry. Everybody knows about the deal between Maou, Yusa, and Alas Ramus nowadays."

"Huh?!"

"Kazuma and Hinako," Laila quickly explained, "told the rest of the Sasakis about our situation. If our families are gonna be *this* close to each other, we have to tell them about Alas Ramus, don't we?"

"Yes, it was quite the surprise at first. But once I grasped all of it, boy, you guys were *really* walking a tightrope back then, huh?"

Kazuma admitted that it took him some time to accept everything, but after the approval of Chiho, Riho, Sen'ichi—and most of all Ei Sasaki, Chiho's grandmother and the spiritual head of the Sasaki family—everyone was willing to accept matters.

"Oh... Well, heavens. I see. I was terrified for a moment!"

"Right? Although the tightrope Maou's walking right *now* is a little tricky, too."

Kazuma's eyes turned toward Maou, who shrugged awkwardly.

"Yeah, sorry about that. Really, I think it's turned out great. If there's any problem, it'll be whether we'll tell Hitoshi about everything or not."

"True. For all we know, by the time Hitoshi's old enough, things might be totally different."

"I hardly think anything can change more than it did in the past three years…"

"You said it."

Suzuno and Maou exchanged an earnest smile.

"But if anything, isn't it you who's changed the most, Chiho? Because Aunt Riho was really worried that you would decide to pursue a career in Ente Isla."

"Huh? My mother said all *that* to you?! Ugh… I'm sorry."

Chiho frowned.

"Well," Nord said, "a parent's always going to worry for their child, no matter how old they are. Especially if that child's going into something the parent has no clue about."

"Put it like *that*, Nord, and it sounds super heavy."

Chiho had to cede the point to him. After all, here was a guy who saw his own young daughter be set up as the savior of an entire planet.

"We didn't actually talk much about work, huh? But I'll be at your office tomorrow anyway, so we can pick it up then. Nord, Laila, Yusa, see you all tomorrow."

"Sure thing. Thanks again."

"You too."

"Keep up the good work, Kazuma."

The Justina family watched as Kazuma walked off into the crowded street.

"What a surprise, though… I never expected you would work with Kazuma again. And buying Nord's wheat, no less…"

The main goal of Kazuma's visit to The Maou Company was to work out a contract for flour made from their wheat, for use in a brand-new bread menu at Yesodd's Family Café. They would discuss costs with each other at tomorrow's meeting, and they'd sign the agreement right there if they came to one.

"My company's still just getting started. I gotta use every

connection and relationship I have. Whenever we can get something at a discount, we gotta bring it in at as low a cost as possible. Then it's on to the next step."

Suzuno looked back at the crowd Kazuma had disappeared into and smiled a little.

"I hardly knew what to expect from you at first, but you seem to be doing rather well, no?"

She gave Maou a light pat on the back.

"Right?" he replied, a bit proud.

"Or maybe it *looks* that way," Emi said with a grin from behind, "if you didn't know how it *really* is."

"Oh, don't wheedle him too much," pouted Chiho.

"So, yeah, that sort of thing. Nothing to worry about, you know? I've had a tight grip on the reins from the start."

Suddenly, the shadow behind Maou's back loomed high in Suzuno's eyes.

"I'm still just biding my time. And someday, all the chains are gonna come off."

"You have been biding your time for *quite* a while. Ever since you came to Japan, the story has never changed, has it?"

Maou rolled his eyes, knowing full well Suzuno wasn't taking him seriously. But now Alas Ramus was tugging at his pants.

"Daddy... I'm tired. I wanna go home!"

"All right, I hear ya. C'mon, guys, let's get going. Alas Ramus is starting to get crabby."

Alas Ramus had her eyes half-open, fatigue crashing over her. It charmed Maou.

"Okay, Alas Ramus... Mommy and everyone else have a lot of baggage, so can you hold my hand?"

"Oh, okay, Chi. But I gotta go to the bathroom."

"Oh, the bathroom? All right. Do you mind if I take Alas Ramus to the bathroom, Yusa?"

"Nope. Thanks, Chiho."

"No problem! Here, give your purse to Daddy, okay? You don't want it getting dirty."

Chiho took the Relax-a-Bear purse hanging from Alas Ramus's shoulder and gave it to Maou.

"Thanks, Daddy."

"Sure."

"All right, there's a lot of people, so hold on to my hand, okay?"

Watching as Chiho and Alas Ramus deftly navigated the crowds, Suzuno looked up at Maou again.

"So. It is all going well?"

What, she did not specify. Maou didn't ask for clarification. Instead:

"The people around me understand, at least."

"...Well, so be it. Perhaps Kazuma did not, but if someone gauges your past history on the surface, they might feel obliged to criticize your ethics more than you need."

"Oh man, if I told the truth to my part-timers, I might be stabbed on the street some late night."

"Ha-ha-ha!"

Suzuno couldn't help but laugh at the idea.

"In your case, it does not seem like much of a joke. The way you look now, you would never have guessed, but..."

"I like to think I'm a virtuous Devil King."

"Uh-huh. You sound human to me, all right. A human too big for his britches."

"Well, *you* don't change at all. What are you even doing? Coming to Tokyo in that pilgrim outfit... It's like your first days in Japan all over again. What would the Archbishops think?"

"I have decided to live freely, and die freely. Work is work, and my private life is my private life."

"Or your private planet, huh? None of the other elders in the Church could pull that off."

As they spoke, Chiho and Alas Ramus came back.

"Thanks, Chiho. Give Chiho her handkerchief back, okay, Alas Ramus? And fold it up nice first."

"Okay. Thank you, Chi."

"You're welcome!"

The child did as instructed. Then she ran up to Emi, a little perplexed.

"Hey, Mommy? Chi's handkerchief is a different color from yours."

"Huh?!"

"Hmm? What's up, Yusa?"

"Oh? Ah, nothing! Nothing… W-wait a sec."

"Hmm?"

"What is it, Emilia?"

Emi grabbed Maou's arm. "You!" she said sternly, in a low voice. "That handkerchief from before…!"

"Huh? Oh, that? Your Mother's Day present or whatever?"

"That one! You didn't give the same thing to Chiho, did you?!"

"…Oh, ummm…"

The thought had never even occurred to him. But now he realized his inadvertent faux pas. It instantly broke him down.

"No, uh, it's not the same thing…so…"

"It's a different color of the same thing! What were you thinking?!"

"I—I'm sorry! I didn't think a handkerchief was any big deal…"

"Will you *please* be more careful? Ugh."

"Sorry…"

Maou put his hands together in front of Emi, begging for forgiveness. And Chiho, who had watched them both from the corner of her eye while chatting with Nord and Laila over the meal, said:

"Yusa just got a different color, huh? Well, that's what I figured."

She placed a hand on her shoulder bag, the slightly damp handkerchief from Alas Ramus safe inside, and exhaled lightly.

THE DEVIL AND THE HERO CHALLENGE THE GOD

It's said that one should prepare as much as possible for the future; but the bigger the thing one is preparing for, the harder it becomes to keep everything organized. Now it was late July, a bit over a week after Maou and company went to the Sasakis to apologize. The day had finally come.

Three days had now passed since the red moon had reached its closest point to the blue moon. The two had reached a stable balance, and once they stopped moving around, the group of Heroes planned to storm in. Maou's party wasn't sure if they were outside the Roche limit Ashiya and Emeralda had worried about, but either way, they set off a week after the demon realms stopped gaining ground over heaven. The storming party consisted of Maou and Acieth, Ashiya and Urushihara, Emi and Alas Ramus, Laila and Gabriel, Copyhara and Amane, and Camio and Farfarello. Amane would not fight; instead, she'd observe and defend herself, while keeping watch over Copyhara.

So Devil's Castle was launched once more from the demon realms— and even when the party plunged into heaven, there was no reaction on the other side. Considering the vast amount of time and effort they'd spent launching from Ente Isla, they ran into no obstacles at all, and after a short voyage through space, Devil's Castle landed in heaven.

"Well, you're just outside the demon realms. How do you feel?"

"I'm fine. Don't distract me."

That was the exchange Emi and Maou had as they surveyed the surface of heaven. Neither of them would ever bring up that night again. They had both decided that, even if they looked at or spoke to each other, they would never rehash the words and memories from that early evening. That was what enabled them to gaze at these enemy lands in full possession of their serenity. They both encouraged each other to act that way.

If Maou had to describe the landscape, the only way was to compare it to a field of ice. The land was a cold shade of blue, one that froze both time and hearts.

"Coming here sure was easy, wasn't it?"

"I suppose there won't be a welcome party. I was pretty nervous about this..."

The quiet surface of the heavens was rocky, a uniform light blue in color. This, they could tell, was why the moon looked blue from the surface of Ente Isla.

"Y'know, this... This is just too weird. I expected something a lot crazier than this...but I don't even see any of the Heavenly Regiment."

Even the normally garrulous Gabriel seemed quizzical as he looked around for signs of life. They had brought along squads of Pájaro Danino fighters, along with a Malebranche platoon led by Farfarello, but it was so quiet that they wondered if it was worth tapping their ranks at all.

"Yeah, so over there is where the Tree of Sephirot is. And over in *that* direction is the administrative research unit Ignora and the rest of us live in."

"Well, Devil King?"

"Obvious, isn't it? We'll check out the Sephirot. Our mission isn't to wipe out the angels. We're here to release Alas Ramus's family... and if we've got Copyhara, that oughtta help us against any other Sephirah."

"Whoa, though," protested Urushihara. "Maybe Ignora trained

more guys like Erone. If she throws all of them except Yesod, Gevurah, and Da'at at us, we're gonna have trouble taking 'em out."

He turned to Gabriel.

"Whaddaya think about that? And what's up with the guardian angels? You took Yesod, and Gevurah was Camael's responsibility. I don't really get the whole guardian angel thing in the first place, but what about all the others? Is there anyone else I know?"

"Ahh… Well, no point keeping it secret now, but there's one more guardian angel. That's 'cause there's just one more Sephirah that's manifested as a 'kid,' kinda."

"…Malchut?" Emi asked.

"Oh, hey, you knew?"

Gabriel blinked, surprised that she had the answer—but this wasn't news to her.

"Well, Alas Ramus has had Malchut's name on her lips pretty much the whole time I've known her. Bright yellow, the symbol of Malchut, is her favorite color. It's funny that the Malchut Sephirah's name is just the same as the Sephirah itself, though, unlike her and Erone."

Alas Ramus had been name-checking Malchut since back when she lived in Villa Rosa Sasazuka.

"Malchut, well… I've never really made contact with her, either. Her guardian is a guy named Sandalphon, but unlike me and Camael, he ain't really suited for battle."

"Sandalphon? I don't really remember for sure, but isn't he pretty old by now?"

"Do angels *age*, really?"

It was a simple question from Emi, but Gabriel gave it a serious answer.

"Well, we've obtained immortality, but we can't turn back the clock on aging, mm-kay? And Sandalphon was already gettin' on a fair bit by the time we left our home planet."

"About that," Maou said, this talk of their planet jogging his memory. "I've been wondering, Gabriel… Why are you able to cast holy magic?"

"Huh? You're askin' that now?"

"If my landlord is correct, humans lose their holy and demonic forces as they mature. Your planet had a huge disease hit it, but it was way more advanced than ours. And if you can cast all this holy magic, why couldn't you use a Gate or something to find another planet?"

"Ahh, umm, I don't know how that whole system works, really. But the reason we didn't open any Gates is easy—we didn't have a Gate spell, and we couldn't use it if we had it. Like, we had no idea at the time where a habitable planet even *was*, y'know?"

"Oh, no?"

"Nah. Lemme tell you guys, you were *damn* lucky to get blown from Ente Isla to Japan. Normally, you gotta define a set entrance and exit for a Gate to work, along with enough force to get you the distance you want. If you don't have control over it, then for all you know, you coulda wound up on Mars or Saturn instead, mm-kay?"

"That's how it works, huh?"

That sounded plausible enough to Maou. Maybe it meant Earth and Ente Isla were pretty close to each other on an interstellar scale. A Gate journey between them took about forty minutes one way— and come to think of it, Olba managed to single-handedly trace Maou and Ashiya's Gate to come here with Urushihara in tow, no angel's feather pen required.

"As for using holy magic, that's a little outside my area of expertise, but we were definitely able to tap it since birth. If I had to guess...I'd say our planet's Sephirah saw that we were gonna have a crisis way before it happened. Maybe they figured we needed some kinda non-standard power like holy magic, or we'd never be able to cope. That's just my guess, though. But we went and killed Caiel and Sikeena, so we've got no way to find out now."

It was rare for Gabriel to talk this soberly about anything, as he stared at the blue lands around him.

"Well, shall we? I know the Tree of Sephirot and our Sephirah administration zone pretty well."

"Ooh, yes, I would *bet*!"

Acieth, who had kept her mouth unusually shut up to now, didn't bother hiding her resentment as she glared at Gabriel.

"We were born from the fragments, too, so what you have done, I don't know. But depending on everybody's condition, maybe you prepare to die soon!"

"Eesh. Scary."

Gabriel, having already lost a very one-sided match against Acieth in Efzahan, quivered underneath her burning rage. It made Maou quiver for much different reasons. If, by some happenstance, the Sephirah children sided with the angels and Ignora in some way, they'd have to face an opponent as powerful as Acieth.

"Calm down, Acieth. Don't kill Gabriel. He's a lot more helpful to us alive."

"Wow, nice of you to actually *sound* like a Devil King for a change! Like, I'm *sure* Ignora thinks I've betrayed her by now. I'm literally between the devil and the deep blue sea, mm-kay?"

"Look, I sympathize for your plight, but even with that in mind, what you did in Ente Isla was horrible. You more than deserve pay-back for that."

"You think maybe my contributions to *this* make up for it a bit?"

"*What?*"

"Okay, okay, they don't. I get it, I get it."

Gabriel's shoulders slumped. One look at Acieth, and he knew almost anything could set her off right now.

✳

"Ughh. What's the deal with *this*?"

It was Amane who first appraised the scene before them. Her voice sounded so disgusted, it honestly puzzled Maou.

"What's wrong, Amane?" he asked.

"This isn't saying anything to you or Yusa at all? What about you, Copyhara?" she asked back.

"Huh?" Maou asked. "No, um… This is certainly a first for me, yeah, but…"

"Me too," Emi agreed. "All I can say is it's just like how Gabriel described it."

"I knew it was like this from before I was born, dude."

"Oh. Wow, really? Maybe it's some psychological thing for me, then," Amane said.

They were in a vast, soundless wasteland, not even a breeze in the air, and in the middle of it loomed a single large tree, the same color as the land. It seemed gigantic in this otherwise flat plain, and from all the many years it had lived, it looked like a lifeless husk at this point, despite all the energy it still contained for the countless years to come. No leaves covered its branches, no flowers heralding the arrival of spring, no fruits symbolizing its living bounty. It was just a dejected-looking tree, sitting here in the middle of nowhere.

Surrounding this giant tree were ten small shrines, each with a name carved into the entrance.

"Acieth says she feels sick…but probably for different reasons than Amane," Maou said.

"*Please* don't take her out right now, okay? I'll be killed before we ever run into Ignora." Between that and the step back he took, Gabriel seemed honestly petrified of the girl.

"So is there some kinda system where there's a guardian angel covering each shrine and we have to beat each one in order to free the Sephirah?"

"What kinda video game setup are you picturing, huh? I just told you, we don't even *have* that many angels. And the fact nobody's even here kinda tells the whole story, mm-kay?"

"So why were you a guardian angel at all?"

"I volunteered. Ignora appointed Camael to the role. And I think Sandalphon volunteered, too, maybe?"

"It was on a volunteer system?"

"Not really a 'system.' I wasn't a scientist or a doctor or anything. I just didn't wanna die from the boredom."

Gabriel gazed at the horizon.

"Emilia… Satan… Gabriel was just a normal person, you know? Not a scientist—just normal. That's why, unlike Ignora and Camael, he didn't truly think it was right to keep the Sephirah this way. That much, at least, I hope you'll understand.

"In the end, I...was just the type of guy who didn't wanna die. I didn't wanna leave my safe little environment. I told myself it was for the team, and it'd keep me fed, too...and that let me ignore the ethical issues. I've always been this kind of conniving peon, so, like, coming this far and getting to live this long... I never imagined it. And even now, I have no idea why I decided to side with Satanael."

"I never heard of a peon who attempted to lead Efzahan and the Devil King's Army by the nose."

Ashiya frowned. But Gabriel seemed to be telling the truth.

"Speaking of which, what *was* all of that? Whatever you used Efzahan and the Malebranche and Olba Meiyer for? I know that you used my liege to deliberately destroy the original plan. But I don't know what the plan was. I don't know what you were blocking, exactly."

Gabriel looked ready to answer honestly for a moment but promptly thought better of it. Instead, he looked at Copyhara, standing behind Ashiya.

"Basically, Ignora wanted it made clear in everyone's minds that angels are higher beings than the natives of Ente Isla. And, you know, I was, like, 'Hang on, is that really right?'"

"It doesn't seem to me that it matters much anymore. Not if it led to Copyhara here," Amane added.

Gabriel was definitely close enough to Amane to hear that. But he didn't turn her way.

"Well, forget about the details for now. Those shrines are still the root cause of the strife Alas Ramus and Acieth have gone through, right? So we take those down first. Then our quiet friends on this planet *have* to make the trip over, right? Then we beat 'em all, and then we win."

"Sounds good to me. Let's get going. Alas Ramus's family needs freedom."

"Yeah. Just watch for the space suit guy. And if that underground base in the demon realms really was Satanael's, that means heaven has the tech to cancel out demonic force, too. If *that* happens to us, sorry in advance," Maou said.

"If it does, I'll scream at you for being so useless, but I'll protect you. Don't worry. I need you to pay Alas Ramus's child support," Emi quipped.

"Wow, I'm about to cry here. Acieth… Let's go."

"Okay!"

The next moment, a Better Half appeared in Maou's hand…along with horns from his head. His legs turned demonic, but the rest of him stayed human.

"I've never actually seen it before… Oh. Never mind."

If Emi manifested her own holy sword with Alas Ramus, she and Maou would be a "pair" in pretty much every way. But she had nothing against Acieth, so she just barely avoided commenting on it.

"Bit too late for all that…"

Chiho, Suzuno, and Emeralda weren't here. Nobody was going to make fun of them for being a pair, and now wasn't the time for it anyway. For just a moment, Emi flashed back to that secret encounter she'd had at the apartment that evening, but she managed to push it deep into her memory and bottle it up.

"All right, Alas Ramus… Let's go. Let's help out your family."

"Okeh!"

Emi's entire body shone. She transformed into Emilia the Hero, with her holy sword, Cloth of the Dispeller, silver hair, and eyes of scarlet. And the moment Alas Ramus's Better Half sword appeared in her right hand:

"Oh, my! Look at you two people, carrying matching swords for the final battle. That's kind of nice! Like a pair of wings being brought together for the first time! Almost reminds me of marriage, in a way!"

"""…"""

At that moment, the two people with the weapons that could change the fate of the world were almost brought to their knees. They both glared at Laila.

"Wha… What?"

She stood there puzzled, unsure why everyone was so angry.

"I had forgotten... You're *that* kind of person, aren't you, Mother?"

"Can you *please* quit with that?"

"Huh? What?! What's gotten into you two?"

Having so much wind taken out of their sails reddened Maou's and Emilia's faces just a bit, for reasons only they knew. It'd be ridiculous to explain matters now, but bringing up marriage made those bottled memories of that night—sealed away by their mutual trust in each other—spring right back to life.

The life seemed to drain from Maou and Emilia a bit as they marched over to the nearest shrine. The sign on it, in writing neither Maou nor Emi could decipher, read KETER—the number one, the color white, symbolized by a diamond. The first Sephirah.

The shrine wasn't large inside, its décor a familiar sight to everyone on hand.

"Oh, right! This looks like the terrarium with the Yesod root."

Emilia's words made Maou remember as well. The shrine was far smaller, but on the far end of it was what looked like a large aquarium tank. Amane winced at it, looking even sicker than before.

"You okay, Amane?" Gabriel asked anxiously.

"*Urp...* I dunno how to explain this..." Amane glared back at him. "But I feel like I'm being shown all my relatives being tortured."

"Ahh... I see. Yeah. It'd be funny to say sorry, but sorry. If you could keep Mikitty in the dark about this, I'd appreciate it a bunch."

"How could I ever *describe* something so cruel? Maou, Yusa... Destroy this at once."

"O-okay. But are you sure? Because I see a little bit of a root poking out over there..."

The big difference between the shrine and the demon realm terrarium was that, while the terrarium had a chopped-off root kept in a tube with soil, this looked more like a capsule that grew from the earth itself. The inside was filled with dirt, and the tiniest tip of a root was peeking out from it.

"It's fine," Gabriel said, keeping a watchful eye on Amane. "These buildings were plopped down over the roots wholesale. We'll destroy them in order…but make sure not to damage the roots, mm-kay? Oh, but leave shrines five, nine, and ten intact. *That* one, *that* one, and *that* one. I think you get why."

Shrine number five was Erone's Gevurah. Shrine number nine was Alas Ramus's and Acieth's Yesod.

"So Malchut, the tenth…?"

"Yeah, keep your guard up for 'er. Like I said, I don't know the girl or what she looks like. The only one who knows the Malchut kid…"

"…Is Ignora, and this Sandalphon guy who might be around here?"

Alas Ramus had clearly "learned" something from Malchut. She and Acieth had obtained bodies as Sephirah children only recently, but based on what they said, they were likely conscious and self-aware well before that.

"All right. Amane can't take much more of this, so let's get crackin', mm-kay? But keep the roots safe."

"We go all the way to heaven and the first thing we do is building demolition? Ah, well. Guess the bad guys aren't gonna make it *that* obvious where they're hanging out."

"*You* sure made it easy for me, Devil King."

"Stop comparing us."

The memory of the Devil King waiting on his Devil's Castle throne for the Hero was nothing but an embarrassment now.

"All right, Acieth! Let's do it!"

Then, deliberately raising his voice, he kicked things off by smashing the capsule in the Keter shrine.

✳

"All this, and *still* nobody? Is that even possible?"

"Hmm… It *is* weird, yeah… I can't see how it's possible at all…but should we bust up the final three while we're at it? I don't *think* it'll be a problem…"

"Well, *I* sure have no problems, and judging by the holy swords, Alas Ramus and Acieth are okay, too. I think we're good, dude."

Copyhara, content with watching all this wanton destruction from a safe distance, seemed awfully casual about it.

"And me, I am the very perfectly fine. Let us do the more of it, Maou!"

Acieth, inside Maou's mind, was out for blood.

"...All right, then. And maybe it's a bit late to ask, but what're these shrines *for* anyway?"

"Ignora said they were sense-canceling anchors," Laila replied.

"Anchors? How so?"

"They function as a sort of blindfold to the Tree of Sephirot, giving it the wrong idea about the world's condition. I heard a long time ago that the capsules were constantly pumped with holy energy to convince the Tree that the planet and its people still require supernatural force."

"Pumped with holy energy?"

"Yes. That's what I heard before Satanael split heaven up. The device wasn't done yet, but that was the plan at the time anyway."

"...So it's deceiving the Tree...? Why would they do that...?"

Maou's head was full of intertangled bits of data about heaven and the Sephirah, but none of the pieces seemed to quite fit together. He couldn't come to a conclusion.

Amane, who had silently watched the shrine demolitions from the side, chose that moment to speak up.

"I think I have an idea of what's happening...and I think their scheme succeeded, right at the point of no return."

"Huh?"

She wasn't looking at Maou. Her eyes were sharpened upon Copyhara. And he, fully aware of what Amane was looking at, had his own eyes on Emi.

"Yeah. It worked, all right. But *she* made all that work moot. Didn't she, Emilia?"

"Huh? Me?" said Emi, blinking at the sudden accusation. Amane gave it a disinterested shrug.

"Don't ask me. It's all somebody else's story. All my relatives come from different situations, y'know."

"No doubt. Anyway, let's get the last three shrines broken up. I think *that* should make something happen. No more half-measures, okay, dudes?"

At Copyhara's signal, the less-than-satisfied group somewhat reluctantly sprang into action, destroying shrines five, nine, and ten. They demolished their bulb-like exteriors, and for the first time in centuries, millennia, or even tens of millennia, the Sephirot of Ente Isla was fully exposed to the atmosphere.

At that moment, the exposed roots began to quiver—and once they did, the entire Tree of Sephirot began to change rapidly. The group's ears were greeted by high, soft sounds playing in staccato, like bubbles popping. They were coming from the edges of the Sephirot's branches.

"It's gotta be the first spring in ages for this guy. As much as it's been saving up, it's gonna come in an instant."

Above Copyhara's head were groups of flower buds—small, but growing in all their countless numbers, in just the hour or so since all the shrines were destroyed.

"Now all the other siblings will be born. But the order's all messed up."

"You mean the Sephirot's flowers?"

"Yeah. They're finally blooming. Without them, there'll never be any fruit."

"Huh? Fruit? The Sephirah, you mean? Why do you need flowers?"

"With Malchut and Gevurah, I think they ripened early in order to protect the Tree. Keter didn't make it in time."

"There's an order to them?"

"Except in extraordinary circumstances, Malchut is the first to wake up. Then, depending on what's going on around it, either Keter, Gevurah, or Yesod will open its eyes first. Malchut functions as a vessel, and based on what the vessel needs the most, you'll either have Yesod's astral energy, Gevurah's defensive traits, or Keter, the sword of the Tree. By the look of things, it's decided to put defense way up high for now."

Hearing it described as the Tree's "decision" seemed to throw Emilia a little. She looked down at her holy sword.

"Well, no point thinking about it now. Trees are living things, too."

This Tree was the "parent" of the Sephirah children, those bright, incredibly diverse personalities. A little bit more mystery wouldn't change the overall picture.

"But *still* nothing's happening?"

By this point, Maou's group had essentially captured the Tree of Sephirot. If the flowers were going to bloom and give birth to Sephirah children, Maou's original mission of getting Alas Ramus's family back was as good as accomplished. By this point, the group wondered if they had to fight Ignora and the angels at all.

"Does the other side even *want* to defend this? Like, what's the point any longer? It's not like we need to keep prodding them if they don't."

Urushihara was an open book as always. Ashiya immediately shot him down.

"No, my liege. If we know the location of the enemy's main base, we should attack it at once. We do not know how long the Sephirah need to grow, or how long it takes for them to become like Alas Ramus and the others. Better to quell any anxieties for the future while we can."

"…Yeah. What a pain, though."

"You really think so, don't you? It's kind of off-putting, dude."

"Look, dude, if you have the same face as me, it'd be a lot easier if you *thought* the same way, too."

"With *you*, it's probably something like, 'Ooh, I don't wanna fight my mom,' right?"

"Me? Not *something* like that, no."

Copyhara, capable of reading minds, visibly winced.

"Watching them banter is kind of funny, isn't it?"

"I don't find it one bit entertaining. But what are we doing now?"

"Ashiya's right. We gotta dive in and attack. They needed to build all this crap to milk the Tree or whatever, and it's all destroyed now, so we can leave it be. It's not like they're gonna destroy the Tree because they couldn't achieve their goals."

"Yeah... But after all that effort, this seems beyond anticlimactic..."

And perhaps the sheer silence of the heavens was what made Ashiya notice.

"...! My liege!!"

Everyone moved at almost the same time as Ashiya's warning. With the whine of solid metal, a large spear was now planted in the wasteland around Sephirot, its blades spread out in a trident.

"Camael!"

"No! Not him! That's...!"

A vast number of figures—angels, apparently, dressed in just as much armor as Camael was—floated in the sky.

"The Heavenly Regiment. Camael's troops are kind of special. Don't write 'em off, or you'll pay for it."

"I know. Suzuno got her ass kicked once by them!"

Once, Camael had attacked Chiho's high school in Sasazuka. When he did, he'd brought along just three of his Regiment—but together with Libicocco, who was more directly fighting her, they had managed to render Suzuno helpless. Considering that Gabriel's three Regiment soldiers were no match at all for Suzuno while the archangel was hijacking the TV signal at Tokyo Tower, the difference in fighting power between his and Camael's troops was clear.

But still:

"So you're finally coming out. Well, sorry, but we're sick of spinning our wheels down here!"

"You picked a funny time to pop up, you bastards. What the hell're you thinking...? It's freaking me out."

Emilia was all but welcoming this army, appearing out of nowhere after they'd destroyed the ten shrines. To Maou, however, something wasn't right.

"Hey, Ashiya, can you keep 'em occupied without killing them?"

"Yes, my liege. You wish to keep them alive?"

Ashiya, given his orders, fiendishly smiled.

"Gabriel, take me to where Ignora is. This is giving me the willies. We gotta whip 'em all and put an end to this."

"Got it. I bet my Regiment's with her. Now's no time to kick back. You sure we're good leaving things to Ashiya here?"

"Don't treat this like Tokyo Tower part two. It's time to show people in heaven what a Great Demon General with all his force back can do."

Before he could even finish speaking, Ashiya transformed into Alciel, the merciless Demon General.

"Whoa, whoa! Your clothes!"

Not only did he transform—Shirou Ashiya tore through all his clothes, without a moment's hesitation.

"A necessary expense, my liege!"

The black shell of the Iron Scorpion shone as he flew up like a shooting star.

"Let's go while Ashiya's stopping them! Gabriel! Where's Ignora's home base?"

"Follow me! It's not far from here if we fly!"

"Gabe! I'll stay here! I really can't leave Sephirot alone like this!"

"Roger that, Amane! And don't worry! I'm not gonna double-cross Mikitty!"

Demonic and holy force clashed violently in the skies behind them as they soared away.

"Watch out! We don't know when Camael may strike!"

"With this many people, we'd definitely spot him! How far away is it?!"

"A bit over ten minutes at this speed!"

"That's crazy close! Why the hell did they just let us destroy their shrines? I don't get it! Laila! Is Ignora that stupid? Is she a science savant and really slow with everything else, or what?"

"No, she couldn't be! It was her strategy that defeated Satanael..."

"Right! This makes no sense at all! But if we're still just seeing

Camael's Regiment after all this, it must mean the enemy's got nothin' left to hide! They already exhausted all their forces on us!"

"Yeah, that'd be real nice, huh? But I think they got a lot of Regiment soldiers in reserve!"

Maou looked up. Several streaks of red light were visible in the skies ahead.

"Okay, I'll take these! Acieth! Waste 'em in one shot!"

"Ready! Time for the death by a thousand butts!!"

"Wait! Actually, let *me* handle it! Also, it's 'cuts,' not 'butts'!"

Whenever Maou started fighting with Acieth's holy sword, this is what she always did. This was a girl, after all, who overwhelmed Camael in a one-on-one fight. If she went *that* hard on the Regiment coming up to them, death was a pretty likely outcome.

"Aww, why?! Let me cut 'em!"

Acieth was starting to sound like a serial killer in a TV show. Maou hid the sword behind his back, focusing his force in his legs and fists. This was neither holy nor demonic force—just like the battle at Sasahata North High, it was pure, coercive *power.*

"Maou! Let me cut them!!"

"...This happens to her whenever I do this. I know it can't be good...for *her!*"

Maou's hooves sliced through the air with a loud roar. He suddenly disappeared—and then the streaks began to fall, one by one.

"So fast...!"

By the time Emilia and the others reached him, all the hapless Regiment soldiers were sprawled out on the ground.

"I didn't kill anyone," he said, sounding like he was making excuses.

"Did I say anything?" Emilia gave him a dour look. "You know, I don't think I've been whining all *that* much at you lately."

"Well," the even more perturbed Maou replied, "it shows all the *trust* we've cultivated, doesn't it?"

Emilia gritted her teeth at that remark, but they knew now wasn't the time for infighting. So they flew alongside Gabriel, now finally caught up, and headed for their target.

"Judging from that, I bet Ashiya will be back with us soon. Are we there yet, Gabriel?"

"Yeah, there it is. Can't you see it?"

On the horizon, past Gabriel's pointer finger, was a large, broad, dignified-looking structure. It didn't clear Maou's or Emilia's doubts at all.

"Man. It hasn't changed at all. Most of the joint's dead."

Urushihara spoke up before they could put voice to those doubts.

"Even in my memories, it was pretty much like that. The lights are out in over half of the place."

A large, abandoned, dilapidated flying saucer—that was the first impression it gave. Just a large, misshapen, Adamski-style UFO half-buried in the ground, covered in a dull metallic sheen. And who knew? Maybe it really *did* wash up on this planet after wandering around the vast reaches of space for years and years.

And Maou recognized that metallic shine.

"So I've been playing Devil King in the hands of *these* guys my whole life? Pathetic."

It was a dead ringer for the stronghold of the ancient Devil Overlord, the place once called Satanas Arc. The domain of the Silverarms, the final enemy in his unification of the demon realms, was the very base Satanael used after breaking from heaven.

"I get it, Maou. It's even harder for me. It's time for me to go independent from my parents."

Urushihara, reaching the same memory, snorted derisively.

"Let's rip it apart before Ashiya arrives."

"He's serious, dude," Copyhara added.

"And *that's* a sign of the trust we've built. No doubting it now. Let's go! Laila! I'm worried about you the most! Don't freeze up when we need you!"

"N-no! Wait a minute!"

Only Laila demonstrated any alarm at Urushihara's eagerness to kill his own parents. All anyone else in the group thought about was storming this crumbling, half-abandoned enemy base in front of them.

"If you don't wanna die, get out of there! 'Cause we ain't gonna stop until we crush all your boss's plans at the root!"

Maou's shout echoed across the skies of heaven.

"Hey, Gabriel! Laila! What do they call this town?"

"Town? We never really saw it that way. It was a research base at first. So we named it something you'll probably find pretty ironic."

"It was the last bastion of mankind," Laila said. "A place of hope and dreams, built to combat the disease that took our home planet..."

The name was, indeed, fairly ironic.

"'All a Lijeh,' we call it. In your language, it means 'Ship of Hope.'"

It wasn't Gabriel or Laila who said it.

Instantly, everyone circled Laila, their noncombatant, and readied for battle. The man in the red armor who gave the answer floated above, looking down at them.

"Finally, some of the main brass? You know who you're aiming for *this* time, right?"

It was the archangel Camael, nothing but sheer black behind his armor and full-face helmet. His aims were nothing short of inscrutable.

*

"Hey there, Camael. Long time no see. You been doing good? We wanna see Ignora about something, but..."

"..."

"...Yeah, I guess you won't let us. And I doubt you're here to negotiate an armistice, but it's not like you can do anything about this force we got..."

"Gabriel, get back!!"

"Huh? Whoa?!"

Seeing the spear Camael had sluggishly readied, Maou grabbed Gabriel by the neck and pulled back hard. The next moment, the spear barely scratched Gabriel's nose, the flame it emitted a completely different color from what they'd seen at Sasahata North High.

"Wh-wha?!"

As far as everyone knew, Gabriel had never been hurt by anything but his own Durandal weapon. Now there was a notable hole in his toga.

"Huh? You... Huh? That...!"

Camael's three-pronged trident was now shining in golden light, something it had never done before.

"His flames have gotten pretty heavy, y'know. I think there's some more backbone to 'em now."

Urushihara, who had his own experience fighting Camael, was showing signs of deep anxiety.

"This isn't gonna be as easy as Ashiya mowing down the Regiment. I'll handle this. I gotta pay him back for Chi's school, and I bet he wants to say something about 'Satan' to me."

Maou motioned the two of them to fall back, prepared his holy sword, and moved forward. He may have overwhelmed Camael once before, but he couldn't underestimate this foe.

"Yo, Camael. Remember me?"

"Devil King... Satan..."

"Right, right. Y'know, I've really been wondering; what's your beef with the name 'Satan' anyway? I think we only met for the first time at Sasahata North High..."

"...Satan."

"What? Are we *ever* gonna hold a coherent conversation, or what?"

"Satan... The name of the betrayer... The unenlightened one that failed to see Ignora's ideals... The man...who killed my wife..."

The revelation spoken by that grating voice came as a shock to everyone on hand.

"I will never forget having to leave my wife's body on the red moon."

"Your wife? What?"

"Those who block our way...who block Ignora's way...must fall.

Every single one of you… Ignora has sacrificed everything for her lofty ideals. I will never let you impede her will!"

"Whoaahh?!"

The next moment, his divine speed closed the distance between them as he thrust his weapon. Maou blocked it with Acieth in sword form, but it still sent him flying toward the ground.

"Ugh! He finally starts talking sense, but that's all he's got?!"

Spreading his wings in the air to stop his fall, Maou flew behind Camael's back, drawing out the edge of his holy sword. Camael easily blocked it with the prongs of his spear, but that single moment was all Maou needed.

"Come on, guys! Let's go!!"

Emilia didn't fail to notice Maou's signal with his eyes. Despite Camael's improved power, the Better Half was still effective against him—that's why he stopped that blade with his spear. He would never let the sword escape his sight.

Emilia, immediately recognizing Maou's intentions, held Laila under one arm as she flew straight for what looked like the main building of All a Lijeh.

"Here's your chance to kill that 'Satan' you hate so much! You ain't gonna get distracted *now*, are ya?"

Maou saw the helmet swiveling his way. He landed a powerful hoof kick on Camael's chest. It didn't seem to cause any damage at all, but it was enough to divert Camael's attention.

"Come on! My main general's gonna be here once he's done crushing your soldiers! Where there's life, there's hope! And it'll be a lot easier for you to live if you surrender like Gabriel did!!"

"I…have long since thrown away my life!!"

"Oh, how nice to hear! So you're ready for me to pulverize you, huh?! All the way…"

All it took were a dozen or so clashes of sword and trident for the battle to be decided.

"You're wasting your life!!"

"Face the death! Hraahhh!!!"

Listening to Acieth's war scream, Maou unleashed a thrust aimed straight for the middle of Camael's chest. But:

"Ngh?!"

A small hand stopped the holy blade.

Maou's Better Half, infused with Acieth Alla, had been completely invincible up to now. It had been halted by a human palm, one that didn't belong to Camael—in fact, the arm extended out from his chest, like an illusion.

"Hey… Hey, hey, hey, hey, what the kind of funny business is this… This is the betrayal! We were gone for little bit, and what you do to us now…!"

"Whahhh?!"

The next moment, the holy sword disappeared from Maou's hand as Acieth decided to separate from him. At the same time, he transformed from half-man, half-demon to his full form, brimming with demonic force—and for the first time since Heavensky, Acieth gave Camael a truly ominous look.

"Maou! This is the little bit of problem!"

"Yeah, I can see that."

The hand that stopped the blade slowly extended, bringing the rest of the body behind it from Camael's chest, as if there was a door made of thin air on the armor. She was a girl who looked a bit older than Acieth, around the same age as Chiho. Her short, crystalline white hair included two-toned bangs—one half bright yellow, and one half a dim shade of black. Her eyes were both that same eye-catching yellow, and she was dressed in a sheer, almost transparent robe of white, the same color as her hair.

"Acieth, I don't know much about theology, but do those colors mean what I think they mean?"

"Huh? What? What do you mean?!"

Now, perhaps, wasn't the time to ask vague questions to Acieth in a situation as charged as this.

"It's her, isn't it?" Maou said, not taking his eyes off the new girl. "It's Malchut."

"Huh? You did not know, Maou?!"

"No, all right? I'm sorry I asked you in a funny way! Just stay focused!"

"You are one who asked me... Ah, but now is not time... Hey, Malchut. Do you have the name? You recognize me?"

"Acieth Alla, younger sister of Yesod," acknowledged the girl, her first words. The voice sounded dry to Maou.

"Okay, sister, then I ask. Tell me your name. Also, you tell me why you protect our enemy. It better be the convincing, or else death by a thousand butts!"

"My name is Eleos. I must protect him. He is the latent force I selected."

"That is the bullshit! Have you eaten the strange thing or something, Malchut—I mean Eleos?! They are the demons! They blocked our growth and tore us apart!"

"I know."

"In last planet of theirs, they did such stupid thing, their own Sephirah nearly kill them all! Why protect them?!"

"I never intended to, until a little bit ago."

"Huhh?!"

"Acieth. I'm sure you must be aware. Da'at flew off with your companions. He is the last member of our family."

"So what?! I do know that! He look just like Lucifer! We all rolling on floor laughing ass off!"

"We didn't laugh that much, you know..."

Satan's rejoinder was ignored.

"Lucifer is the problem, Acieth. Do you know what kind of being he is?"

"Yes! He unemployed bum!!"

"Well," Maou interjected, "I think he's actually been working pretty hard lately..."

"Then what else do I say to her?!"

This time, Acieth bothered to react to him. But Maou didn't know what to say next.

"...Look, what's going on? Because Amane looked pretty floored by Copyhara taking on Urushihara's look, too. Is there some important meaning to it?"

"Da'at is the result of the selection."

There, for the first time since Eleos's appearance, Camael spoke up.

"Ignora had waited long for that selection. She spent many months and years, blocked by so many obstacles, betrayed by so many people, almost fully giving up. But…after this near-infinite span of time, we finally have a place of our own again."

"The hell does that mean? A place of your own? We smashed up all that junk you attached to the Sephirot. You're not getting your way in Ente Isla. You can try fighting us now, but you know it's just a matter of time. You seriously think Malchut alone is gonna change anything? How can you be sure of that…?"

"Da'at picked Lucifer, leader of the second generation of angels, as the primary race of human beings on the planet affiliated with this moon. It has been decided that Lucifer and his kin are the race that will evolve and commandeer the planet."

That stopped Satan's childish taunting quickly.

"Your companions may be traveling to Ignora…but killing me, or killing Ignora… It does nothing to threaten our victory."

For the first time, Maou thought he saw Camael's face exhibit a genuine emotion. It was a cruel sneer, showing total contempt for his enemy—but it was vacant, withered, and a sense of resignation seemed to rule over it.

✳

"Devil's Castle is sure a lot nicer than this. I mean, just *ewww*."

"I can't believe what's happened to it…"

In the central core of All a Lijeh, Emilia and Laila winced as they looked around. The area Gabriel called the "research unit" didn't look anything like the home of the world's greatest enemy or the mastermind leading the world's angels. The air was dank and moldy. Thick layers of dust occupied the corners of the hallways. The shine to the metal used to construct this certainly spoke of an advanced civilization, but the sheer lack of maintenance meant this setting was like nothing they'd pictured for the final "assault on heaven."

"Was it always like this?"

"I don't think it's changed much since Satanael took part of the research unit to the demon realms. But..."

Laila hesitated a bit as she looked around the entrance.

"It was definitely a lot busier. I left here a long time ago...but even that was after All a Lijeh landed here. I can't believe everyone disappeared in such a short time... Gabriel, what happened in here?!"

"Yeah, I'll admit that the maintenance wasn't exactly first-class... but this is just weird. I've only been involved with you guys for the past year. The first time I went down to Sasazuka, it was nothing like this... Hell, it hasn't been half a year since that battle in Efzahan... Hey, and where's my Regiment...?"

Gabriel could no longer hide his agitation. If he had gone down to Efzahan, he must have been ordered to. At that point, All a Lijeh was still in its normal, familiar state. Or it should have been.

"So where would Ignora be?!"

"Well, up to now, she had her own floor in the general research unit, but..."

But if Gabriel was acting this concerned, it was safe to assume his assumptions about All a Lijeh no longer applied. After all, no matter how well-built this research unit was, they were non-military buildings—they'd fall quickly if subjected to intense warfare.

"Where's Raguel? Or Sandalphon, even. They'll know what's going on here. I'm sorry, Emilia, can I go look for Raguel and my Regiment?"

"...You want to go solo?"

"Please," Gabriel replied, expecting this. "Like I told Amane, I'm never gonna double-cross Mikitty."

"Maybe I could join him? I could probably handle Raguel by myself if I needed to, and Gabriel's Regiment wouldn't try to defy me."

"All right," Emi said, Urushihara's offer quelling her concerns.

"You do that, Lucifer. But if you find out anything, come back to me immediately."

"I'll join them, too. If I follow the internal voices of the angels, maybe I can find where people are."

"Okay. Thanks."

Emilia, not wanting to waste a single moment, accepted Copyhara's request as well.

"Oh, good. I might look the same as him, but you actually trust me, huh?"

"Stop reading my mind."

"Okay, Gabriel, let's go."

"Right. Thanks, guys. But, really, what's going on...?"

Watching Lucifer, Copyhara, and Gabriel disappear into the research unit, Emilia turned to Laila.

"We should look somewhere else. Gabriel acted like nobody's around, but we just ran into Camael's forces, so watch out for others."

"Yes... I remember here very well, too, and I think I know where people would be. There's a residential floor adjacent to the research unit. This way!"

Emilia let Laila guide her along. They snooped around, carefully looking for signs of life. But all they found were the classic signs of abandonment—damp, heavy air, and clouds of dust rising with every footstep.

"Why is nobody here?! It's so strange... Walking this far, and not running into anyone..."

"Gabriel said there weren't many survivors in the first place, right?"

"Yes, but we still numbered nearly a thousand living here. They didn't all have the power of Gabriel or Camael, but most of them were at least strong enough for space travel and long, healthy lifespans. And there were just as many Heavenly Regiment members called in from Ente Isla."

"Seeing this so deserted *is* weird, then. If it's a research unit, you'd think they would at least clean it...?!"

In a flash, Emilia caught up to Laila, grabbing her waist and pulling her to a halt.

"Look out!"

"Ahh?!"

Then, with a loud roar, a giant hole opened in the wall Laila was just walking past. Satan and Acieth barreled into the corridor.

"Damn it... What a punch..."

"What on the earth is going on?!"

"Satan!"

"Devil King?! Acieth! What happened?!"

"Emi, get back. He's become a pretty decent fighter. Don't bring Alas Ramus to the front..."

Satan slowly hefted his large body up from the rubble. The scratches and bruises here and there indicated he was struggling.

Emi, sword at the ready, carefully peeked through the hole to the outside. There she discovered two figures floating in the air.

"Who's that next to Camael?"

"Yeah, that's a problem. We gotta rescue her."

"So is that Malchut?"

"Her name's Eleos, apparently. She's way more of a handful than Camael."

"Wanna tag out?"

"Acieth's pretty helpless. I think Malchut's a measure stronger than Yesod...but they're still just the foot soldiers. You guys need to find Ignora now!"

"Why she joins their side, I have none of the ideas! Eleos! Please, open the eyes, you!"

"All right. Acieth! Take care of the Devil King for me!"

"Aye, the stick, I drew short end of it! Eleos! Round two! *Hngh!*"

Acieth got up before Satan, zooming toward Camael—but Eleos stepped in between, parrying her closed fist. There was a loud thunderclap, but even Emi could tell that Eleos was overwhelming Acieth. She tried her best to target Camael, but Eleos refused to give her an inch.

"So Camael is fused with Eleos?"

"Maybe. But let's leave this to those two and find Ignora! We can worry about other people later! I have to make Ignora tell us what's going on!"

"Y-yeah... You're right!"

Emilia gave Laila a hand over the rubble as they ran for the research unit. Acieth and Eleos were behind them, and they could hear what were likely the sounds of Satan and Camael fighting.

"Ugh, I'm completely lost! What is Ignora thinking?! What's going on?!"

Laila was almost in hysterics.

"Hrraaahhhh!!"

"Speed and power are important...but without technique and a cool head, the moment you are surpassed, you lose."

"Ohh?!"

Acieth unleashed a flurry of fists, faster than even Satan could keep up with. But Eleos stopped them all then pulled Acieth's leg out from under her.

"You see? If she wasn't fighting *me*, Acieth would be in trouble."

And so Eleos lunged for Acieth's wide-open side...

"Hyee-hee-hee-hee-hoo-hee?!"

...and nimbly began tickling her.

Even as she dopily laughed, Acieth's face twisted in anger, her arms blindly swinging around. But she never had any chance of hitting Eleos that way.

"Acieth. If you are a child of the Sephirah, you have to realize—there is no point fighting Ignora any longer. Da'at has already given his judgment."

"Who cares?! My sister, how long was I separated from you?! Gevurah, Erone, how terrible was it for them? I know you know!"

"..."

"If you help angels, then you betray everyone! Eleos! If you not join us, at least let me hit *this* angel!"

"No."

"Why?!"

"Acieth. Have you seen a mirror?"

"Huh?! What is…?"

"If Yesod, with its astral energy, is as polluted with demonic force and negative emotion as your eyes are, any Sephirah would stop them."

"What?!"

"You have a deep affinity for that demon. If Yesod is taken by negative emotion—the hatred that drives the power of any demon—it will hurt all of the Sephirah. No matter how much I hate the angels, if I let you have your way right now, you and that demon may destroy all of them."

"So what?! I use this hand, and I take them all…!"

"Da'at has chosen the form of Lucifer. If you are Yesod, then please consider that. Listen to me, Acieth the Yesod…!"

"Gah…!!"

Without any advance warning, Eleos brought her palm to Acieth's forehead. That was all she needed. Acieth's vision faded with her consciousness, the power draining from her body.

"Our Sephirot has chosen Lucifer. Angels shall be the 'humanity' in Ente Isla."

"What…are you…!"

"And I can't have a Sephirah like you kill the angels when they've only just been chosen."

Just before the light fully faded from Acieth's eyes:

"Mm?"

Her body disappeared.

Eleos looked away. Satan was there, hand in the air. Fusing with Acieth, he was half-Satan, half-Maou again, his glowing red eyes glaring at his foes as he growled.

"You… What the hell are you doing to *our* girl?"

"She is my sister first."

"Shut up. Ignora, the Ente Isla humans… Even you Sephirah… You all look down upon us, don't you?"

Spitting out some blood from the side of his mouth, Maou readied himself.

"Why are you guys actin' all bossy after choosing *Urushihara*, of all people?! Why're you leavin' the future to some guy who sits in the closet in the middle of summer and plays games all day?!"

"Mngh!"

With an explosive sound, Maou shot off from the rubble and lunged for Eleos.

"I know the truth! No matter what kind of special power you guys, or the angels, or I, or the Hero have…!"

"Ngh… This power…!"

"You all still have to eat and sleep to be healthy! You're all just *humans*!"

"What are…you…!!"

"And humans shouldn't *dare* look down on other humans! You're just a little brat lettin' the angels use and abuse you!!"

Maou grabbed hold of the right side of Eleos's head and slammed it against the ground. The powerful, deafening force put a small crater in the hard surface of All a Lijeh.

"Kahh!"

"*Wait… Maou, it is too much…!*"

"This is still the only way I know how to make a bratty kid listen to me!"

"*No, but…*"

"I *want* to know some other way, but all these bastards…!!"

"Ngh!"

Before Eleos could get up, Maou shot back into the sky and confronted Camael.

"These kids keep getting into trouble because *you're* not setting a good example for them! If you're gonna try conquering worlds, do it *without* enslaving these goddamn kids!!"

"Silence, Satan! It all began when Satanael sided with you demons…!!"

"You got a beef with my dad, so you're gonna make little kids settle the score? Don't give me that shit!!"

Weaving out of the way of the golden trident's tips, Maou connected his fist cleanly with the chinstrap of the helmet. With a surprisingly soft sound, it came flying off.

"Gnnnh…!!"

Under it appeared, for the first time, the face of a crazed archangel—a stout, masculine man, with silver hair and red eyes. Nearly half of it was covered with painful-looking burn scars.

"So the helmet hid that? If you're gonna explain, now's the time!"

"You… Satan… Satan!!"

"If this is about some battle in the past, I'll hear you out after it's all over! I just wanna get this over with, go home, eat, take a bath, and go to bed!!"

Camael, deflecting Maou's follow-up punch, swept ahead with his recoiled trident. Maou stopped it with his re-manifested holy sword.

"So I guess you're Malchut's latent force? Well, I'm Yesod's latent force. We're even. Right, Camael?!"

"Satan! I'll kill you! I swear I'll kill you!!"

"Yeah! Do it! And let's hope this is the last death duel this world ever sees!"

Satan's holy sword and Camael's trident collided, a murderous clang echoing across the starry sky.

The reclining seat looked hard and uncomfortable. That was Emilia's first impression of it.

"What a fine morning, Laila."

The woman looked up at a transparent ceiling, hazy in spots due to the lack of maintenance. Watching the cold night sky, a virtual copy of the heavens' blue earth, the figure called it "morning."

This figure, rising from the hard reclining chair meant for stargazing, was a far cry from the "angel boss," the "puppet master ruling over history," the "god that must be slain" that they had pictured. She was gaunt, and no strength was in her eyes. All the angels they had seen before—Sariel, Gabriel, Raguel, Camael—they all had their own self-serving drives, something they strove to fight for. Why did they ever take orders from someone like this?

"Your name was Laila, correct?"

"Huh?"

"Well, Laila? How does it feel to be a mother? Isn't having a child wonderful? No matter how hard things get, it always feels like you can overcome them, doesn't it?"

Her voice was scratchy, difficult to decipher; she spoke the words slowly.

"And do you see how, when you lose that, there is so much despair...?"

"Ignora, listen. I..."

"But the more despair you face... When the moment comes, that hope wells up anew..."

"Nngh?!"

"The happiness you feel is infinite."

"M-Mother, what are you...?"

Ignora pointed a wispy hand at Laila. That alone brought Laila to her knees, making her cry out in pain.

"Emi...li...a...?"

"Mother?!"

"Emilia? I'm sorry. Your mother and I are having an important conversation. Can you go play over there for me?"

"Wha... Ah!"

The next moment, Ignora turned back the clock. Her body looked young again, like a dry sponge dipped in water. It wasn't a transformation—her form blurred, overlapped, and separated.

"Nyx, play with Emilia for me, please."

"Yes, Mommy."

A little girl, with golden eyes and two curls of olive and reddish brown over her forehead, appeared in a burst of light.

"Huh?!"

"Emilia, you should introduce Nyx here to Alas Ramus. Last time..."

"Mommy! Here I go!!"

"...! Mommy!!"

"...she couldn't play with you at all, so..."

The moment Nyx, another child of Malchut, confronted Emilia, a ball of purple light focused itself upon Emilia's forehead, stopping Nyx's fist from hitting it.

206 THE DEVIL IS A PART-TIMER!, Volume 21

"*Nng!*"

"Ah!!"

Wincing, Nyx shook her hand to ease the stinging. There were tears in Alas Ramus's eyes, but she refused to cry as she stared the other girl down.

"No mischief, please. Laila, over here."

"Ah, ah..."

Maybe it was telekinesis. With a wave of Ignora's arm, Laila lost her freedom, floating into the air...

"Mother!!"

...and then, before Emilia's eyes, both of them vanished.

"Gnh!"

"Mommy, she told you. Play with me! You too, Alas Ramus!"

"Nyx... Are you a Malchut, too?"

Acieth had already confirmed for them that Eleos, the girl with Camael, was Malchut.

"Yeah! Eleos is my big sister! I'm the little sister!"

"Alas Ramus, are you okay? Is that really Malchut?"

"I dunno. The Malchut I know is Eh-os. But..."

"But she's like you, too, huh? It makes sense. You and Acieth are sisters... It's not like Yesod is the exception."

"So what're we gonna play?! Mommy said to play 'tag' with you."

She never intended to take her eyes off her for a moment. But after a single blink, Nyx was right at Emilia's side, a hand placed on her breastplate. At once, her entire Cloth of the Dispeller glowed purple and disappeared into a swarm of particles—and the next moment, Nyx's hand contained a small stone, just small enough that her tiny fingers could grasp it. It was the largest Yesod fragment Emilia had seen yet—silver, the color of Yesod, but with just a tinge of purple, like Alas Ramus's bangs. It was the Holy Silver that powered her armor.

"Aww, now look what happened... But Da'at has already appeared, hasn't it? So...you'll be back to normal soon."

"Just one touch took the Cloth... The fragment... Nyx, are you...?!"

Nyx smiled. There was no light in her eyes. She seemed to be watching some point far, far away from Emilia.

"Uh-huh! This is the third time I've met you, lady."

Only a fellow Sephirah could cancel out a fusion or latent force with another Sephirah.

"*You* were in the space suit!"

"My mommy puts it on me 'cause she doesn't want me touching anything icky outside our home! So, lady..."

Nyx played with the Holy Silver in her hand, flashing a dry smile.

"You think I can have Alas Ramus and the Yesod back?"

"I don't want to comment too much on other people's children... but I think you need to learn some discipline."

"Alas Ramus was part of our family. Besides, do you think you can keep me from taking her back?"

Nyx's plastered-on smile battered Emilia. But:

"Taking, being taken... Why don't any of you understand this? It's so obvious."

Everyone had feared the possibility of Alas Ramus being captured. When they didn't know who was in the space suit, it was a clear and present problem. But now—well, all right, Laila was gone, but Ignora and Camael weren't here, either.

"Alas Ramus... I'm going to save your family. You mind going over to the corner and being a good girl?"

"Mm?!"

Purple light shone on Emi's and Alas Ramus's foreheads. The child was instantly, awkwardly teleported to one corner of the chamber.

"Uh... Ah!"

Nyx, attempting to touch Emilia again, blinked helplessly. Emilia seized that moment's hesitation, focusing her holy energy on her palm.

"Explosive Light Blast!!"

"Gaahhh!!!"

A strong light exploded directly before Nyx's eyes, generating a shock wave that made her turn somersaults in the air.

"It's so bright, Mommy!"

"Sorry, Alas Ramus. Are you okay?"

"Yeh!"

Then Emilia and Alas Ramus voluntarily split apart. Concerns that Alas Ramus and Acieth would be kidnapped were, in the end, more a worry about them being taken from Ente Isla or the demon realms over to heaven. The way Emilia saw it:

"There's no way Alas Ramus or Acieth would do anything to betray me or the Devil King. If we're fighting in heaven anyway, it doesn't matter whether we're split apart or not. After all…"

She gently picked up the unconscious Nyx, her eyes lolled back in her skull.

"We came here to save you the whole time, so we're not going to kill you. I don't have the power to do that anyway. But if we can neutralize you, at that moment, we win."

This move was something she'd learned from Albert in the past—holy magic that rendered a foe powerless without killing them. The spell summoned shock waves of light to blow enemies away, but before the light was set off, Emilia pointed the shock waves at Nyx's chin. Based on experience, no matter how powerful Alas Ramus, Acieth, or even Erone were, their physical structures were still those of human beings. And no matter how much more steadfast their internal organs were than your average Ente Islan's, Emilia's "full force" was perfectly balanced to "go easy" on the awesomely powerful Sephirah children. It was a nonlethal blow to the brain. The moment Nyx was sure she had taken Alas Ramus's power and nullified Emilia's, her sight was blocked by the light, and then she'd received a de facto concussion.

"But now what should I do? I want to know where Mother and Ignora went, but I can't just leave Nyx here…"

"Mommy?"

"Yes, Alas Ramus?"

"Nux is off."

"What?"

"Eh-os is with the angel. But Nux is off."

"Um... You mean this child isn't fused with Ignora right now? So what?"

Alas Ramus smiled warmly and placed a hand on the forehead of the fallen Nyx.

"Mommy, over here."

"Huh? What are you... Ah!"

Invited over, Emilia brought her face closer to Alas Ramus. The child's right hand was on Nyx's forehead, and now she placed her left on Emilia's. Then, her body glowed a golden yellow, while Alas Ramus's glowed purple, as if serving as a conduit.

"Uh... Ah! Wait!"

Emilia could feel it. She could see that Alas Ramus was going inside of her...with Nyx in tow.

"W-wait a second, Alas Ramus! What *is* this?!"

"...*They can split us up. But...*"

Alas Ramus's smile came through in her voice.

"*Only Yeffod can bring them together. Connect heart to heart.*"

"No, um, I understand the logic, but *should* we do this?!"

Certainly, nobody ever said that only one Sephirah could lodge itself inside a person's body. And certainly, they couldn't leave Nyx lying there. But considering how life with Alas Ramus currently worked...

"*Owww... Ah... Huh?! Wait! Who am I in?!*"

"*Nux, this is my mommy.*"

"You, you're...!"

The voices of Nyx and Alas Ramus bickering echoed in her mind.

"*Whoa! You can't just do that, Alas Ramus! I'm together with Mommy! Take me back to her!*"

"*Mm-mm. Let's play together. Let's have snacks.*"

"*We're not at the supermarket, Alas Ramus! Snack time's later...*"

"*Quiet one minute, lady! Alas Ramus the Yesod! Get me out of here!*"

"*Nuh-uh! No bein' selfish!*"

"*Let me out, let me out, let me ouuuutttttt!!*"

"Mommy! She's bein' selfish! Don't let her out!"

"Ah, um, o-okay… Sure… But can you keep it down…?"

The human body might not have been limited to one Sephirah, but having multiple personalities screaming and shouting in your brain would make anybody's mental health suffer.

"A-Alas Ramus… Um, once this is all over, she can separate from us, okay?"

"Nuh-uh!"

"Ugh, none of *that*, please! I gotta find Ignora and finish this! Umm…"

"H-hey! You're trying to hurt my mommy! Stop, stop, stooooopppp!!"

"Argh! What is… This is gonna drive me crazy!"

She knew it was futile, but she covered her ears with both hands as she all but fled the chamber. The hunt for Ignora and Laila was on.

✳

When Ignora stepped into the large room, she never expected it would be occupied. By three people, no less.

"Uh-oh. You came here ahead of us, huh?" she quipped.

"Nngh… G-Gabriel…"

The only people that could've gotten ahead of her were Gabriel and his team.

"…Ignora. Can I ask what the heck is going on?"

Gabriel, ignoring Laila's pain, approached Ignora, a frantic look on his face.

"What's going on? Just what we've always been doing, isn't it? I had everyone pitch in to help us through a difficult situation."

"Wait. Wait, Ignora. If you've done something like *this*, then…!"

Raguel was right behind Gabriel. But he was unconscious and stuffed inside a capsule, much like the ones that had once housed the Tree of Sephirot's roots. Next to him was another capsule, and inside was an old man, clearly a generation or two older than the other angels.

"Why'd you do this to Sandalphon, too...?! He was one of the moderates who supported you to the end! What do you expect to accomplish doing *this*?! Look! Look at this! After all this... After Da'at finally did what you hoped for...and picked *us*!"

"..."

Was it Urushihara who reacted silently to Gabriel's words? Or was it Copyhara?

"Gabriel... What are you talking about?"

Ignora lightly smiled.

"Aghh...!"

Then Laila fell to the floor, groaning. Nobody else paid her any mind.

"Doesn't our *true* challenge begin once we're selected? I'm certain you know what kind of shape Ente Isla is in right now. You've seen just how many of the 'unchosen' run rampant over that planet. Don't you? And you, too, Laila."

Ignora grabbed the hair of Laila, who was crawling on the ground away from her, pulling her up.

"Right, Laila? It was you, wasn't it?"

"Wh-what... Ah!"

"I had everything set up just fine, and you used me as a front. How very nice of you! Without that, I'm sure this would have been done far sooner... Nobody would've had to suffer like this."

"Ow, owww!"

"You...and maybe Gabriel, and *these* people..." Ignora flashed an abject, brittle smile as she peered at Laila behind her. "I really didn't need any of it... All they needed was a little glimpse, but *you* had to grow the Church into this big thing...and it's cost us so much. Right?"

"Ah!"

Ignora let go of her hair. She placed a foot on her back, lifting her head high.

"Right, my boy?"

There was no expression on Urushihara's face as he said:

"Maybe so, Mom."

◊

"Hmm?" "Huh?" "Oh?"

"What's up?"

On the way back from Tokyo Station, as they switched to the Keio Line at Shinjuku, Maou, Emi, and Chiho all let out little yelps of surprise as they looked at their phones. When Laila asked why, the three of them exchanged glances before Maou dared to ask the question:

"Urushihara called you, too?"

"Yeah. It would've been right when we left Tokyo Station."

"He called me then, too. A few times."

Urushihara's phone number had called all three of them.

"Yeah, mine, too. Some kinda emergency? Lemme call him back."

Stopping Laila and Nord for a moment, Maou called Urushihara's number. Nobody picked up.

"Well, huh. After calling all of us ten minutes ago..."

"Did you get any texts?"

"No. But I'm kinda worried now. This isn't like him."

Although even Maou had upgraded to a smartphone by now, Urushihara was still going around with an old-fashioned clamshell phone. Maou had bought it for him, of course, and Urushihara certainly had a number of complaints about not being given a smartphone. But he wasn't in the habit of reaching out to people in general; as a rule, he and Maou spoke over the phone only for urgent matters. Emi and Chiho had known him long enough to have his number, but they had never talked on the phone. If he was trying to call *them*, too, that seemed like a real crisis.

"What should we do?"

"We can't do very much here. Why don't you call him when we reach Sasazuka?"

"Yeah, that sounds good."

But neither Emi nor Chiho looked too concerned.

"All right. I'll text him just in case."

Maou didn't have any faster way to physically reach Urushihara, so they stuck to their original plan, boarding the next train bound for Keio-Hachioji. It was midafternoon, so the train car was nearly empty—even the Justina family (with all their luggage) and Suzuno (in her pilgrim's outfit) had no trouble finding seats.

"Come to think of it," Suzuno said, "if you were in Kobe, did you visit Rika? How is she faring?"

"Yeah, she's bursting with energy as much as ever. She said she'd be in Tokyo soon, so you oughtta go out to eat when you're free, Chiho."

"That sounds great! I'd love to visit her, too. I've never been to Kobe."

Urushihara was forgotten after they boarded the train, as the conversation turned toward other topics. Once they had reached Akebonobashi, the next station, Maou's phone started vibrating.

"Damn it, don't call back just as the train's about to leave…"

It must have been Urushihara. They didn't have time for a long chat, though. Maou looked around to ensure the coast was clear then took the call.

"Hey, sorry, I'm on the train. I'll call back once I'm at Sasazuka."

"No, wait…!!"

The panic bounced off his ears, but Maou mercilessly ended the call. They were on a train, and the signal was about to drop out anyway.

"Hey, y'know, I've never been to Kobe, either. Kobe beef's supposed to be really good. Didja eat any steak?"

"Mostly I was out sightseeing and visiting Rika's family house, so all the Kobe beef I tried was in this boxed lunch I bought at the station. But their other Western-style food was really good…"

Once again, Urushihara vanished from the conversation, as Emi discussed all the restaurants in Kobe she'd gotten to try out.

A little while later, once they had reached Sasazuka Station, Maou called Urushihara back.

"Dude, didn't me calling Emilia and Chiho Sasaki give you any clue how freaked out I am?!"

He'd picked up before the first ring ended.

"I'm at the yakiniku joint by the station! Get over here right now!"
Then he hung up, leaving Maou helplessly looking at his phone.

"What's with him? What kind of emergency is *yakiniku*? And also..."

Maou's eyebrows furrowed as he stuck the phone back in his pocket.

"Since when was he back in Japan?"

Chiho, meanwhile, gave everyone a concerned look.

"Wouldn't Urushihara have Acieth with him...?"

Suddenly, the words "emergency" and "*yakiniku*" linked together in their minds.

"...Let's go."

Maou, head hung low, began to worry about how much money he had in his wallet.

"Ooooh! Maou!"

"Laila, Nord... Hey."

"Oh! The Devil King! Whoo-hoo!"

"...Hello, Alas Ramus. Guys..."

Leaving the others to wait outside, Maou entered the *yakiniku* restaurant by Sasazuka Station, only to be greeted by a scene straight out of hell. At a six-person table, Acieth, Erone, Nyx, and Eleos were all cooking their own meat—and at the far side, Urushihara was slumped against the table, a mug of oolong tea in his hand. A tower of plates was stacked by the lone empty seat.

"Urushihara... What made you think taking *these* guys out to *yakiniku* is a good idea? You knew full well this would happen."

Clearly, Urushihara's attempts at resisting them had failed.

"Dude, you know none of them listen to me," Urushihara said, his face a bit hollow. "And lemme warn you, I'm broke."

"Huh? I know you get a salary."

"Yeah, but I don't make enough to cover Kobe beef courses the way *they* run through them!"

"A-are you serious?! How much did they eat?"

Kobe beef returning to the conversation this fast staggered Maou.

"I stopped counting midway through...but all those plates are Kobe beef. The good parts."

Maou shuddered. The dishes suggested they had gone through an entire cow all by themselves.

"Guys... Can you hold back a little? You're not the ones who have to pay for all this."

Even he had to complain to them about it. But:

"S-sorry."

Only Eleos seemed apologetic at all. The other three barely even slowed their chopsticks.

"Boy, I feel the sorry for Iwaki, but me, I'm a little sick of MgRonald, so..."

"If we're going to another world, it's just boring if we eat the same thing every time, isn't it?"

"Yeah, I wanted to eat something besides MgRonald, too, so... Hee-hee!"

Acieth and Nyx were shameless. And Erone smiled, much brighter than he used to be, as he chowed down on some white rice.

"Hey, Urushihara, you think we can split this? Is this the tab?"

Maou snatched up the receipt slipped tableside. Then he felt the blood slowly drain from his upper body.

"How's it look?"

"I can't cover all of it...but hey, good news for you. I'll call for help."

Leaving the anxious Urushihara, Maou went back outside and dragged the reluctant Laila back in.

"What? What's going on?!"

"You're responsible for 'em, too. You help cover this. I'm not gonna let you say no."

"What happened in here? ...What?! Four of you?! Huh?! Where did this check come from?!"

The four members at the table shocked her. The tab shocked her again.

"Divided by three, I think we can manage."

"...Guys, please, make this the last round."

Laila's shoulders dropped in defeat. In the end, a pretty impossible amount of 10,000 yen bills flew out of their wallets—far more than an average Tokyoite's meal would normally be—but the culprits still complained about wanting more.

✳

"But why the hell did you take *four* people here?"

The three grown-ups, pale and not even getting to eat anything, began marching straight for Villa Rosa Sasazuka after leaving the restaurant.

"It was *supposed* to be just Acieth, dude. She fired that hunger beam again."

Those purple beams Acieth shot out when she was peckish had acquired a rather ominous name over time. Even after the assault on heaven, they had never stopped.

"Eleos and Copyhara said that three years aren't enough for the Yesod to fully adapt to the current Ente Isla, so it's not gonna go away that easily. But if we're managing her, having stuff destroyed every time it happens is kind of a bummer."

"You should've eaten something, too."

"I was worried they'd take a bite of me if I tried taking anything."

It didn't sound like a joke. That was the scary part.

"Erone, did you say thank you to Urushihara?"

"Yes, Nord. I've always been saying 'please' and 'thank you,' haven't I?"

"Yeah. He and Eleos. The other two are animals." Urushihara shrugged after chiming in. "So anyway, Acieth was in bad shape, so I tried to sneak her out, but then that idiot Nyx found us, and... Agh!"

"Oh, come *on*, Lucifer! Don't call me an idiot!"

Suddenly, Nyx jumped on Urushihara's shoulder from behind.

"Y'know, I always *thought* something was up! Acieth would just disappear on regular occasions, and so would you at the same time,

Lucifer. Erone seemed to know what was up, so I pressed him, and *now* I know. Stop spoiling the Yesod all the time!"

"He is not the spoiling me! This is valid treat! Based on trusting relationship!"

"She's talking as crazy as ever..."

Acieth was being so outlandish, even Emi felt obliged to join in.

"Acieth, did you have a lot of meat?" asked the sleepy Alas Ramus in Emi's arms. Her sister smiled back, her lips still a little glossy from the grease.

"The Kobe beef, it was so good! The *Wagyu* grease, it is sweet taste! True!"

"Hmm... Mommy, can we have Kobe beef for dinner...?"

"Didn't I say we were having ramen?!"

Acieth's review sounded more like a taunt to Emi—and Alas Ramus's urgent plea floored her. Chiho, meanwhile, was taking an apologetic tone with Urushihara.

"Let me cover some of it, too. It's partly my fault for introducing Acieth to MgRonald in the first place..."

Urushihara seemed ambivalent about it. After a great deal of thought, he shook his head.

"You're fine, dude. I get to expense Acieth's food bill, so it's all good. And Nyx finding me is my fault as their supervisor."

"It's my fault, too. As Nyx's elder sister, I should have stopped her...but I've never tasted anything so good before, so my instincts kind of took hold."

Only Eleos demonstrated even the slightest hint of remorse. But:

"Let's come back again soon."

"Yeah. I wanted some more."

Already, Erone was readily agreeing with Nyx.

"...Considering your 'expense account,'" Maou blurted out as he listened to the Sephirah, "you sure racked up a huge bill. We got one more wallet we can hit up, y'know."

"Oh. Yeah, perfect. Hell, I shoulda called him first."

Urushihara, realizing who this "wallet" was, smiled grimly.

"Besides, logically speaking, *he's* the one who needs to take responsibility for this."

He took the receipt out from his wallet, playing with it between his fingers. There was a glint of pure evil in his eyes.

"Man, oh man, oh man. This is a mean prank to pull, mm-kay?"

Emerging from Room 103 of Villa Rosa Sasazuka, looking like he just got out of bed, was Gabriel, being rather immodest with his T-shirt, boxers, and hair flying every which way.

"If you wake me up in *this* heat with *this* tab, I'm liable to have a heart attack, y'know."

"Have it *after* you cover your share, dude."

"My share...? How much can four kids even *eat*? I ain't gonna cover *you*, Lucifer."

"All I had was oolong tea! This isn't the *yakiniku* I wanted!"

"Hey," interjected Maou, "next time, take them to my favorite *horumon* place, okay? I'll tell you where it is."

"Yeah, I know it, dude. We already got banned from there! And that was a *solo* trip for Acieth!"

"It *was*?!"

"But all of you guys went together? If it was all of *you*, it can't be *that* bad if you split it."

If Emi, Alas Ramus, Laila, Nord, and Chiho were there, then yes, a *yakiniku* party split evenly wouldn't break the bank. But before anyone could set Gabriel straight, it was (for some reason) Acieth who first took offense.

"No, this price, it is the *true blue* what four of us eat. When I eat, I not rotten enough to take help from others!"

"What are *you* talking about?" Gabriel asked. Everyone else could sympathize for him, but Acieth couldn't.

"Now, you pay the money we eat! In full!"

"Not even demons are *this* cruel, you know. Ugggh..."

Resigned to his fate, Gabriel took out a long wallet atop the stand by the front door—brand name, much to everyone's chagrin.

"Is 20,000 yen all right? That's all I have on hand."

"Tch! How the broke you are! Okay, Lucifer, thanks for lunch!"

Acieth snatched up the bills and politely gave them to Urushihara with both hands.

"Dudes…don't try pulling this act with anyone else, okay?"

Even Urushihara, who had eagerly come here to take Gabriel for all he had, felt a little guilty. He felt it proper to turn around and give the other three Sephirah a warning.

"We won't, I promise. I'm not *that* much of a dummy, Lucifer."

"Acieth, I really don't think that was very nice to do."

"I felt bad for Gabriel from the start."

Watching Nyx, Eleos, and Erone plead their cases, Urushihara breathed a sigh of relief. The others looked at him.

"Urushihara's sure matured, too, huh?"

"Yeah, despite it all, he's become a good caretaker."

"I'm glad to see that. I mean, Lucifer, of all people! What an amazing person he's become…!"

"It's really true, isn't it? The worse a kid is, the happier you are when he grows up."

"Lushiferrr, you're like a big brother now!"

Chiho, Emi, Laila, Suzuno, and finally Alas Ramus all showered Urushihara in warm praise.

"I *totally* regret taking this job, dude!!" was the reply.

"*Yawwwn…* What a terrible way to wake up. On my day off, too…"

"What's it like upstairs, Gabriel?"

Gabriel winced as Maou pointed at the second floor. He followed the finger upward, one eyebrow raised.

"I think it was quiet. I didn't hear any noise. Hope she didn't die in this heat…"

The building had been fairly extensively renovated, but it was still decades old, so the first floor could hear almost everything that went on upstairs.

"All right. Thanks. I know she's eating, but…"

"Is she? Hopefully that'll make *my* shift easier, starting tomorrow."

"I'll go check on her later. Sorry to spring that on you. Rest up, okay?"

"I don't have the nerves of steel to go back to bed after *this*. *Yawwwn*… I'm all sweaty, too. Maybe I'll go to the bathhouse. When I'm helping Mikitty with her work, I barely have enough time to bathe."

The gutted-looking Gabriel waved a hand at Urushihara and Acieth, shooing them away, and promptly closed the door.

"Keter's been growing little by little lately. Sandalphon says it's just a matter of time now. But that makes Acieth hungrier, and that's what led to today. I dunno what to do, dude."

Maou, talking alone with Urushihara in Room 201 for the first time in a while, offered him some iced coffee from the fridge.

"Is that from your café?"

"Kind of. It's a blend of beans I've been testing out for sale."

"Oh. You're sure dedicated."

Urushihara noticed an unfamiliar machine sitting in a corner of the kitchen. It wasn't there when he was still a resident. Picking up the glass (straw and all), he took a sip and nodded, convinced.

"It's good, yeah, but do you really need to go through the trouble? You can get something this good in the refrigerator aisle at the supermarket, if you don't mind payin' for it."

"That's not really the point, man. This is a hobby, but it connects directly with the work I'm doing. It's a hobby like the video games you've been playing since the freakin' moment you came here."

"Oh. Yeah, it's not nice to make fun of people's hobbies. I've really come to think that lately."

Urushihara looked out the closed window, peering into the backyard.

"I never thought I'd keep up the gardening Bell taught me for so long, dude."

"Yeah, and I doubt Suzuno thought you'd be taking care of the Sephirah, too." Maou sipped his own iced coffee. "I thought trees and vegetable gardens would be totally different, but I guess the fundamentals of plant care are the same anywhere. When Keter began growing little fruits, I couldn't help but think they looked like the eggplant at Komagane, kind of."

"Yeah. And Kazuma threw out the eggplant that didn't make the grade, right? I think about that a lot lately. You can't coddle these guys too much."

"You don't think? Because I don't think you can group Sephirah with eggplant."

"Sure you can. Keter's been growing fine since I've been managing it, right?"

"Mm… Yeah, I guess so."

Maou didn't have anything particularly convincing to dispel Urushihara's pet theories with. And if he was the one dealing with the Sephirot every day, that must've been backed up by experience.

"But it's really true. Gardening *is* a good way to get off your ass and start working. You can do it at your own pace."

"Ahh, shut up."

Urushihara finished the remaining coffee, then turned back to the wall behind him, over toward Room 202. Suzuno used to live there.

"But how's she been?"

"Hard to say yet. She's eating now, but… You worried?"

"A little," Urushihara said, giving him an honest nod.

"…Yeah. But maybe you bringing Nyx here will be a good influence on her. She's really her only ally, in a way."

Maou tried to cheer up the slightly downcast Urushihara. But his reply wound up surprising him.

"Huh? So how about we just bring Nyx back to the other side, then? I don't want her recovering *that* fast."

"Huh?"

"When my work's going *this* well, it'd be annoying if she recovered and started griping at me."

"…Yeah, sounds true to me. I don't need to be Copyhara to see that."

"*You* lie a lot more than I ever did, Maou."

Maou put a hand to his head. "Wait… You're not actually Copyhara, are you?"

Urushihara attempted to deny it, but seeing Maou's confusion inspired something within him. His evil grin was there as always.

"Well, who knows, huh? If you think I am, you'd better not think anything too mean, y'know?"

"Stop it, you asshole."

No, he couldn't help but implicitly threaten his old master.

THE
DEVIL
AND THE
HERO
CLOBBER
THE GOD

A human wall. That was the only way to describe it.

It was the same setup as the shrines and the Yesod-root terrarium, or the room with the relic capsules underneath the demon realms. Large numbers of angels were "sealed away" in them, Raguel visible among them.

"You're kidding me, Ignora... These many? Most of the survivors...?"

"I'm not kidding. You saw Nyx earlier, didn't you? I needed them for her."

"Needed them...! All your comrades except for Camael?! Just for that...?"

"It's going to take a long, long time for the rest of the Sephirah to manifest anyway. Better to have them sleep for now and awaken them once everything is ready, isn't it?"

"B-but not like this...! Ahh!!"

Just then, Camael and Satan once again came barreling in through a wall.

"Ow! *Damn* it! Emi, stop screwing around! And, whoa, what kinda gross room is *this*?!"

"Graaaahhhh!!"

"Give the hell *up*, god damn it!!!"

"Shut up! Be a little more mature already!"

Through the giant hole left by the two giant men, Acieth and Eleos rolled in like a gumball, engaged in what could only be described as a catfight—a brutish, unrefined brawl.

"Aaaah, just shut up! Hurry up and finish that already! I gotta get this kid out of me… Shut *up*!!"

And behind them, Emilia—hands to her ears, and eyes shut tight—just walked in like normal. Behind her, they could see all the carnage and rubble Satan and Camael had caused outside.

"Huh? Where's this? Ah! Mom, are you okay? The Devil King's fighting over there!"

But Emilia, her mind full of feedback from the fused Nyx, sounded all but desperate as she spoke, ready to land a few blows of her own against the two giants grappling with each other.

"Well, perfect! This building looked like it fit the bill, so I had him blow the guy in here, and bingo! Ignora! I really don't think this can go on! Just give it up and surrender!!"

"You 'don't think'? You wanna *be* any less committal—*urgh*!"

Turning his eyes away made Satan groan, Camael's broken spear slamming against the side of his head.

"Shut up! I've just about had it with all of this! Based on Nyx, I can tell that Ignora's nothing but a bastard! I don't know what she wants to do with Ente Isla, but if it results in more kids like Nyx and Lucifer, we're all doomed!!"

Her words were on a grand scale, but she was referring to something incredibly tiny.

"First you fly in here, then you berate all of us, and now you're pickin' on my upbringing, dude?"

"What, Lucifer? Don't tell me you're homesick for *this*?!"

"No way. It's just, you know, you're treating this the same as everything else… But anyway, the boss we gotta beat still doesn't seem too concerned at all. We have her so outnumbered, but…"

"Yeah. Looking at this room, it's really messed up, but if we put our minds to it, we could easily destroy all of it… No, shut *up*, you!"

"Huh?"

"There's another Malchut inside of me! And she won't shut up! Zip it, damn it!"

Even as Emi spoke, Eleos was scuffling with Acieth, and Satan was trading blows with Camael. But amid all this din, nothing seemed to affect the nameless, faceless angels that lined the walls of this massive chamber. Emi looked up at them, even as Nyx continued her griping. There were young people, old people, but none of them seemed to have the "holiness" of an angel. The only one Emi recognized was Raguel.

"...Raguel..."

His trademark Afro had unfrizzed itself. But seeing him—and Ignora, holding Laila down but not looking too ready for battle—Emilia sensed something.

"Ignora, you... You've accomplished your mission? Is that why you're not trying to resist much?"

"You're not going to kill people for no reason, are you, Emilia?"

Ignora didn't answer the question Emilia asked.

"Look at that! That Da'at, taking the form of my own boy!"

"I got a few things to say about that, but what about him?"

"To be honest, it didn't matter much to me who it was. But he picked *him*... He picked Lucifer. Nothing could make a mother happier."

Her words were nothing but a stream of consciousness.

"I suppose children love a grown-up who doesn't act his age, don't they?"

"Stop implying all this stuff."

"After being chased off our home planet, this new planet's Sephirot recognized us as the valid successors. And the proof of it...lies in that wonderful boy...that he and I had."

"..."

Urushihara and Emilia were uncomfortable with the term "boy" for differing reasons. They sneered as Ignora continued, trancelike.

"I know that you, a limited number of 'Ente Islans,' are angry about what we've done to the Sephirot...but it's not that I want to destroy you all. In fact, we're using our powers to watch for danger across all of Ente Isla, managing the Sephirot so we may create a planet and people that will never perish. And to do that, we have to show that we are the superior presence on this planet..."

"The superior presence?"

"We protect this planet, and its people. Everything was a battle toward that end. Satanael's group defied us, trying to stop us...but look! The Sephirot has finally judged us to be correct. It has manifested itself as Lucifer!"

"...Calling someone 'superior' over others takes a lot of guts."

Emilia listened to Ignora's long speech, more exasperated than surprised by it. Then she asked the woman herself.

"So, what, is *that* what you're like?"

"Apparently I am sometimes," Copyhara tossed out. "That's why Amane Ohguro was in such a panic. She's the daughter of the Binah of Earth, right? So seeing me, the descendant of the angels she fought, appear instead of you Ente Islan natives must've scared her. The Sephirah of Earth must've sided with you because they thought you were on the right side of this argument. But then here I am, taking the form of the angels' descendant."

When Copyhara appeared at the Sasaki residence, Amane gathered as many of the Earth Sephirah as she could and laid out a dragnet for him.

"So they saw me as 'the enemy of their friends.' They must've figured there might be war between two Sephirots. They were panicking, so they all filed in to take me back here—and they had Amane Ohguro watch over me, too, because they were still anxious. So, yeah, Ignora does kind of have a point."

"...You're still obliquely implying a bunch of stuff. The Devil King and Acieth are about to get pretty awful with us, so I'd really like to end this conversation already..."

Even as they spoke, Satan and Camael, and Acieth and Eleos, continued to fight. Both appeared evenly matched, which meant neither side had a definitive finisher to break out. It was more of a bar brawl or fracas than a real battle. And while the Devil King and Camael were one thing, Emilia was reluctant to have two young girls like Acieth and Eleos get permanently scarred or bodily disabled.

"Ah, sorry, sorry. What she said—what Ignora said—is generally right. But she's reading the situation a little wrong. Yes, the Sephirot and Sephirah came to a consensus, and that was Lucifer, the child of Ignora and Satanael. But they didn't choose an *angel*."

The next moment, before Emilia's eyes, Copyhara pressed a small piece of metal against her hand.

"I'll lend you my powers for a little bit. If you have a Yesod *and* Malchut inside you, then it's a simple story."

The hand of Copyhara that touched Emilia's had a small ring on it—the ring with the small Yesod fragment that Chiho Sasaki wore.

"You, the Hero Emilia, have obtained the power your mother pulled out through Chiho Sasaki, whether she meant to or not. And that makes *you* the strongest in the universe."

There was no light. It was so different from fusing with Alas Ramus or Nyx, and Emilia didn't know what to do for a moment—but then all became clear.

"W-wait! No...!!"

"Alas Ramus... Nyx... I'm gonna borrow some of your powers!"

"Three people...!!"

Now there were three different consciousnesses in her mind, alongside her own. That alone was enough to potentially drive her insane, but the next moment allowed her to gather her wits, forgetting about it all.

"Mommy, your right hand."

Alas Ramus, against Emilia's will, had appeared as a holy sword. But it wasn't the usual sort of metal blade. From the tip to the edge of the handle, it was a sword of light—composed of nothing but purple illumination.

"This..."

The sight of a holy sword like none other stunned her...but she had seen this happen once before. She looked back at Raguel, locked inside his capsule. It was almost like he was ensconced up there to remind her of that moment.

"There are lots of crazy coincidences in the world. But that's all they are. Coincidences. There's no meaning to them. I was born from

the Yesod fragment Chiho Sasaki had, and that's why I'm giving this power to you. I am the Da'at, and the Yesod, too, and that makes me the one who decides the Sephirot's future. The one who wants peace for the planet's inhabitants more than anyone else. And a world where the Sephirot and Sephirah children function correctly once more...!"

But Emilia could tell she had been acting of her own volition. It was what anyone would do to correct a world that wasn't heading in the direction it was supposed to. A perfectly natural, human thing to do. And even before they attacked heaven, Emi herself had decided to use this power to "put an end" to this.

That was why—at this moment in time before anything had been settled—she didn't hesitate to test the true value of this holy sword of light.

She leaped forward—like a fencer beginning a match, her sword pointed straight ahead of her. The target was Camael.

"Devil King! Get back!!"

That, too, was a warning Emilia gave because she wanted to.

"Ngh... Ah! ...Huh?"

When the Acieth-fused Satan smashed Camael with everything he had, not even that was enough to destroy his armor. Now it was like a knife slicing through tofu. The sword of light slipped right through, with no resistance at all. But no blood gushed from the wound; no bits of broken armor flew away from it.

"E-Emi, what are, you...?"

Satan's eyes opened wide at this sudden bout of violence.

"It's fine... This is fine... This should end it all... The astral energy...in humans, that Yesod controls...flowing through me, the one she's bonded with the most... With this..."

It happened immediately.

"Wha-ah..."

In terms of time, it was around three seconds. Camael, after overwhelming Satan in a clash for the ages, suddenly fell to his knees, shaking. The sword of light was already pulled out of him.

"H-hey, Emi..."

"Watch."

Emilia didn't move. She was looking down on the fallen Camael, sword down, defenseless.

"Wh-whoa, watch out! He's still..."

Emilia sadly shook her head at Satan's warning.

"No. It's already over."

"Huh?"

"N-no... This can't be...!! Sata... Laila... Satan... *Ngh!*"

"Wha—?!"

Satan's eyes flew open in surprise. With a muffled scream uttered by Camael, white light began to burst from his body, head to toe, before disappearing. Then, with a blast like all the holy force in him being expelled, Camael's body shot into the air and then fell limp. The crimson armor vanished, and all that remained was a silver-haired man in the prime of his life, dressed in a toga and lying on the ground. There wasn't a single drop of holy energy, or spirit, or stamina left in him.

"N-no way... That..."

Satan wasn't the only one shocked by this. Eleos, still grappling with Acieth, suddenly stopped. Acieth, not getting the message, lunged at her from behind and landed a blow to the back of her head—but Eleos was so shocked by these events, the pain didn't even register.

"Hey! Come on! This battle, it is not over yet! C'mon!!"

"Wh-why...? We've been separated..."

"Huhh?! Separated?!"

"Camael...is no longer Camael. The power I instilled in him is lost... What did you do...?"

The sight of Eleos acting so absentmindedly flustered near her enemy puzzled Acieth. Emilia gave her a sad look.

"Don't you see, Eleos? ...When the people of a world watched over by the Sephirah truly mature... When they can truly protect them-selves...the holy force and the demonic force leave them."

Emilia lifted her blade and pointed it at Raguel's capsule.

"The answer was already before us. That astral blade, the one that removed the miracle housed within his soul. The blade of Yesod light banished his holy force."

"Raguel, and the purple blade of light... Ah!!"

Satan shouted, eliciting another exasperated look from Emilia.

"Tokyo Tower? Chi, against Raguel?"

As Satan recalled, when Gabriel and Raguel had hijacked the Tokyo Tower transmitter, Chiho—controlled by Laila—was the one who had defeated Raguel. When he was struck with an arrow made of purple light, he was drained of holy energy and unable to fly. It was a "fall" for the angel—and Satan and Emilia knew someone else that term applied to.

"Wait. Do you mean...?"

"When we go back, we're gonna have to stop by Ente Isla and have that guy take an eye exam. If it was Satanael who broke the Yesod, there'd have to be lots more fragments than the ones Laila and Gabriel know about."

The angel of judgment, the one who could emit purple beams of light from his eyes that made angels "fallen," was no doubt breezily working in Hatagaya right now. There was a Yesod fragment in those eyes, in all likelihood.

"The Yesod had made up its mind long before any of this. But it was in fragments...its roots cut off and crushed. It couldn't execute the role assigned for it until now."

"...So we're gonna have to go on a fragment hunt after this?"

"Yes. I don't think collecting them all would make Alas Ramus and Acieth go away...but I think we're going to be busy for a while."

"Okay, you guys get the gist now?"

Somewhere along the line, Copyhara had come out of Emilia's mind, carrying Nyx in his arms.

"Yes. Loud and clear."

"*We* chose *them*. And all that means is we recognized that they were the human race we needed to protect. And the 'human race' we have recognized for Ente Isla..."

Copyhara and Emilia's eyes turned toward Ignora, still holding Laila down.

"…will someday all lose their miraculous powers."

"…What…was…that?"

Ignora groggily gazed at the fallen Camael.

"Can I ask you one question, Copyhara? Has Camael lost his immortality?"

Copyhara had a clear answer for that.

"Immortality is a scientific breakthrough, discovered by Ignora's team based on hints taken from our distant brothers and sisters. It is not a miraculous power, like holy or demonic force. Thus…we don't know."

"Oh. Well, that's too bad," Emilia jeered. "Then we're gonna have to let them live, won't we? To see if they've lost it or not."

"What a scary Hero *you* are," Copyhara replied.

"No… That's a lie…" Ignora croaked. "Camael? No—Malchut! Da'at! Didn't you choose us…?"

"Weren't you listening?" Copyhara said. "Yes, we did. And that's why this happened."

"L-Lucifer…"

"Finally calling me by name, huh?"

Too stricken to keep Laila down, Ignora took a step—only to find Urushihara waiting for her, grabbing her with a bear hug.

"Lucifer, you…"

"You know, I kinda like the life I've had. But when I recall the past, there's something that struck me about it…"

"Wha…?"

"Knowing that I wasn't loved… That actually hurts a lot."

"L-Lucifer…"

"Mom only cared about research. Dad was all about politics, and saving the people. And unfortunately for me, they only saw me as a way to prove they were right. I think I have the right to be a little upset."

"Lucifer, that was…!"

"But I'm grown up now and all. I know you were both dealing with really important stuff. But that's that, and this is this. Both of you locked me up in one of those capsules for so long—Mom for her

immortality research, Dad so she couldn't take me back. No matter what kinda rationale you had for it, to me, it wasn't much more than abuse."

Urushihara constrained Ignora, preventing her escape.

"Now I get why I was so attracted to Olba when he said he could take me back to heaven… I wanted to get back at you for what happened to me as an infant."

It was those most personal of emotions that drove Urushihara to seal the fate of a god that wrecked an entire world. But—this time, at least—Emilia couldn't find it in her to sass him back. She plunged into battle herself, after all, because she cared for her parents—and it was those parents who sapped her will to fight.

"Alas Ramus?"

"Yeh?"

"Time to break the source of everyone's pain."

"W-wait. That, that can't be…"

Emilia's sword of light retained its power, even with Copyhara and Nyx away from her. She pointed it at Ignora's throat, making sure Urushihara wouldn't get caught by it.

"…"

Wordlessly, she closed the distance in a heartbeat. Ignora had the power to make legions of angels do her bidding—even to seal them away like this. But she stood there helplessly, waiting for the tip to reach her. The assault on heaven, after countless hours of preparation and hard work, seemed ready to end with little more than a whimper. Just as the thought crossed her mind…

"Stop, Emi."

"That's enough, Emilia."

…the tip was stopped in front of Ignora's forehead by the hands of two demons.

"What are you doing?"

She glared at the large hands holding her arm and shoulders.

"The battle's already over, isn't it?"

Satan pulled her arm, moving the sword away.

"…And it's not a good idea to banish her powers right now."

Alciel, accompanied by Camael's Heavenly Regiment, had his hands on her shoulders. The demons had stopped the human Hero before she could kill the god.

"...Camael's Regiment told me a great many things," he went on quietly. "Sandalphon, the elder of the angels, has been sacrificed by Ignora to the Sephirot, and as a result, only she knows how all of this machinery works. The angels who have slept here for hundreds, thousands of years—or even before then—did so to await the Sephirah's 'day of selection,' just as Ignora aimed for. Now only she knows how to release them. Our mission here was not to massacre the angels. Put it down for now."

Emilia gave Alciel a sidelong glance then lowered her sword.

"All right. I knew this...from the start."

"You didn't *really* wanna do it, did you? You wouldn't have given up so easily once we stopped you otherwise."

"What do *you* know about me?"

"I know more than anyone alive what you're like when you're out for *blood*."

"Good point."

Emilia softly sighed and transformed out of her Hero appearance. Her hair and eyes went back to the old Emi Yusa, her sharpened holy force and murderous rage out of the picture. Once they were sure the transformation was complete, Satan and Alciel let go.

But not everything was normal. As Emi undid her transformation, Alas Ramus manifested herself from the sword of light. Toddling over to Ignora, she grabbed the stupefied woman's hand and placed it against her own forehead. The moment she did, Ignora's bluish-silver hair turned purple, and she fell limp.

"Oh, that's *it*?"

Urushihara shrugged as she let go of Ignora. "Well, geez. I thought you'd kill her, but... You guys are such pushovers."

He was being pretty brazen about his mother. Emi shot him a glare.

"Stop using me for your own revenge. If you have a grudge over something, use your own power to deal with it."

"But I get why he would say that. It definitely ain't the most satis-fying ending."

Satan turned toward the wall behind him. There were more angels sealed up there than he'd ever want to count.

"And *we're* being left with all the cleanup work, too. It's *such* a pain when killing them all doesn't end it."

"You're right."

Ignora was in a trance on her knees, Camael on the floor in a per-manently altered state. Eleos was unable to accept Copyhara's and Camael's current states, Nyx was a bit dazed after separating from Emi.

"Conquering the Devil King was a lot easier. Just kill and forget."

"No doubt," Satan said, flashing a tired smile.

◊

Emeralda and Albert each held an Airenia gold coin. These they transferred to a large, pudgy hand, where they were further exam-ined with the receiver's monocle.

"Yes, yes, everything looks in order. You may go back at any time within the allowable period, but if you want an extension, let me or Amane know, all right?"

"Okaaay, dear. Thanks as alllways."

"Money makes the world go round, huh? Or worlds."

Miki Shiba put the gold coins in a jewel box on the table, opened the door in the dark room, and invited the two of them through it.

"You have Japanese yen with you, right, Emeralda? Do you need any money exchanged?"

"Oh my, no, I exchanged a lot the last time I was here."

"Very well. And I should also tell you—Urushihara returned half a day ago, with Acieth, Erone, Eleos, and Nyx."

The sheer number took Albert by surprise. "Oh, he brought all four along? What for?"

"Acieth seems to have had another episode, but this time Nyx caught them in the act, so..."

"Ohhh. So nothing *toooo* new, then?"

"Well, there is one thing. I hear that Keter is about to bear fruit."

"Bear fruit, huh? Well, you never know what'll happen before a Sephirah child is born. It doesn't lead to much change that *we'd* notice, so it's hard to drum up much tension for it."

"Indeed. But while we cannot see the sun or moon actually move with the naked eye, everything in the sky is constantly in motion. You know all the facts, and that makes you the cornerstone of world peace. Make certain you do not miss any change, no matter how small. Have a nice stay!"

The sound of the Shiba household door closing seemed louder in their minds than it actually was.

"...Eesh. Now I see why the Devil King finds her so creepy. Are all the Sephirah like that?"

"She can hear you, dear."

"She probably could no matter where I was. Better to be an honest man, I'd say."

"Ms. Shiba is helping guard Emilia and the others for us. As long as we're bothering her with our own affairs, we should try to stay on her good side, dear."

"Yeah, and that's what the Airenia gold is for every round trip, ain't it? Money sure makes the world go round. Oh, that's an expression from *this* world, huh?"

"Oh youuu..."

"But let's get going. This heat is awful." Albert winced at the midsummer sunlight as he walked ahead.

"Ahh! Do wait a minute! I'll tell Emilia that we're here."

Chasing after the loping man, Emeralda took a smartphone from her shoulder bag and turned it on. Albert was in a polo shirt and chinos; Emeralda, a sleeveless high-necked blouse and denim pants. Taking a glance at the adjacent Villa Rosa Sasazuka, they passed it for the time being, opting to walk to Sasazuka Station instead. From there, they took a Keio New Line train for Shinjuku and got off at Hatagaya, the first stop.

"I hate to walk in this weather..."

"Me too. So, anything unuuusual?"

The Hatagaya Shopping Arcade, visible when they climbed the stairs to the surface, looked unchanged from before. The same was true for the Hatagaya Station franchise of MgRonald.

"It all looks okay at first glance." As Albert gazed up at the sight, they heard an engine approaching. The pair moved to the side of the road, figuring it was a car or bike—and there, they saw a familiar face.

"Oh! Hi, Emeralda! Hi, Albert!"

"Hellooo. Good to see you again, Ms. Iwaki, dear."

Kotomi Iwaki, manager at the Hatagaya MgRonald, was just back from a delivery, her face a little sweaty under the top of her Honta Gyro-Roof.

"Ahhhhh, I feel like a new woooman…"

"Yes, it's been a real heat wave this past week. Here's one for you, too, Albert."

"Thanks. I appreciate it."

Invited to the staff room in the back, they both quickly finished the iced coffees offered to them.

"So for the first half of the year, I really don't have much news to report to you."

"Oh, nooo?"

"Well, that's always reassuring news to hear on these trips, but is that really true? It feels like you have more folks from foreign lands comin' in these days, but there aren't any of *our* guys mixed in?"

"Yes, we're certainly seeing more of an international clientele now. I had Libby keep an eye out at first, but he says he hasn't spotted anyone, and I'll have to take his word for it."

"I see. So all is well on that front, but you know, if we could discuss the food bills for the Sephirah children, dear…"

"Oh, um, to tell the truth, Acieth's gradually been coming here less frequently over the past three years. The subscription fees Ms. Shiba and Mr. Urushihara pay us are fully covering the costs these days, so there's no need to pay us extra this time."

"Ohhh? I wouldn't want to disappoooint you..."

"No, no, it's really fine. I don't want to receive *too* much and arouse suspicion."

"Ah. Sorry..."

"It's fine. As an employee, I really shouldn't be offering that system, but it does make handling Acieth and the other children easier, so if anything, we'd gladly have them over more often. Kawata and Ohki step away from their current jobs to help out, even, so it's fun for me as well. However..."

Only then did Iwaki's face darken a bit.

"I think I'm going to receive a transfer order soon."

"Really?"

"I've been managing this location for three years, you know. And thanks to your and everyone else's support, we've managed to maintain the sales figures we reached during Ms. Kisaki's era. But still, we're going to need to be more careful from now on."

"Hmm, that's definitely bad news for us, yes. They're not coming as freeequently, but I think Acieth and the rest see MgRonald as part of their regular diets, you know, so..."

"True. So I'm going to take kind of a pushy approach with this. That'll allow us an extension for just a little bit longer."

"A pushy approach?"

"Yes. I think he'll be back soon, but... Oh!"

As if on cue, the staff room door opened.

"Oh, you're seeing someone? Excuse me... Huh?"

"Wh-whaaaa?!"

"Whoa, whoa, whoa, whoa, are you serious?!"

The sight of the man who walked in shocked Emeralda and Albert.

"Oh, it's *you*, huh? Albert Ende... Were they outta clothes *your* size?"

"Don't even start with me, Libicocco!"

Even in his XL polo shirt, the muscular Albert didn't look particularly comfortable.

"And ain't that a *business suit* on ya?! That looks *so* weird! That fancy getup on that ape-like face!"

Libicocco, meanwhile, was dressed to the nines in a well-tailored business suit. It took the words out of their mouths. Only Iwaki acted like nothing was amiss, greeting Libicocco with a smile.

"Hello, Libby! How's training going?"

"Nothing too concerning so far. The other female crewmembers seem a little intimidated, I think..."

"Yes, as you know, it's easy to misjudge someone by their looks, so..."

Libicocco in a suit seemed like the premise for some kind of comedy sketch. Emeralda and Albert had no idea where this was leading.

"Ms. Iwaaaki, when you say you took a *pushy* approach..."

"Yes, I've arranged it so Libby will be named manager of this location."

"You can *do* that?!"

"Ohhh. So you mean the manageeerial training the Devil King took before? He's going through thaaat?!"

Iwaki and Libicocco exchanged an awkward chuckle.

"Ummm...?"

"Well, about that..."

Then Libicocco revealed the astonishing truth.

"I...I already passed the managerial exam. The 'training' we're talking about is a company internship that'll prep me for signing on full-time the next fiscal year."

Silence.

"Whaaaaaaaaaaaaaaaaaaaaaaaaaaaaaaaaaaaaaaaaaaaaa?!!"

"*Dahhh*-ha-ha-ha-ha-ha-ha-ha-ha-ha-ha-ha-ha-ha-ha-ha-ha!!"

Emeralda screamed. Albert laughed.

"Huhh?! Really?! That thing the Devil King couldn't get into...?"

"*Yes*, all right? That's why I'm embarrassed about it! Stop laughing!"

"I gotta know how the Devil King reacted!"

"He made this crazy face, and then he treated me to a *horumon* restaurant to celebrate."

"*Gahhh*-ha-ha-ha-ha-ha-ha!!"

"You're laughing too *much*, Al, dear. They'll hear you in the dining room."

"Aww, Eme, how could I not? Man, I can't *wait* to tell Rumack the good news. For the first time, a demon from the demon realms is a 'full-timer' on another world, to use the local parlance. I bet that'll inspire the demons we got all around, too, huh?"

"...This is why I didn't want to say it. You should've told me they were coming if you knew, Manager. I would've gone out for a walk or something."

"Now, now, this is an important event to report on, isn't it?"

"Well, yeah, but..."

"Definitely so, but this," Emeralda said, "This is just beyond anything *imaginable*."

"Yeah, I don't get to see Eme truly shocked like that too often. Now I'm glad I paid so much to come here!"

"Knock it off. And don't go blabbing about this to all the other Malebranche chieftains! Anyway, Manager, my shift's coming up, so can you kick those two out before I go on break, please?"

Without another word, Libicocco disappeared into the changing room. In another minute, he was in his familiar red crewmember shirt, not even nodding at them as he went out on the floor.

"Ms. Kisaki was considering her own restaurant, but she's still working hard at corporate. That's why I'm hoping that the three of us can figure out a system to allow Acieth and the other Ente Islans to keep patronizing us."

"Ah, yeah, I see. But... Sorry to ask this after I laughed so hard, but I'm amazed they brought him on full-time. He's not even meant to be *from* Japan, is he?"

"That turned out to his advantage, actually. Like you noticed, our international customer base is booming. Even a lot of brand-new college grads working in the area were born or have citizenship overseas. So while it's a bit late, we're implementing more of a global strategy to earn those kinds of customers. And he's 'Italian,' so..."

The idea of Libicocco being from there was still one of the most magnificent jokes in the world. But then the eyes behind Iwaki's glasses turned serious.

"But even if he's appointed manager here, Hatagaya Station may not have the freedom it's enjoyed up to now. There's a good chance he might be taken off location management and moved into some corporate department. Ms. Shiba's obstinacy has been a great help to us so far, but by my estimate, I'd say that Libby and I can have MgRonald provide you all full support for, at most, two more years. I've been discussing this with Maou, too, hammering out takeover policies in case of emergency."

"...Ah, yes, I've heard about that. Thank you."

"I have to say, thooough, it would be faaar safer to have them relax at this restaurant than at any other nation in Ente Isla, you know, so... We'll need to work out some measures pretty fast."

Acieth's binges and hunger beams had come to be called "episodes" within the group, and they tended to accompany assorted types of growth or change to the Tree of Sephirot and its Sephirah children. But if one of those Sephirah came to depend on one nation of Ente Isla or the other, it might lead to one of the summit members attempting to craft them into a second or third all-powerful tactical weapon, similar to the Better Half or Hero Emilia. As a result, all summit participants agreed that Sephirah children should be restricted from mingling with Ente Islan nations, if at all possible.

Acieth herself obtained her body and personality in Japan, and she was far more used to Japan's cuisine than Ente Isla's. Thus, they figured, Japanese food was the best way to quell her episodes—and it was Urushihara managing and overseeing her, along with the Tree of Sephirot and the rest of its children.

"All riiight. We will bring this information back with us and debate it over therrre, I suppose."

"...Oop. Hey, Eme," Emilia responded. "It sounds like a fair number of folks are meeting at Villa Rosa Sasazuka."

"Oh, *are* they? Well, that's just perfect. All right, Ms. Iwaki... I'm afraid it may be without much warning again, but we'll be back soon, I *promise*. Thanks again for the coffeeee!"

"You will? Well, you're welcome anytime. Outside of your work, even."

Iwaki walked out of the MgRonald to see them off. Libicocco joined her out there, once he was sure Emeralda and Albert were far away and back at the train station.

"You really don't need to worry about them, Manager."

"Oh, it's fine. I do this because I like it."

"Well, if you say so, but you don't earn anything out of it, do you? The company makes money, but it's not filling up *your* wallet."

"It's not about money, Libby. I think you know the expression by know—it's 'work worth doing,' you know?"

"Work worth doing? Is it?"

Even underneath her UV-resistant lenses, Iwaki's eyes were sparkling. "I mean, look at me. I'm just your average 'salaryman,' with a completely average Japanese upbringing, and I get to make friends with all these powerful people from other worlds. They *rely* on me, even! What other kind of work would be so gratifying?"

"…I can't say a demon like me sees much in it, but if you like doing it, then great."

"And I do. Right, then, let's go back to regular duty."

"Yep."

The human and demon, finished with their otherworldly work, fled from the sunlight and ran back inside.

✳

"One Airenia gold coin *each*? Dude. What a rip."

When he heard how much Emeralda and Albert had paid Shiba, Urushihara immediately winced.

"Well, we have no alternative, do we, dear? Think of it as a border crossing fee, and it seems *reasonable* enough, no?"

The two of them had dropped in on Maou and Urushihara's deep discussion on the Tree of Sephirot. They quickly realized that Emi, Chiho, and Suzuno likely needed to get in on the Acieth food-sourcing issue, so before long, Room 201 was seeing its largest crowd in a while. Considering all the racket they had heard from the Sephirah children down in Room 101—which Nord and Laila were still renting as their Tokyo base—Maou and Suzuno awaited news about Room 202 with bated breath.

Once Maou had passed around the iced coffee blend he'd tested on Urushihara earlier, Emi spoke up first.

"Well, maybe this was good timing after all. We all knew that we couldn't rely on Ms. Iwaki and MgRonald forever. We're planning to hold an emergency meeting on this tonight—would Eme or Al mind joining me at work for a bit?"

"At *your* work, Emilia dear?"

"Yeah. Well, more like Father's and *his* work, but…"

Maou grumbled at Emi's signaling. "Yeah, yeah… That's the best option we have. I've been keeping in touch with Iwaki about this the whole time, so it's a good opportunity. We'll see how things are at our Eifukucho café, and if it'd be tough to stick with that, we're talking about a second location, too, so we need to think about handling it that way as well."

"Would you hire new employees, then?"

"I don't have the cushion for that, sadly. Either I'd move Aki over, or I'd cover it the whole time."

"That'll put more work on you, though. You can't have *that* much free time."

"If we're doing this to handle Alcieth, it's gotta be someone who knows, so I can't hire my way out of that problem. Honestly, instead of trying to force it into our location structure, why don't we just cater it each time?"

"You saw how the Kobe beef worked out. Maybe it's fine now, but if this goes on for years, we'll need staffing and raw ingredients each time. Isn't that gonna be tough to budget? If anything, I think we should consider bringing on some new demons."

"Demons, huh…? I'd really like them to adapt to life in Ente Isla, not here. That, and I'm afraid of what the landlord would say, so I don't want too many of them fleeing over here…"

All this talk was just about how they'd keep Acieth fed going forward—but to Emi and Maou, it was serious stuff. They continued talking about it on their end of the table.

"Chiho, dear, are you *okay* with that?"

"Oh, are you dredging *that* up again?"

"I'll bring it up as *many* times as I want, dear. After all..." Emeralda's eyebrows arched lower as she motioned toward Maou. "She's totally *dominating* him, no?"

"I can't do very much about that, Emeralda. Besides, isn't that partly *your* fault?"

"Ooh, I just *hate* to be reminded of that...but I didn't think he would turn out like *this*, you know..."

Emi frequently gave Maou her two cents about how The Maou Company managed their storefront. She occasionally debated at length with the supposed "president" of the firm, and sometimes she even followed orders he gave her.

"Well, if you and Saint Aile can stop with *that* stuff, Emeralda, I think that'll pull Yusa and Maou apart, at least..."

"...You say that because you *know* we can't do it, riiight?"

"Right. Because it'll take the reins off Maou and make Ente Isla and the summit members all nervous."

Chiho smiled warmly.

"Ooh... Out of the frying pan, into the fire..."

"I'm not completely sure that applies here, but anyway, that's how it is. You'll have to give it up. *You're* the only one who's not accepting it, you know."

"Oooooh... This is so *unbelievable*..."

"Besides, we have Alas Ramus to think about. Nobody's going to allow Maou to do something as irresponsible as completely sever ties with Yusa. Plus..."

Chiho smiled at Maou, currently being cowed into silence over one topic or another.

"I like to watch those two."

"Hmmm... And that's why, Chiho, dear. Because you *act* like that."

"Mm-hmm. Because I act like this. Thanks to everyone here, this is how I've turned out."

"Arg!"

There was no malice, no ulterior motive to Chiho's smile. Emeralda had no choice but to bite her tongue.

Meanwhile, Emi finished her tirade against Maou with a familiar refrain: "Well, don't *you* have a nice life for yourself! I tell you, it would have been *so* much better if I'd killed you instead of letting you go, way back when!"

"Sooo," Emeralda asked as she fell silent, "what are you taaalking about?"

"Well, The Maou Company's thinking about launching a restaurant that's focused around bread and grains, and the wheat Father's growing at the Sasaki's Nagano farm is one candidate for their flour."

"Huh? Candidate?"

Albert picked up on Emi's odd wording.

"Yeah, it's not decided yet. Today we need to discuss all the costs involved, and then tomorrow, we'll rent out an industrial test kitchen and try a few recipes. Father will be there, along with Chiho's cousin Kazuma Sasaki, and they'll make a final presentation. Kazuma's staying at a hotel in Tokyo somewhere on other business tonight."

"Ahhh… Keeping a sharp eye on work, are you, Emilia, dear?"

"Hell yeah I am," Maou interjected. "I'm not gonna hire 'em just because we got a connection. I gotta pick good stuff, and then I gotta figure out how to sell it!"

Thus, all the luggage Nord and Laila were carting around contained material for their upcoming presentation.

"But Nord has been cultivating wheat for a very long time. I hardly think he will fail to make the grade."

Maou pondered that a bit. "Well, we'll see when we get there. We did a test bake over in Komagane, and we wound up with some really sour-tasting bread. Maybe we could sell it as healthy, but if we want it to be our flagship, we're gonna have to work on the yeast, and on making it a good match with our cookware, and stuff. If we need to invest in a more expensive oven, that's gonna affect our price points, so…"

"Oh... I see. So it is more than a matter of Nord and Kazuma producing good food?"

"When you're making something, the ingredients ain't the only cost you have to worry about. There's the cooking costs, the work costs, the equipment maintenance costs, the supply costs, the storage costs... You gotta calculate all that, plus all the other work and customer rates and so on, and *then* you gotta pick something you're willing to serve. That's what craftsmanship is. On the other hand, even if you have a cost overrun somewhere, if that element is good enough in my eyes, sometimes I still go with it. And of course, the food's gotta be 'good,' as you put it—and if customers see a lot of value from it, then we can sell them on other products, too. And so on."

He paused, satisfied with his speech.

"And I tell you, when it all comes together right, it feels *so* great. You really feel like you did a good job."

Maou truly looked invigorated, not an ounce of malice on his face. There was no doubt that he put his heart and soul into his job.

"So to sum up," Emeralda whispered to Chiho, "he's saying that Emilia's making correct choices?"

"Yeah," she whispered back, "I think so. Oh..."

Then, hearing a dull thump, Chiho turned around in her seat.

"Excuse me, guys..."

Attracting everyone's attention, Chiho put a finger in front of her lips.

"...I think we're making too much noise. I hear something from inside the closet..."

"Oh...?"

Maou, eyes open, turned toward Room 202. Suzuno (the former tenant) and Urushihara did the same, mixed emotions on their faces.

"Anything new?"

"Well, the landlord barged in there this summer to install an air conditioner...but I haven't seen it running too much."

"But she's eating, isn't she?"

"Oh, yeah."

Suzuno seemed a tad relieved over it.

"You see," Urushihara casually tossed out, "how tenacious she is. She wants to keep living *real* bad. She's not the kind of wimp to let her heart break over something like *that*. I'm sure she'll have some other nefarious scheme in mind before long... Maou?"

"Huh?"

"Keep a close eye on her. I *really* don't need anything messing with my current work."

"...Gabriel, Amane, Laila, and I are watching her in rotation. Stop acting so haughty about it."

Maou gave Urushihara a kick.

"Ow!"

"She's *your* mother, y'know. *You* take care of her."

"Oh, like that's my duty? Not like she ever took care of *me* as a kid. You oughtta thank me for taking care of the Sephirah, dude. Doesn't that kinda make up for it? ...Oh."

She must have heard Urushihara's complaining. Because Ignora—forced into Suzuno's room after the assault on heaven three years ago, after Suzuno had to move back to Ente Isla to serve as an Archbishop—languidly knocked on the wall a few more times before she fell silent.

THE DEVIL AND THE HERO SETTLE MATTERS

As much as he feared the cleanup, Maou's group didn't actually have many things to address. Mostly, they needed to oversee Ignora and Camael to ensure they didn't spark any more trouble. But after being run through with that holy sword of light, Camael's holy force showed no sign of returning—and after she'd witnessed that, Ignora was in such a trance that she barely even bothered to move.

"…Should we restrain them?"

"With what, you think?"

Satan and Alciel exchanged somber glances as they watched the pair. Ignora hadn't lost her powers (Camael was another story), so they weren't sure tying them up or whatnot would accomplish much. Ignora hadn't even fought, for that matter. Was anyone here capable of holding her back?

"Nyx is separated from her. But considering how Camael, Raguel, and all the other angels took orders from Ignora without question…"

It was an issue on Emi's mind as well.

"Whether acting purely as a leader or joining the battle herself, we need to think of her as a primary threat."

"But you saw how bold she acted once she was sure she'd won. And no matter how strong Nyx and Eleos are, Copyhara and Acieth can stem them off. So it's no biggie if she causes a ruckus, is it?"

"Well, um, probably not, no...so, again, what'll we do with them?"

They had captured the enemy ringleader—one more powerful than all the sorcerers on a single continent combined.

"I bet this is how Eme and her team felt when they captured Olba... You know, Devil King? I think we will need to restrain her somehow. If we didn't come here to kill her, then maybe we can put her somewhere in heaven, or the demon realms...or someplace where she'd have no idea where she was..."

Emi, realizing she was starting to sound a tad abusive, trailed off before starting again.

"Just for now, you know? I mean, she *did* try to fight us..."

"Yeah, I mean... Sure, but..."

"No!!"

The protest came from a surprising source.

"Nyx?"

"I heard from Alas Ramus that Mommy was doing mean things to us...but to me, she's the one who guided me when I was born! The Sephirah Malchut... A Sephirah that wasn't supposed to produce anything but my big sister Eleos... It also made me, and it had a reason for it."

"..."

"So please... I wasn't born for no reason! Our Sephirah let me fuse with Mommy because it saw a good reason for it!"

"Now this is getting even harder to deal with. What do you think of that, Copyhara?"

"I'm not exactly the leader of them all or anything...but if Nyx says so, she's probably right. She's not lying, either. Eleos should've been guiding Alas Ramus and everyone else by herself, but a second Malchut was born ahead of Keter. Maybe..."

Copyhara looked through the hole Maou and Camael had made in the All a Lijeh wall, to the point far beyond, where the Tree of Sephirot grew.

"The Tree gave me Lucifer's form, and...you know, maybe it had pitied the circumstances the angels were in. So when it comes to all the terrible things she and the angels did to Ente Isla... I'm not going to let that slide, but I hope you won't go overboard with the punishment, either."

"…This isn't giving me much to work with. We didn't come here to torture her to death, but we can't just say 'nice try' and let her out, you know."

"You were here to free the Tree of Sephirot, right? You even found more of Alas Ramus's siblings. What more could you ask for?"

"A bright future for the kids. And she's done a lot to threaten that over the years."

"Huh?" Copyhara gave this a quizzical look. "Lemme just say, dude, *you* guys count as Sephirah, too, so you're part of the equation. And if *you're* a Sephirah, then you're siblings with Alas Ramus."

Maou turned back toward Emi, who, something dawning on her, manifested Alas Ramus.

"Daddy?"

"Yeah."

Alas Ramus, capable of clear, grown-up intelligence during important battles, must have accurately understood Maou's words and thoughts.

"This assault on heaven was meant to be a Christmas gift for Alas Ramus last year. We're over half a year late on it, and now it's also her birthday present. Along those lines, I *really* couldn't half-ass this."

"Oh… It was? Wow…" Copyhara fell silent. Maybe his mind-reading skill surprised him. "Well, in that case, there's nothing else I can say. I'll respect your decision."

"Yeah, thanks… Hey. Ignora."

Ignora surprised the audience by turning toward him.

"…Satan…"

"*Please* don't start doing a Camael impression, okay? Listen, we're not here to kill you, but if you're gonna meddle with these kids, I can't make any guarantees."

"…"

"What was your endgame here anyway? It looks like your plan went off the rails somewhere, but if we let you live and the plan gets fixed somehow, you *know* that's gonna be trouble."

"..."

"And if you're gonna stay silent, *we're* not gonna be reasonable with you."

"Mommy..."

Nyx's concerned voice irritated Maou further.

"...*Tch!* Hey!"

"Hold on, Maou. Can you stop right there?"

It was Amane Ohguro who stopped Maou from grabbing Ignora and shaking her around.

"I'll take possession of her."

"Amane?"

"I looked around the shrine ruins a little, and I got questions I wanna ask about them first. Otherwise, we might have Acieth and Erone going out of control again."

Amane was dead serious.

"Maou, Yusa... You know how you two treat Alas Ramus as your daughter? Well, I'm not heartless enough to abandon one of *my* own relatives to the wolves. Right, you?"

Amane grabbed Ignora by the collar, her cold eyes and voice upon her.

"We're both grown women. Time to spill the beans, okay? And *we're* all 'separated' from our parents, too. We aren't gonna be as nice to you as Nyx, and we're not gonna go easy on you like Maou's group."

"...Ah..."

"You better not think we're gonna be like the kids *you* took control of."

Back at the plain with the Tree of Sephirot, they summoned Alas Ramus and Acieth in front of the flowering tree. The two sisters held hands as they looked up at it.

"Nyx, Copyhara...and stupid ol' Malchut."

"Who are you callin' stupid?" Elos shot back.

Ignoring her, Acieth kept her gaze on the tree.

"Everyone... It will take the more time, yes?"

"Yeah. But I came out *this* fast, so I really don't know what's gonna happen next. It all depends on that planet."

Copyhara pointed at the moon's horizon—to Ente Isla, rising above the blue land in the starry sky.

"Hmm. Funny shape."

"The Land of the Holy Cross... The land looks split apart because the Devil Overlord Satan's disaster broke the moon and changed the tidal patterns, apparently. I'm sure there weren't any civilized nations down there at the time...but to everything living there back then, it must've seemed like the end of the world."

"Wow. So when demon realms come here, that not affect anything?"

"It'll affect *something*, I'm sure...but based on how Ente Isla's still flying around with its two moons, I don't think it'll be any kind of big disaster."

"You heard him, big sis."

"Mmm?"

"The big birthday present from Maou and friends... Maybe you have to wait long time for it, still."

"No I don't, Ash-eth."

"No?"

"I know Mommy an' Daddy love me a lot. That's good enough."

"Ooh. Maybe so, yes."

Acieth smiled at her tiny big sister.

"So, you grow and get big now?"

"Yeh."

Then, as if Acieth had just given the signal, Alas Ramus's body began to glow. They had seen this phenomenon before, around when Maou had moved into Emi's apartment—but the small toddler grew just a little bit larger in height, this time, before she stopped.

"Mommy, Daddy..."

Alas Ramus let go of Acieth's hand, ran up to Maou and Emi, stopped, and stood up as tall as she could.

"Thank you for helping them all. I love you!"

For just a moment, Alas Ramus kept a stern look on her face. Then, her cheeks glowed as she broke into a big smile.

*

"…And that's about everything that took place in heaven."

"Um…so you hardly did much real fighting at all?"

One week after they had all stormed heaven, Suzuno was visiting Chiho's room at her family house in Sasazuka, giving her the not-exactly-triumphant circumstances behind the assault's conclusion. She was sitting properly at her low table, wearing her usual *kamawanu*-pattern kimono and tucking her legs under her body. It was a common sight for Chiho to see, but that just made her story all the more fantastic and unique.

"The most injured out of any of us was Acieth and the Malchut girl, Eleos. Both of their faces were quite a mess—but it appears they will escape any permanent scarring. And Alciel did not kill any of the Heavenly Regiment."

In terms of casualties, the nations of Ente Isla had suffered far more in the sporadic Central Continent skirmishes that took place during the Crusade just before the summit.

"Ignora's original goal was to make the Tree of Sephirot recognize the angels as the 'first' species of mankind that belongs in Ente Isla. That would let them stand above us natives and create a perfect world for their perfect species. That was why she engineered all the miracles and mythologies that formed the cornerstone of the Church."

"Oh? Didn't Laila build the Church? I think Yusa mentioned something like that when we were talking about Yesod fragments…"

"What Laila created, in order to compete against Ignora, were the legends about holy swords—the folklore related to the Yesod fragments, and how to use them. She waited for the religion Ignora established to gain a firm foothold, and then, as the weaker opposing force, she deftly spent years and centuries spreading the word about the holy swords. That, and the concept of Ignora, the heavens, and the angels being a different race from humanity. This led to differing religious sects, and to different people in Ente Isla devoting themselves to the angels in different ways. That, it seems, was one major reason why the angels were not recognized as the 'main' species by the Sephirah until that moment. That is what Copyhara said, at least, and I cannot ascertain how true it is."

Suzuno didn't seem too confident about it as she spoke, occasionally pausing midway.

"Their home planet, you see, was stricken with a genocidal disease they could do nothing about. They escaped before the species was wholly wiped out, but I would assume there is no life remaining there. And when Caiel and Sikeena began to oppose their research into immortality, that was the deciding blow that led to Ignora's current situation. It was a denial of the idea that supernatural aid was something to ever expect… A denial of God, essentially."

"A denial of God…"

"Did it ever strike you as odd, Chiho? We are the Church, and figures like Lord Sariel, Gabriel, Raguel, and the Sephirah appear in our holy scripture…but the name of Ignora, the 'God' herself, never does."

"But she's still the primary figure, isn't she?"

"No. The name appears in the scripture zero times. It remains only in the ancient name of a body of water, but not in our own words."

"It doesn't?"

That surprised Chiho.

"Our scripture talks about the legends of multiple higher-plane figures, but never about anyone leading them. That is why our ancient theologians and clerics theorized the existence of a 'great ruling God' that governed the world and its heavens, and that idea permeated the Church. That, too, was something Ignora failed to anticipate."

God, in this religion, was not a person. And Ignora had already gone through the trauma of being judged for blocking the natural evolution of a human race. That was why she'd laid the foundation of the Church so a God could never be born. But it was Laila who foiled that—her, the angels on Satanael's side that defied Ignora, and…

"…and the ancient Ente Islans, who clung to the concept of a God."

At this rate, the Ente Islans that dominated the world would be recognized as the planet's official, Sephirah-approved human race. The angels would once again lose a potential planet to settle on and perhaps even be persecuted by the Sephirah. And now, when multiple civilizations were flourishing in Ente Isla, Ignora was feeling the heat. Her solution: a Devil King Satan–driven invasion of Ente Isla, so that the human race would taste bitter defeat.

Ignora had taken a two-pronged approach to using Satan's world conquest, as well as the Church that failed to develop as she meant it. First, she would create a Hero, someone born from the power of heaven and the angels. This would help advertise the angels as higher-level creations, the defenders of mankind. It would be an effective way, she thought, to root out Laila, who had long since left heaven by then. The result of all this: Emilia Justina, the girl with a Yesod fragment in her body.

But here, too, Ignora made a miscalculation. Emilia Justina was not purely Ente Islan. Her body reacted to the holy sword, and to the Cloth of the Dispeller driven by her Holy Silver, and it was "transformed." She adopted the genes of the angels and their trademark look.

They reasoned quickly that the Hero Emilia had inherited blood from the archangel Laila. And the potential fallout from this made Ignora shiver in fear. To her, Emilia's existence proved that the still-immature civilization of Ente Isla was hereditarily homogenous with their much more advanced civilization. If Emilia went on to save the world, would the Sephirot recognize the angels' pitch that *they* were the higher beings?

So the heavens engineered the most chaos the world had seen since the Devil Overlord Satan's disaster. Ignora's faction, seizing the initiative in the race to keep the angels alive, just slightly outnumbered the others, but many of her peers began to posit whether her approach to Ente Isla's Sephirot was the wrong one. The opposition was led by Sandalphon, who had long supported Ignora up till then.

In an even greater shock to Ignora, Lucifer was part of the Devil

King's Army invading Ente Isla. To Ignora, who had never forgotten the face of her child after all this time, seeing her own descendant—the epitome of the "higher race"—side with the lower classes of the planet's natives and broadly impact the whole world came as an intense shock. Even worse, Lucifer lost to an inexperienced girl of a Hero, from an inexperienced human race. Now, not only would they never get the Ente Islans to see angels as the superior species—slander could go around that they were just a greedy race of tyrants seeding chaos worldwide.

So, through an old contact of Emilia's named Olba, Ignora secretly had Lucifer recovered. She reasoned that one of the Six Archbishops, the highest echelons of the Church that followed the angels, would be easier to manage—but, once again, her hopes were betrayed.

"But Olba wasn't anything like that, was he?"

"No. He was the sort of man who had grave doubts about the existence of any god. He also questioned the existence of Emilia, and the truth behind the holy sword and Cloth of the Dispeller. And while he didn't confide it to Emeralda, he had a direct connection from heaven, and that is undoubtedly what drove him over the edge. The rest, you know well, Chiho."

So the Hero Emilia dispatched the Devil King's Army at breakneck speed—but then she let their leader escape before disappearing into another world herself.

That ensured peace in Ente Isla, more or less, but the personification of the angels' miracles was now in some far-off planet. That, however, marked a good opportunity for the heavens to do away with Emilia, this half-angel, half–Ente Islan who proved an inconvenient obstacle to their colonization plans.

But every attempt at eliminating Emilia ended in failure. The reason? The Hero Emilia and the Devil King Satan had installed themselves into the society of this land Japan—and they learned how to work together, in public and private. If the Hero and the Devil King were to come to terms, that would bring peace and development to the people of Ente Isla…and that might tilt the Sephirot's judgment.

"Alciel's kidnapping in Efzahan and Archbishop Robertio's assassination triggering a Crusade were both preliminary attempts to make angels the 'approved' race. They truly *were* trying to restage the melodrama of the Church receiving angelic protection to defeat the Devil King's Army and save humanity. And with the Tree of Sephirot in her custody—and with it, Erone and Eleos—Ignora must have seen that as her last chance."

But thanks to Gabriel's secret betrayal, and Satan working together with Emilia in all possible ways, it fell apart. Olba was no longer a valuable pawn, an Archbishop was appointed who knew God's real identity, and then the demons, angels, Hero, and humanity joined together to deny God herself.

"But Da'at took the form of a descendant of the angels anyway. Why was that?"

Suzuno began by warning Chiho that she could only say what Copyhara had explained to her, plus some of her own deductions.

"Lucifer was the first angel born in the 'second generation,' the one after they left their home planet. In terms of his lineage, he was from that former planet, but to him, his native world was Ente Isla and nowhere else. And with Emilia being born between an angel and Ente Islan human, the Sephirot must have concluded that even if it selected Lucifer, angels and Ente Islans were nothing but the same species, apparently. So the angels lost all of their superiority, and then..."

"...And then Camael lost all of his power."

Chiho recalled the ring that used to be on her right hand. She, too, had shot down an angel once with that ring's power. She could recall it with a cool mind now, but—really, that arrow shot down Raguel, a fellow human. When Raguel's holy force–driven wings disappeared and he fell, she sweated it out quite a bit, worried she had actually taken someone's life. But in the end, the Ente Isla Sephirot must've looked into the future and discovered that while humanity would continue to develop, angels would lose their miraculous powers over time.

After essentially losing to Maou and seeing his power drain, Camael was taken by his Regiment to the Malebrache homeland in the demon realms. There, she heard, remained the vestiges of a certain someone important to him, someone who drove him to despise Satanael and lose himself in the process.

"So what's going to happen next?"

"We will stick to the plan. The members of the summit will make careful observations to see whether the holy force will truly fade from the world. Nyx and Eleos are under Copyhara's supervision for now, but they are still rather shaken, so Amane is making an exception to her rules and providing care as an elder Sephirah family member."

"...Sounds like there's still a lot to do."

"There is. From now on, the world will enter a phase of preventive maintenance. It will be plain, simple, inconspicuous, and painstaking...but it is vital work, deeply intertwined with Alas Ramus's and Acieth's futures. I intend to treat it quite seriously."

Chiho closed her eyes, looking conflicted.

But in the end, she gave Suzuno a light bow. "Well, thank you so much for all of this... I'm sorry I wasn't any help at all in the end..."

"Of course you helped."

Suzuno's strong tone made Chiho open her eyes.

"Without your power, Chiho, the summit, and the ensuing assault, would never have worked. Even now, many summit members are complaining to me about wanting you to lend a hand."

"...They're giving me way too much credit. I'm just a regular teen now. I have college exams."

There was a lonesome tone to her voice, and the reason was clear to Suzuno: Even now, at this point, things had completely drifted out of Chiho's hands. She couldn't influence events in heaven, in the demon realms, or in Ente Isla. She couldn't be involved in things, and she didn't need to be. She should've been cut off from all the goings-on of Ente Isla, in fact. It was true that some were clamoring for her uncommon talents, but they had all given up on her coming to live there as Chiho Sasaki, a girl from another planet.

"Chiho, I...I, well..."

Suzuno leaned over the low table and took her hand.

"Suzuno?"

"I do not think we can allow that."

"Huh?"

"Without you, we would all drift away. Our worlds were apart at first. Nobody could have been saved. But the idea that you would not, or could not, turn to any of us after everything is done with... A silly concept, is it not?"

"Umm..."

Chiho wavered. For some reason, Suzuno looked about ready to cry.

"To tell the truth, there is still one problem left unsolved."

"Wh-what's that?"

"The world wanted this. It wanted you, and all of us...to have this beautiful thing happen. And perhaps it is not vitally necessary any longer, but still...if it can happen, the world will be able to take one more step forward."

"Beautiful...? Huh? What are you...?"

"..."

Suzuno seemed lost. She looked thoughtfully at her for a moment, then changed the subject.

"Ignora will be in the custody of Amane and Shiba for the time being. We have decided to keep her in Villa Rosa Sasazuka."

"What? Even *God*'s moving in there?!"

She couldn't help but shout it out. Suzuno talked over her.

"No matter the scope of her power, it won't be enough to defy the mature Earth Sephirah. She is answering Amane's questions and behaving in there, so that much is clear. The problem comes after that."

"After that...?"

"Ente Isla has lost a god—one that never existed in the first place. That, and there is one other thing that must also be banished from Ente Isla for all eternity."

Tears were now forming in Suzuno's eyes. In them, Chiho felt she could see her resolve, and that of the many others she kept in her heart.

"The path and plans have already been laid out…and what comes after, as well."

Chiho reflected on all the events leading up to today. After a moment—

"When are you going to do it?"

—She arrived at her answer.

*

It was a quiet late night in Sasazuka, the traffic of the Shuto Expressway clearly audible in the background, as a man and woman walked slowly home, letting the warm air soothe their work-weary bodies. It was now a month since the assault on heaven. Most of the troublesome decisions had been made, and with all the other miscellaneous questions left to other people, Maou and Emi were back to the normal grind.

Iwaki and Kawata didn't say much upon their return. Akiko did, and Maou and Emi handled all of them—although talking to your fellow MgRonald employees about how you defeated the god of another world and helped lead it to peace, they realized, sounded incredibly stupid now that they were actually doing it. It was the truth, but it was incredibly stupid. That's how faraway a tale it was, this story of war in another world.

"Man, I am *spent*. Delivering to the same apartment building three times in a row…"

"Yeah. We all had a laugh when you left the third time."

"The groundskeeper was totally giving me the stink eye the third time…"

They were discussing the day's events, just like after any other work shift, laughing over them as they walked toward the home they shared. They were the Devil King and the Hero, two people who had once warred over the fate of an entire world.

It was a little past midnight. The sky was overcast, and now thick clouds covered the moon and the stars, making things dark. The Devil King pushed his bicycle along, the Hero carrying a large shoulder bag—and on the way, they spied a deserted intersection. The neon sign for the Italian restaurant on one side was shut off, the streetlights and stoplight the only things illuminating the two of them.

"Brings you back, huh, Devil King?"

"Here? Yeah."

Maou knew exactly what Emi meant.

"It was around this time, wasn't it? I was on my way home then. And then you threatened me with that 100-yen knife."

The crosswalk light turned red.

"I was *so* humiliated when they thought I was your girlfriend."

"Yeah, that was hilarious. Even funnier how we're treated as a pseudo–married couple now, huh?"

"It sure is."

Emi smiled a bit.

"But…that's all over."

Maou dodged the blade tip suddenly swinging at him by nothing more than sheer luck.

They had been chatting along, on their way home like always, and right in the middle, she'd broken out her holy sword of light.

Maou was stunned. "What…what is this, Emi?"

"The assault on heaven is over. It ended in a place where nobody knew about it. But there's something still going on in Ente Isla."

Emi still smiled softly, affectionately, as she spoke.

Maou immediately knew what she meant. "Slaying the Devil King, huh?"

"Yeah." Emi nodded. "Last time, you fled to another world. This time, it's somewhere up in the sky, on that rocket. To the people of Ente Isla, you're still a symbol of fear, one that might still be alive somewhere. Are you aware of that?"

"Well, yeah, more or less."

"Isn't that hard for you? I ought to rid you of that baggage already."

Maou put up a barrier. That way, if anyone happened to pass by, they wouldn't get all huffy about the blade in Emi's hand.

"You're serious, huh?"

"I've got to get over this already, or I think I'm gonna be dragging it along forever."

In their little world under the barrier, time frozen for everyone except them, the Devil King danced around, continually avoiding the Hero's holy sword. She was fused with the Sephirah Yesod, wielding a sword like none he had faced before in battle. All he had was demonic force and his own body. The difference in power was clear.

With divine footwork, the Hero got behind the Devil King, the edge of her sword flat against his back.

"You know, Devil King…"

"Hmm?"

"When you saved me in Efzahan, there was one thing I couldn't remember."

"What's that?"

"The words we exchanged when I first saw you."

She had encountered Satan, the Devil King, as he fought in Heavensky to save the cornered Great Demon General Alciel. The words she screamed back then, driven by hate, came to her lips once more.

""Hello!""

They both said it at the same time. It made them both crack up.

"And that's how your journey's gonna end?"

"Yeah. The Hero Emilia's slaying of the Devil King is over, as of today."

Maou stood up, still feeling the blade at his throat. His gaze turned away from Emi and the holy sword, instead examining the darkness behind him.

"Well, tell Ashiya I said hi. That I apologized to him. He'll understand."

"All right. I will."

The next moment:

"Maou!! Yusa!!!"

The shout that ripped through the night came just as the sword of light stabbed through Maou's back.

"Hey, Chi."

Before Chiho, gasping with her hands at her mouth, Maou was on his knees, head against the ground. Vast clouds of dark fog seeped from his body, quickly dissipating into the air. Behind Maou, who had collapsed and was immobile, Emi dispelled her sword and let out a deep sigh.

"Hello, Chiho. Pretty late for a walk, isn't it?"

"Yusa... You..."

"I had to," she calmly said to the lone eyewitness. "Think about it. No, I don't hate the Devil King any longer... But...still, he... What the Devil King's Army did to the people of Ente Isla was unforgivable."

Chiho's legs were too shaky to move. Instead, Emi knelt and pulled Maou's top half up for the other girl to see.

"Even if I defeat our god, even if I save the world, that still won't calm the souls of the murdered. You see?"

"But... Why... At this point?"

Emi gently caressed Maou's hair. His eyes were closed, his face serene.

"Now was the best time. Now, when everything is over... Everything with me and the Devil King's battle... Now, I had to settle things."

Before Chiho, her face straining to withstand the waves of despair, Emi brought her face to Maou's and whispered into his ear:

"Hello...Sadao Maou."

The barrier disappeared. The clouds spread out in the sky above the Hero and the Devil King were gone, the bright moonlight illuminating the town of Sasazuka as if it were a beautiful flower.

Character

SADAO MAOU

EMI YUSA

CHIHO SASAKI

SHIROU ASHIYA

HANZOU URUSHIHARA

SUZUNO KAMAZUKI

ALAS RAMUS   ACIETH ALLA

MAYUMI KISAKI   RIKA SUZUKI

EMERALDA ETUVA   ALBERT ENDE RANGA

RIHO SASAKI   SEN'ICHI SASAKI   AMANE OHGURO

OLBA MEIYER   SARIEL   CAMIO   PÁJARO DANINO
GABRIEL   RAGUEL   LIBICOCCO
KAORI SHOJI   YOSHIYA KOHMURA   MAKI SHIMIZU
TAKEFUMI KAWATA   AKIKO OHKI   KOTOMI IWAKI

ADRAMELECH   MALACODA   CIRIATTO

FARFARELLO   BARBARICCIA   CALCABRINA

DRAGHIGNAZZO   SCARMIGLIONE   RUBICANTE

CAMUINICA   KINANNA   HU SHUN-IEN

DHIN DHEM WURS   HAZEL RUMACK   ROBERTIO IGUA VALENTIA

EZRAMHA   TAJAH   RAJID RAHS RIAN   CERVANTES REBERIZ

GARNI VIDOU   ARVAIM WELLAND   PIPPIN

VERDIGRIS CHIRICO   CESAR QUARANTA   MAURO VALLI

KAZUMA SASAKI   HINAKO SASAKI   HITOSHI SASAKI

EI SASAKI   MANJI SASAKI   YUMIKO SASAKI

HIMEKO TANAKA   YUKI MIZUSHIMA   KANAKO FURUYA

KEIKO YUSA   SILVERFISH   TOMITAKA YONEYA

KAZUKO MAEYAMA   MITSUKI SARUE   KOTARO NAKAYAMA

WATANABE   TAMURA   HIROSE   KURYU   ONDA

SATO   ANDO   KIMURA   KUSUDA   NITTA

IRHIEM   GINGAM   BELYANZA   DELGRIFF

GEORGE   HARIANAK   TIMMY GOLDMAN

CAIEL   SIKEENA   SANDALPHON

ELEOS   NYX   COPYHARA

NORD JUSTINA   LAILA·JUSTINA   ERONE

SATANAEL NOIE

IGNORA

MIKI SHIBA

One two three four

From where does the morning come? The quiet sky,
the pinky promise I pretended not to see, that fingertip?
If it's the moon that was laughed at, it's going away in the direction of yesterday.

A liar, a coward—
collect all that and I'm the result;
if I was blooming, it must have been within a dream.

I hid it in the moonlight, but you know, the truth is that I was crying.
My tears won't flow anymore—has the well run dry?
If everything could be forgiven, maybe they'd flow again,
but there are so many things I want to protect.

How long have you been able to hear my voice?
Was it really shaking that much? That's so weird.
All I was doing was singing, "I am here," in the direction of tomorrow.

Memories, a disordered room—
if I don't even have a place to stand,
I'll leave everything behind, bringing just my body.

I wrenched open the dark door and set out on an ending journey.
Even if I get lost on a detour, good-bye, this place is fine.
If I acknowledge everything, I might be able to find it,
but there are so many things I can't protect.

Empty as I had become, even though it was so precious to me,
it all crumbles down with a single touch of a fingertip.

Alternatively, I'd obtain it and clutch it so hard, it would break,
or I'd plug my ears with a love song, then get scared and let go—
and it repeats.

I hid it in the moonlight, but you know, the truth is that I was blooming.
Please don't tread on it at the corner and let it wither away.
To let go of everything and be able to protect the one thing that remains—
thus I pray to the dawn.

"Moon Flower" / nano.RIPE
Words: Kimiko   Music: Jun Sasaki

Special Thanks

Akio Hiiragi   Kurone Mishima   Oji Sadou
All contributors to the Official 4-Panel Anthology

Director

Hitomi Araki   Taku Onodera

Character Design

029 (Oniku)

Author

Satoshi Wagahara

EPILOGUE: THE DEVIL, NOT A PART-TIMER

The night before his momentous business discussion:

"Hey, Ignora?"

Maou leaned against the door to Room 202. There was no answer.

"Everyone's starting to move. You're gonna have to get going, too, someday."

"…"

"I think the world, and everyone in it, has forgiven you. So come on out already. You could go back to Ente Isla, you could live here in Japan… Someone can help you now."

"………This…" The voice was muffled, and not because it was coming through a door. "How could I ever recover at this point?"

"Recover, huh…?"

"You have it good. You're loved by everyone, forgiven by everyone. But I…"

"Don't be stupid. This happened to me because I'm *not* forgiven."

Maou cruelly declared it to the brooding woman on the other side of the door, who had tried to become God in another world and failed.

"The people you've encountered experienced all kinds of things before they appeared before you. That's how you are to us, too."

"…"

"There's something in your life you wanted to accomplish from the heart, and that's what made you stand up, isn't it? So…I know you can walk. All those strong memories are still left in your mind, and your body. So…"

Maou stood back up and repeated the words for the nth time.

"No matter how ugly you get, come out while there's still an environment where someone will help you. Then you'll find the path to create a new world."

There was no answer.

"Anyway, I gotta visit this super-scary sponsor. It's gonna get a little loud again, but deal with it, okay?"

He walked off toward…not Room 201, but Room 203 of Villa Rosa Sasazuka. On the door was a small nameplate reading:

THE MAOU COMPANY, LTD.

＊

"All right, let me see your monthly report, for starters."

Room 203 had four small computer desks shoved inside it. Emi sat down at one of them, leaning back. Maou sat at a desk on the other side, and as he did:

"Here's your coffee, president."

With a studied hand, Chiho poured some instant coffee from a pot in the kitchen and brought it out to him.

"Ah, thank you… Um, what was it? The report?"

Maou booted up his old laptop and launched his spreadsheet software. Synchronizing his files with Emi's PC (via the tower machine that was a little too weak to be called a company server), he waited as Emi loaded up the images.

"Looks like you're attracting fewer customers to the upstairs parenting space."

"Yeah, we're getting a lot of single customers lately. There's been feedback that Yesodd's is getting too popular. It's always crowded, and there's no space to work your way in."

"Ah. Guess you really *don't* have days when it's not full, then."

"So I think our new location focused on bread should adopt the Yesodd's format as well, and I think it should be within walking distance from the main location. That way, we can point customers to the second location and keep from losing them."

"...But that way, they'll gradually start to clamor for reservations. That system makes it easy to gauge customer sizes, but it reduces the flow. Yesodd's isn't a day care center. The concept works only when parents are casually stopping in with their kids. If I'm going to build a new Yesodd's, it needs to be at least one rail stop away, I think. If we're going to start a new place within walking distance, we gotta mix it up a bit, not just offer the same format. Maybe low-allergen bread, or no-sugar bread, or someplace where Yesodd's customers can stop by to eat or pick up bread on the way home with their kid. That'll build more synergy."

"Well, I don't think we can do that with the bread we'd make from Nord's wheat."

"...Yeah. The taste isn't exactly geared toward young children."

"Adding honey makes it more versatile, but it also ups the price fast. We could make it a premium offering from the get-go, but then staffing will be a problem."

Chiho lent half an ear to the discussion as she poured out some of the black tea Emi had brought to the office, offering her a cup. Then she sat down on a folding chair in the corner. Just when she was about enjoy a cup of her own:

"Well, look, I keep on *telling* you, we only *get* this rent on the main location because my landlord owns it! If we try to rent another space this big in Eifukucho, I don't see how we're gonna budget it!"

"I *told* you we'll pay out whatever you need!"

"It's *my* job to give you a *return* on that, dumbass! The whole *point* of a traded company is that it *can't* go blowing all the money it has! *Your* approach is insanely irresponsible! We'll be drowning in red ink before we can expand our size at all! I'm gonna build The Maou Company into a major firm in one generation! That's what makes the beginning so important!"

"Do you think I'm not considering any of this?! I looked at all the rental spaces near the main café with fixtures, and I finished the preliminary inspections on them last month! I have lease estimates right here! Look at this place! We can finish the buildup for twenty percent cheaper than our first place!"

"I *told* you, I don't *want* any fixtures! It just proves the previous tenants ditched it for a reason! Stop deluding yourself into pretending we're gonna find some hidden gem of a storefront that way! We gotta build up our staff and make the second location of Yesodd's our second step to success! And if we bring in wheat from Kazuma and Nord, that'll make it cheaper and easier to read the initial response! Come *on!*"

"What *point* is there to reading the initial response?! It's directly proportional to the location's size, so if you're making comparisons, then opening the exact same location is just gonna get you a clone of our first one. And if we open up *this* close to it, what if one location starts declining? They'll knock each other out!"

"Well, the bank supports *my* concept!"

"Oh, don't tell me you're gonna take out a loan?!"

"Look, the interest rates are gonna plummet from here on in. If we're a publicly traded corporation, I got a duty to make profits for my stockholders. All *you* have to worry about is making money from the stock you hold, all right?! *I'm* running this company!"

"Oooh, '*I'm* running this company!' You know what a death knell that is?! That's it! I'm bringing Akiko to tomorrow's employment conference and then we can *all* duke it out! You and she are the only *real* full-timers in The Maou Company anyway."

"Bring it on, girl!"

And so it wound up turning into that.

Chiho snickered. This, really, was how Maou and Emi should be. It was what she wanted and what Emi wanted. The ideal.

"Um, president and main stockholder? Your helper needs to step out for a bit. If you need dinner, let me know, all right?"

Leaving the bellowing Maou and Emi to themselves, Chiho made a motion for the door of Room 203.

"...Hang on. I'll join you."

"Huh? A-are you sure?"

Maou left his seat, heading for Chiho.

"Hey, where are you going?"

"The new FriendMart toward the station!"

"Then buy me a chicken curry plate!"

"Curry? You *always* ask me for curry!"

"It's important to stay fed at times like these. We gotta go in hard on this, so would you *mind*, please?!"

"Tssh… All right. But I'm keeping the receipt. Meeting costs."

"Fine! Just go! And make sure he doesn't buy anything stupid, Chiho."

"Yes, yes. See you later."

Chiho snickered again as Maou pushed her out of Room 203. Once the door was shut behind them, he sighed.

"I swear, she comes in for the first time in a while and *this* happens."

"I kinda want to say the same thing, in a way…"

"Ahh, I'm sorry. But it's still gonna be hairy for a bit, so you mind staying just a little longer?"

"Hmm… But when you get *too* heated up, you stop listening to me… Well, how about I type in the receipts for you, and you can pay me with FriendMart's new dessert?"

"For that much, I'd be glad to. And I'll pay your work rate, too."

Walking down the stairs and away from the apartment, they were greeted with a sky not quite blazing with stars but still remarkably clear for a Tokyo night.

"No progress with Ignora today, either?"

"Nah. No reason to corner her that much. But I'll be patient. If we keep screaming at each other like that, maybe she'll get sick enough of it that she'll leave."

"Yeah, maybe." Chiho nodded as she walked by Maou's side. "Emeralda got angry at me."

"Huh? What'd you do?"

"She said that I needed to capture you, or else Yusa's going to start feeling affection for you."

"She does *not* give up, does she?"

"Right? Even though we're all on the same page."

"Well, like I told Kazuma, from a Japanese or Saint Aile perspective, I can't help it if people raise their eyebrows at us. But still…"

Chiho held Maou's hand, a look of from-the-heart joy on her face.

"You and I…and Yusa, and Suzuno, and Urushihara, and Ashiya… We all risked our lives working for that child, after all."

282 THE DEVIL IS A PART-TIMER!, Volume 21

"Emeralda would call that being spoiled, wouldn't she?"

"I'm truly, honestly okay with this, so that's tough to hear."

Chiho joyfully attempted to put more concern into her face and failed.

◊

Maou, run through by the holy sword of light, stood right back up as if nothing were amiss. But it was more than nothing that had happened. Chiho instantly realized that the dark fog from his body was demonic force.

"Yusa... That holy sword... You used it on Camael...?"

"That's right. Did Bell tell you about that?"

"Yeah... I—I was really surprised. I didn't think you'd actually do it at this point..."

"It *would* be way too late. I can't kill him with a sword that has Alas Ramus in it."

She tried to make it sound like a joke.

"This is just settling matters. And Alciel's on board with it, too. This was the final concern from the summit meeting."

To them, the Hero Emilia was a human being. Despite her supernatural skills as a tactical weapon, they recognized her as a human who could be reasoned with—and that's why they allowed her to live beyond worlds, in Japan.

That wasn't the case for the Devil King Satan. Unlike Alciel, with a proven track record of running things in Efzahan, the summit member Satan was still a symbol of fear, someone who could bare his fangs to the world at any moment. Many were those who looked at this fear with pure hatred and malice.

"And those feelings become demonic force. If we want to have the demons work things out with humans in Ente Isla as soon as possible, that's not a necessary force for them to have. So...I had to avenge your crimes."

Emi shook her head.

"The Devil King is no longer a demon."

"...Huh?"

This cascade of revelations made Chiho gasp.

"Based on what Ms. Shiba and Amane have found, the immortality that Caiel and Sikeena created no longer exists in Camael's body. And everybody knows that if the 'Devil King Satan' loses all of his demonic force..."

Chiho couldn't have felt more shocked.

"He...becomes human?"

"*That* is the punishment given to the Devil King who attempted to conquer the world. Normally, he could've lived for centuries and seen how the demons turned out, far into the future...but now he's human, and he's not even gonna live a hundred years. He's got no power to fight with. This man..."

Emi embraced Chiho.

"He's the man you love so much that you saved a faraway world for him."

"...!"

Chiho's eyes were filled with tears of joy and shock. They darted between Maou and Emi several times. Emi, watching her, gave Maou's back an irritated slap, inspiring a coughing fit.

"*Hrrgff!* Hey! I lost my power? What did you..."

"Shut up. It doesn't matter. Just wrap up *your* stuff already, too. And Chiho!"

"Y-yes!"

"Stop using me and Alas Ramus as an excuse. It's not like you at all, letting that stop you."

"...Yusa..."

"But outside of *that*, I'm hell-bent on making him step up for Alas Ramus, right up to the end...so forget the excuses and work that into your decision. Good night."

Before anyone could react, Emi turned around, her pumps tapping against the sidewalk as she disappeared into the Sasazuka night. She almost seemed to disappear into the mist beyond, perhaps because she had left the barrier.

"..."

Maou and Chiho spent a few moments watching Emi's back.

"...Hey, Chi...ah, no."

Maou made the first attempt before correcting himself.

"...Chiho."

It made her heart leap. It had never beaten harder in her life.

"We've been through a lot, but I can finally give you an answer... I'm not a demon any longer... I can only protect you with the kinda power any human man would have...but if you're okay with that..."

"..."

Chiho silently nodded.

"...You know, though, I'm really not that courageous. With me, I've always been a coward bluffing his way to the top. So..."

Chiho stood there, waiting for the words. He placed his hands on her shoulders, eliciting tears in her eyes.

"The man I love isn't a demon, or a human. It's a man with two names—Satan and Sadao Maou. And he's the most wonderful man in the world."

"...If that's what you have to say, then I better fulfill the other promise I left unattended. It's you, Chiho, who gives the final reply... and..."

Maou's face cast a shadow over Chiho's. The wind had blown the clouds away, the moonlight illuminating the two of them, locked in the barrier.

"...Let me give you the 'reward.' The one I've been keeping all this time as Devil King."

And the power from their lips touching was neither demonic force, nor holy energy, but simply the warmth between two people.

◊

"I'm all right. Back then, you were only looking at me. You selected me as your partner. I became your number one."

"Chiho..."

"And I have no intention of giving up the number one spot. But I'd never want to take Alas Ramus's daddy away from her. To her, Yusa

is Mommy, and you're Daddy. She'll never give *that* up. We risked our lives, trying to do so much. You went through a lot of pain to make it here. You had to work so hard. So...why can't we be a little selfish for a change?"

After saying that, Chiho turned around.

There stood the old Villa Rosa Sasazuka apartment building. Now, at this point, it was truly packed with dreams—dreams she wanted to keep going as long as she could.

The Maou Company was in Room 203. That fake firm that Ashiya had made up alongside Suzuno, trying desperately not to blow Emi's cover with Rika, was now a full-blown corporation. Its president was Sadao Maou, and its chief shareholder was Emi Yusa. The only full-time employee for now was Akiko Ohki, manager at the inaugural Eifukucho location of Yesodd's Family Café; Takefumi Kawata was an outside observer, Kaori Shoji and Yoshiya Kohmura were part-timers who signed up out of curiosity more than anything, and Mayumi Kisaki and Sariel were their first regulars. Chiho would come in to help with meetings, mediate between Maou and Emi, assist with basic data entry, and occasionally swing by Room 201 to cook a healthy meal for the nutritionally unsound Maou.

"I'm happy enough now, but no matter how much time passes, or who goes in and out of our lives, I want you and Yusa and everyone else to be happy together. I wanna be able to be selfish around them. And someday, I'll convince Emeralda about that, too."

"Well, if she didn't give her that stupid 'Hero Pension,' maybe I wouldn't have to worry about that so much, huh?"

"Ah-ha-ha! That's true. But I don't think Emeralda would've accepted the idea of Ente Islans giving her no reward whatsoever."

Not long after Devil's Castle had blasted off from the Central Continent, Emeralda went all the way up to the demon realms merely to have Emi review some business documents. That, it turned out, was a letter of intent for Emi to accept a "Hero Pension" drawn regularly from Saint Aile's national budget, the result of Emeralda pulling a lot of strings. Even by then, Emeralda predicted that Emi would settle in Japan for good after the assault on heaven. The pension was paid out in metals exchangeable in Japan, and as Emeralda put it, she planned to pay out enough to let her enjoy life and play around, even if she was reincarnated three more times.

Emi, of course, wasn't about to choose the "play around" option.

"Yusa is a Hero. Even in this other world, that truth is never gonna change, huh?"

When Emi realized the Yesod holy sword of light sucked the supernatural powers out of people, she used it to "slay the Devil King"—and what's more, to prevent any more antics from him, she proposed the founding of The Maou Company. That was way too much for Maou to swallow; his past dreams of conquering the world were crushed, and he even failed at his shot at a full-time position. Starting up a firm would be insanely reckless—but Emi put the hammer down.

"Look, when you marry Chiho someday, how are you gonna save any money with your current career? Because no offense to Ms. Iwaki and Ms. Kisaki, but if you stick with MgRonald, you have no future."

She was completely right. Maou felt no anxieties about his future prospects at MgRonald because he had powerful demonic force, supernatural strength, and a safe spot to retreat back to. All the human Maou had was his body and a rented one-room apartment. Could he really make Chiho happy as a part-timer? Maybe, according to Sariel's tenets of love, but he'd likely hit the ceiling pretty fast.

"Maybe the public's accepted you, but the summit members aren't gonna believe me if I just say I defeated you. But if you work at a firm where I have managerial decision-making rights, and the summit chairman Chiho is there, too, I won't let any of them bitch at me about it. I already had Ms. Shiba help create a draft business plan, and we've already found a space, too. So come on..."

Emi Yusa, still calling herself a Hero despite residing in a wholly different world now, smiled a devil's smile.

"Like I told you at the start, if you're willing to stay here till you're dead and buried, I'll let you live."

That was the temptation the Hero offered to him—a sweet, devilish, merciless taste of the happiness of regular life. One that featured the Devil King fully defeated, peace spreading worldwide, and a very happy friend of theirs.

"Emi and Emeralda make me suffer so much..."

"That's the *last* thing I wanna hear you whine about."

"*You've* been acting pretty confident lately, too, I think."

"Well, thank you. And...I've never tried to confirm it, and I think she's just keeping quiet about it out of respect for me...but Yusa loves you."

"Huhh?!"

This bomb, dropped out of nowhere, turned Maou's eyes into little dots. But after being with Chiho for three years, he had a sharpened sense for little subtleties like that between men and women. Now he was reminded of that one night just before the assault, when he fell ill.

"No, that..."

"That just reminded you of something, didn't it?"

Chiho didn't overlook Maou's hesitation. She gleefully prodded at it, draining the strength from him.

"...There's just no beating you."

"Of course not. I mean, can you imagine Yusa happy with some guy she doesn't know at all? At *this* point? It's only when you and she and Alas Ramus are together as a family that she'll find happiness, I think."

"And you're fine with that, Chiho?"

"Totally fine...even if it's hard to make anyone besides Copyhara believe that. But it's better for me if I fully understand everyone, like Suzuno. There's nothing particularly strange about all this. After all..."

Chiho brought both hands up to her temples, sticking out her pointer fingers to simulate devil's horns.

"You're the most reliable, hardest-working Devil King we know."

"You sure you wanna be caught saying that?"

"But in exchange for that, I'm not giving up the number one spot. I won't, and so I'm fine if you have lots of wives! Like the Devil King of another world should!"

"Being an ex–Devil King isn't a get-out-of-jail-free card. When I picked my number one, I knew what I was getting into."

"Yeah. Thanks."

"Besides, now isn't even the time for that. Why're you painting me like some polygamist? There're times when I can't even devote time or money to you already. I can't think about anyone else."

"Well, give that some serious thought. Because realistically speaking, you're Alas Ramus's guardian. You're thinking about putting her in a Japanese preschool or elementary school, aren't you?"

"Yeah, I did mention that we gotta talk about that soon, didn't I? ...Man, the work just never stops. There's no way this company's gonna go smoothly if Emi and I are running it... Hmm?"

Maou's whining was stopped by his phone vibrating. He took it out. It was a notice from his main bank's smartphone app, notifying him about a withdrawal from his account.

"Oh crap... The account for my petty cash is gonna be empty by the end of the month."

The bank account had been wrung completely dry. The reason couldn't be simpler: He had used up all the money. What on earth? Well, first, there was the "entrepreneurial spending" on that meeting in the soba restaurant. That, and transferring Alas Ramus's child support payment to Emi. *And* the payment on the card they used for little day-to-day purchases. He had a lot of expenses this month in particular, business *and* private, and so the account was looking pretty lonely.

Then, like it was aiming for that moment, a voice rang from the top of the stairs.

"Can't you plan your spending a little more carefully?"

Maou scowled in the voice's direction. Chiho gave it a joyful smile.

"Oh, you want my work to get tripped up? You want me to fall behind on Alas Ramus's child support?!"

"That's not what I am talking about," the calm voice said as it traveled down the stairs. "Even if you're short on *that* account, you got a company off the ground, and you're making good earnings from it. You're guaranteed an income from next month forward. Couldn't you have paid that off in installments?"

The overbearing voice belonged to Shirou Ashiya, former Great Demon General and current Devil King, who had just come back to Japan.

"Look, you *know* I hate taking out loans..."

"No, listen to me..."

"And I already *got* enough monthly payments. Emi's been pretty merciless about making those deposits on time lately. She's already my chief stockholder—I don't want her griping any more than she is about money."

"But..."

"I hate having debt, all right? If I can pay something off, I do. And *this* is the result."

Here, in this old apartment building like any other, Maou and Ashiya began the same argument about money they had conducted a million times before.

"Well, Your Demonic Highness..."

Even after assuming leadership over the many demons residing in Ente Isla right now, Ashiya still addressed the powerless Maou like royalty.

"If *that* is your financial approach, how you will ever save enough money for the wedding?"

"Wha-what, you...!"

"Ms. Sasaki has taken that tone with you precisely because she sees you as reliable, my liege. For us demons, if Emilia is keeping quiet because she thinks you are tied down by your company, I couldn't feel more relieved...but I predict a long journey ahead for you otherwise."

"Hey! When did you eavesdrop on that?! And don't say stuff like that around Chiho!"

"You must have a different sense of time from before. A human being's lifespan is far below that of a demon. Earning enough wealth to enrich your life is a difficult task! And there is not that much time before Chiho graduates from college. Have you made any plans at all along those lines?!"

Ashiya was bearing down on him more than ever before. In his current position, taking the Azure Emperor's place in managing affairs across Efzahan, he couldn't find much good to say about Maou's financial situation. But that's just how it was for now. In

Maou's current plan for his life, he would achieve a bare minimum of stability within five years of Chiho's graduation.

"Look, I had bad timing with my bank account this month! It's just one of those things!"

"*Such* a wretched state of affairs!"

"Why are you two screaming at each other after dark? Sadao, where's my curry?!"

"Ah! It's Al-cell!"

"Why are you people arguing about money outside? I can hear you up in my apartment."

"Yeah, dude, y'see? When you use a credit card, it doesn't feel like you're spendin' money, right? Everybody's like that."

They must have been loud indeed, because Emi from Room 203, Alas Ramus from Room 101, and Urushihara and Suzuno from Room 201 all came outside.

"…Hee-hee-hee!"

Chiho, seeing this unfold, smiled from the heart once more. Here was the man she loved the most in the world, alongside the friends and companions she cherished the most. This view—featuring everything that was number one in her life—made her happier than anything else.

"Hey, Sadao?"

Chiho took up the flustered Maou's hand.

"It's all right. I'll be earning money, too."

That only added fuel to the fire.

"Ms. Sasaki! That is not the issue here!"

"You better not spoil Sadao too much, Chiho!"

"Oh, man, Maou's gonna go on a downward spiral…"

"That lucky dog…"

"Stop, stop! What are you doing?! …Whoa!"

Maou, unable to withstand any more of this, rather deliberately took out his phone and put it to his ear.

"Oh! What's up, Ohki? Shoji and Yoshiya? Wow, that's bad. Okay, I'll be right there!"

Ending the maybe-fake, maybe-not call, he shoved the phone into his pocket.

"I got a work call!"

Then he all but fled to the bike parking lot.

"D-Devil King, wait! We need to talk…!"

"Shut up, shut up! You can lecture me when I'm back!"

He got on the locked bicycle parked next to his bright yellow scooter. Although the MgScooto (so named by Alas Ramus, because the yellow body reminded her of MgRonald) was his first pick, the bicycle was still his go-to for little neighborhood errands.

"Onward, my intrepid Dullahan II!!"

With a war whoop, he flew off into the city. And as Chiho Sasaki saw him round the corner and go out of sight:

"Good luck. We're all waiting for you back here."

The bell on Dullahan II pierced the night sky, echoing away as if answering her.

"See you later, my Devil King…working for all of us."

— End —

THE AUTHOR, THE AFTERWORD, AND YOU!

When families, friends, lovers, and acquaintances communicate with each other, it's common for them to talk about what they did, where, and when. The udon I had for lunch yesterday was good. I obtained a rare item in this new game I'm playing. I learned a few new recipes. I went out with my school friends. I bought a new game. At work, I ran into this guy, and he opened me up to this new world. I spent time with my family and friends this or that way.

Meeting each other and catching up like this lets you know how your companions have been spending their time while you haven't seen each other. And while your family, friends, lovers, and acquaintances can tell you what they were up to, they sadly can't share those times with you themselves. However, the next time you meet them, those family members, friends, lovers, and acquaintances will have had all kinds of new experiences and felt all kinds of feelings, and they'll bring them all over to you.

Think of it that way, and the people you cherish are, essentially, just a small part of your life. And, oddly enough, the more time that passes—and the older you get—the less time you'll have to see those cherished friends. Still, though, there's no doubting the fact that those family members, friends, lovers, and acquaintances are using their valuable time to live out their own lives, building those experiences over time, and always advancing forward.

The characters that appear in *The Devil Is a Part-Timer!* are just the same. And thanks to all the readers beside them, they've been truly blessed by the time they've spent with each other. If the readers ever cherished any of the people in *The Devil Is a Part-Timer!*, then even after the story ends, they'll still exist somewhere out of sight, living their lives, passing the time—and today, as well, they're sharing that time together.

This story I signed a deal with the Devil King to write, one that has taken up a lot of readers' time as well, is the tale of a bunch of people who struggle every day to make their lives as fun as possible. Perhaps that one person in *your* neighborhood is a visitor from another world. And if you ever happen to see that gang living out their lives somewhere, please say hello to them. I'm sure they'll wave and smile back at you.

This is the last volume of *The Devil Is a Part-Timer!*, and the first thing I want to say is: Great job, Wagahara...! And to Hiiragi, Mishima, Sada, the editors, and the readers, thanks so much for your support, your cooperation, and your readership.

Ten years seems like a long time, but it's really short.

Checking the manuscript for each volume, I've been gladdened and saddened in equal turns by the text and dialogue. I've been struck in the heart, tears in my eyes. I love all the unique characters, as realistic as they seem, and I love the world setting. In my art, I went through a trial-and-error process, hoping to bring the scenes across as accessibly as possible to readers. There were times when my skills weren't good enough to express what I wanted—but each time, I received aid and support from the people around me, and on the comic side, they did an amazing job of expressing themselves as well, without breaking the atmosphere of the original. I can't thank them all enough.

If I'm no longer reading manuscripts and drawing illustrations on a regular basis, that means I don't get to interact with the characters as much, which is always a sad thing. But this work will stick around my whole life, and I can always read it again—that's good enough! (And I guess that means *The Devil Is a Part-Timer!* is now a firm part of my life...!)

Wagahara told me once that "Chiho was supposed to be a one-off guest heroine, but when I saw your design for her, I decided to make her a regular." I never really thought the characters I've designed would come to play such a pivotal role in the story...! I suppose this is a job that gives you more blessings than you really deserve—and if I helped create synergy that improved the story Wagahara told, that makes me pretty happy.

I've met a great deal of people through this work, and receiving direct feedback from readers at events and on social media has provided a lot of good memories and inspiration. If I'm ever blessed with another chance to depict the world of *The Devil Is a Part-Timer!*, I'll work on my drawing skills and try my best at it, right alongside The Maou Company! So to wrap up, thank you all very much for your support over the years!

niku

THE DEVIL IS A PART-TIMER! IS COMPLETE! CONGRATULATIONS!

THE DEVIL IS A PART-TIMER! HAS FINALLY COME TO AN END! IT FEELS LIKE IT'S GONE BY IN A FLASH..! DRAWING THIS PIECE REMINDED ME OF ALL THE SUPPORT I RECEIVED DURING THE DEVIL IS A PART-TIMER! HIGH SCHOOL! I'LL ALWAYS REMAIN A FAN OF THIS SERIES. TO WAGAHARA, 029, AND MAOU AND THE GANG, CONGRATS ON A JOB WELL DONE...!

KURONE MISHIMA

THE DEVIL IS A PART-TIMER! COMPLETE!

THE SERIES REACHES ITS CONCLUSION. CONGRATS ON COMPLETING THIS EPIC TALE! BEING INVOLVED WITH THIS SERIES WAS SO MUCH FUN! I ALWAYS LOVED DEVIL'S CASTLE WHEN IT'S AT ITS MOST CROWDED.

OJI SADAU